Echoes From Heaven

by

Tammy D. Thompson

Bloomington, IN   Milton Keynes, UK
authorHOUSE

AuthorHouse™
1663 Liberty Drive, Suite 200
Bloomington, IN 47403
www.authorhouse.com
Phone: 1-800-839-8640

AuthorHouse™ *UK Ltd.*
500 Avebury Boulevard
Central Milton Keynes, MK9 2BE
www.authorhouse.co.uk
Phone: 08001974150

This book is a work of fiction. People, places, events, and situations are the product of the author's imagination. Any resemblance to actual persons, living or dead, or historical events, is purely coincidental.

© 2006 Tammy D. Thompson. All rights reserved.

No part of this book may be reproduced, stored in a retrieval system, or transmitted by any means without the written permission of the author.

First published by AuthorHouse 11/1/2006

ISBN: 1-4259-6939-9 (sc)

Printed in the United States of America
Bloomington, Indiana

This book is printed on acid-free paper.

Other titles by Tammy D. Thompson

Buried, But Not Forgotten

The *Dream Mountain* Series, including

Dream Mountain
A Dream Come True
Lessons of the Heart
Echoes From Heaven

Dedication

I'd like to thank God for giving me the patience, the will and the spirit to be able to express myself in such a way. My heart is in the midst of every word and I am so very thankful to be able to live my dream. Also, I'd like to mention several good friends. There are few people that you come across in your lifetime that never fail you. There are few people that touch your heart in everything they do. And there are even fewer that will stand beside you no matter what the cost. These two people are those type of friends. So, to Melissa Burns and Lisa Friday you're both angels to me in every way, and I'm thankful for you every moment. With friends like that, I know I'll never be alone. Lastly, as I finish this series, my family still plays a major role in my life. If it weren't for the support they always give, I wouldn't have the courage to do all I've done. Thank you, and I love you all. "Always let love lead you down life's pathway."

1

My mind started flying back into the past as it had done quite often in the recent months to pass. I guess because I wanted to remember what had gotten me to the point I gladly reached. I could clearly see my wedding day. I was dressed to a T and my husband to be, Lonnie was looking more than just plain ole handsome. It was a day I thought would change my life forever, and I suppose it did, but not in the same way I thought at the time.

Then when the day came I had to say good-bye to my beloved so soon after we were joined to live with one another forever, I saw my life as over, but with that, I was forgetting one thing. I was carrying the child that was created in the midst of all the love Lonnie and I shared so openly.

Whisking to a happier time, I saw my son for the first time. His face was red as a beet and he was so tiny, I was 'bout near afraid I'd break him in two just by holding him, but I was completely wrong. That day made all the negative thoughts I had rolling around in that confused, mixed up brain a mine, turn positive, at least for a while.

That's when Evan showed up. He stood there tall, sexy and right handsome if you don't mind me sayin'. Anyway, amongst all my fears and rude behavior towards him, little by little, in just a moment, I relived everything he did to impress me, bringing me to the moment at hand...the moment where a pure, perfect happiness seemed to be prevalent above all the hardships my heart had been through and recovered from.

I looked up; reality taking hold abruptly, and there stood my two favorite men...Evan and my sweet little Cody Lee, my son. He held him as if he knew what he was doing. It amazed me how his eyes glimmered in the way he talked to that tiny human being I carried inside of me for nine months. Strangely enough, at that moment, in that very light shining on them, they favored. Cody was staring up at him in a way I don't ever recall him looking at anyone, and the expressions he revealed, was a sign that he liked this man as much as I did. They were almost immediately drawn together, as were he and I at first glance.

Evan was making silly faces and it was entertaining to watch my son try and imitate such expressions. With all of the coos he was making, it made Evan continue talking in the baby language...least wise that's what Pa always called it. He always said babies had their own language. I didn't know if that were true or not, but Evan sure was speaking to my child where he understood, or it appeared so anyway.

"He's a manly sort," Ma said, nudging me slightly.

"MA!" I replied, afraid Evan would hear.

"Well dear," she replied in a playful voice, "Ain't no use in lyin' now...is there?"

Shaking my head at her, "I suppose not, but just don't go embarrassin' me."

"That's your Pa's department Betty Jean. He's a pro at that when it comes to you and his little girl's fellas."

"Don't *I* know."?

"Of course, " she continued. "Douglas does a pretty good job himself."

"Yeah, well if he tries to run this one off, I got somethin' for 'im Ma."

"Oh stop you're talkin' crazy. You know don't nobody take Douglas serious…least not nobody 'round here," she retorted quickly.

"They got no reason to," I replied. "Shoot that little brother a mine is got so many wild hairs, I'm surprised he ain't got this whole town wantin' to run him out."

Laughing together, we noticed Pa starting in on Evan. Pa had his arms crossed in a manner that clearly said "I'm gonna ask your intentions boy!" His look was all too familiar with that serious face and squinting eyes as if he were interrogating him, or getting ready too. That's when I stepped in before he could get started good. I went over and took the baby from Evan. His hand immediately fell to the middle of my back. He held it there as if he were trying to keep me from stumbling backwards or something. Regardless, it was a simple gesture I thoroughly enjoyed. Just his touch was heaven sent.

Pa stared at both of us…looking at one, then the other, and then shook his head.

"What is it Pa?" I asked, my head tilted a hint sideways, curiosity clinging to my thoughts.

"Just thinkin' Betty Jean," he answered. "I was thinkin' how we're probably lookin' forward to another weddin' here b'fore too long."

"But Pa…"

"Now I ain't got much money. So don't ya'll be goin' all out this time."

"Pa…"

3

"But do as ya like. I suppose as long as you two care 'bout each other that's all that matters anyhow," he finished, disregarding my pleas for him to hush.

"We ain't talked a marriage Pa," I replied, wondering what his reaction would be.

The look on his face was beyond bewilderment, then it transformed into his normal expression.

"Well, whenever you two do decide," he said. "Make it cheap. I ain't got no money tree growin' in the back yard ya know."

He went inside and all I could do was laugh. I never did know of my Pa to pay any mind to what we're saying, at least not when he was on a roll and talking about what was on his mind. Besides, I figured Pa was right. I was sure marriage would be the next logical step. I just hoped Evan felt the same way.

"Night Ma," I said, still chuckling a little from Pa's outburst about marriage.

"Night dear. You too Evan."

"Sweet dreams Mrs. Cole."

"Call me Gertie," she said. "Or Ma...whichever suites you son."

"Yes ma'am. Night Gertie."

She nodded and began to go inside, catching Douglas as he started to come out and see what was going on. He was throwing a fit to start in on Evan, but I sure was glad he didn't. I was positive he'd run for the hills if he met my brother first off. I know if I was him I would've.

With nothing but smiles, we traveled the short distance back to my house. The sun was getting brighter and brighter, but the cold was evident. Just to look outside, it would seem summertime was already here, but we knew better. The dead of winter approached and the wind was so chilling it would 'bout near cut you into, so we didn't hinder to go inside

Cody had been up for some time from what Ma told me, and his eyes began to flutter, closing more and more, showing how tired he was. It didn't take long to get him fast asleep. Evan just stared at him as if he were in awe of the miracle I gave birth to. He stroked his arm and face and seemed to study every bit of what made my handsome little boy.

"You're lucky," Evan said about the time I got up to go lie the baby down for a nap.

Turning to him, again I smiled, "I know Evan. And now I'm even luckier."

His eyebrows raising a hint, "Why's that?"

"Now I got two handsome men in my life," I answered, going ahead and putting Cody down for his nap.

Evan didn't say a word, but I would swear he started blushing. That gorgeous, sexy and tough exterior soon turned embarrassed just by a few words from little ole me. That surprised me more than you know. Here was a guy who was in the service who came into my life out of nowhere just because he was Dean's cousin, my sister Lizzy's husband. Lizzy and Dean had been so worried about me after the death of my husband Lonnie, and they immediately jumped on the chance to get Evan and me together. Somehow they saw it as an everlasting relationship. Even though I didn't see it at the time, I had to admit...they were right, or seemed so for the time being.

I guess my thoughts were apparent in my eyes and in the expression painted evidently across my slim façade. Evan just sat there staring at me, almost as much as he did with Cody. Not even blinking, his look towards me was as if he were staring at something utterly priceless and unforgettable, which I didn't feel I was any of the above.

"Now what?" I said. "Do I got somethin' on my face or somethin'?"

He looked down, laughed and looked right back up to me, placing two fingers under my chin, his eyes shining radically. Just the touch from the tips of his fingers was enough to run a passionate electrical shock through me, reaching every vessel, every muscle, and finally shocking my heart once more.

"You don't have anything on your face but somethin' beautiful."

Shaking my head, I got up, "I'll tell you like Lizzy used to tell Dean. You're a sweet talker and a half, Evan Bain."

"Now why do you always use my last name?" he asked.

Shrugging my shoulders, I thought for a moment, not sure of the answer myself. " I don't know," I replied slowly. "I guess it just got to be habit when we first met."

"Hmmm," he countered, nodding his head.

"What?" I asked again, wishing I were tiny enough to where I could go inside his brain and read his every thought.

"Nothin' BJ…I was just thinkin' about that day we met."

"You was…was ya?"

Letting out a short sigh, "I swear, you was about unruly as they come. I tried my best to impress you, but didn't none of it work. You were as cold as ice and after a while, I didn't figure nobody could thaw you out."

"Now wait just a minute here, Evan. Think back," I questioned. "You came on a bit strong if I do say so myself."

"Strong?" he replied, as if he had no idea what I was talking about.

"Yeah! You picked up my hand and commenced to kissin' it like you was some prince lookin' for his princess."

With a short pause, he replied, "You were right about one thing BJ."

"And what was that?"

"I did find my princess. The prince part...well that might be going a hair overboard."

Trying not to sound too mushy, "I think you're a prince."

"Is that right?" he remarked, scooting closer to me.

His lips began gracing my neck tenderly. Nibble after nibble, I knew where it was leading. It wasn't that I didn't want him. I wanted him more than anything in the world at that point, but I didn't want to make the same mistake I'd done so many times before. For once, I wanted to hold off sexually long enough to make sure what he and I had was real, honest, and true.

I pulled away just enough to show him I didn't want to go any further, then I laid my head on his chest, letting my hand rest on his perfectly shaped abdomen. I could feel his chest moving up and down, and his heart was racing to a speed I'd never heard before. I was sure he and I were thinking the same thing, but then again, I knew what was best...at least for the time being.

It was strange, but there was a moment I could tell he wanted to say something, but then he just didn't. I peered up at him, letting our eyes speak to one another, hoping I could figure him out.

"What was you gonna say?"

He got up, went to the door, reached in his bag and started to pull something out. The entire time he was steadily glancing over at me, making me even more interested in what he was hiding. Then he got up, put whatever it was behind his back and walked in my direction.

"Evan, what are you hidin'?"

About that time, he pulled the poem in the frame I had bought him, from behind his back. He looked at it as if he were reading it all over again.

"I believe you dropped this in the hospital didn't you?"

Suddenly I was the one turning embarrassed, "I suppose I did."

"It was for me right?" he asked, confirming his thoughts.

Shaking my head as if were only trying to pry a compliment out of me, "Why yes. I was just so mad when I saw you with that woman."

"My sister remember…my sister."

Sighing hugely, I smiled, taking it from him and reading over it again, as if I had forgotten what the words said. As I did so, he got up again.

"What now?" I asked.

"Hold your horses, I got somethin' else," he replied with a wink in the most sexy way.

I sat down the poem I had gotten him and when he came back over, he pulled something else from behind his back. This time it was one he had gotten me. The frame was earth tone colored with tiny flecks of gold all through it, and the poem was written in the most elegant and beautiful writing I ever recalled seeing before.

"You didn't have to…"

"Just read it BJ," he interrupted, anxious as I was when I brought him his that night at the hospital.

"Okay…okay. I'm readin'" with no more hesitation, this is what it said:

"MY PERFECT ROSE"

I used to wander in the midst of gardens,
Searching for my perfect rose.
Some were pale and withering,
And others I would not have chose.
I'd linger looking at every one
Finding flaws wherever I looked,
But the moment that I saw you,
My perfect rose, I then was hooked.
You weren't the liveliest you see,

But the one with hope, I knew.
And as time passed that very rose
Blossomed a smile I see in you.
No longer afraid to pick such a flower,
I took a chance and picked your stem.
I wrapped myself around you,
And realized I held a gem.
I used to wander in the midst of gardens
To find my perfect rose you see.
But when I finally knew…that rose was you.
The perfect rose for me.
Your skin is like soft petals,
And your scent, a heavenly bouquet
The way your smile makes you bloom,
From day to day to day.
I used to wander in the midst of gardens,
But I now hold the rose I need.
To you, my love, my perfect rose.
To love me, that I plead.
To my perfect rose from the one who wants
to be the sun that nurtures you!
I love you…Evan

Letting it fall to my lap after being hypnotized by each and every word, I was in shock that he went through so much trouble to find something that described his feeling for me.

"Did you write it?" I asked, pretty sure he didn't.

"Believe it or not, I did. I always was interested in expressing myself with words. Of course in the military, there ain't much use for such things," he replied in a caring way.

"Nobody's ever…I mean, I never had…"

I couldn't help myself, but a few tears began to trickle out because of how touched I was that this man had done something so terribly romantic for me. There was a time when I believed nothing would get better in my life, but after reading those words, I had no doubt in my future...my future with Evan. Even though I knew things wouldn't always stay so perfect, it didn't matter. Moments such as the one that just passed were moments that would remain in my mind forever...one I'd never ever forget.

Caught up in the moment, I almost didn't hear the cries of my little one in the very next room. When I started to get up, Evan stopped me.

"I'll take care of him," he said tenderly, again winking as he left the room.

The safe feeling of being with him was unlike any other feeling. Just knowing he was there, gave me the most intense sensation of peace and reassurance. And the fact that he wanted to show Cody attention like a father would, only gave him more points on top of the ones he'd already scored with me in his sentimentality.

In just a moment, the baby had stopped crying and I tiptoed to the room where he was, stopping just outside the door so I could hear what Evan was doing to pacify my little man. He was humming and singing softly. If I didn't know any better, I would think he had children of his own, but I knew that wasn't true. Then I heard him talking in a whispering manor, assured not to wake him. I was impressed in the words he spoke to my child.

"Listen Code Man," he said softly. "You're mama loves you a whole lot and I see why. But if I got anything to do about it, you won't be alone anymore. I know I can't take your daddy's place, even though you never knew him, but I'd like to try. I always wanted kids, and I can't think of a better son to have than you."

My emotions took my entire body over and I didn't want to hide outside the door any longer. I stepped in the room where Evan was so lovingly holding my child and walked up to him. He glanced up and

I knew he was about to say something. I could see it in his eyes and I could feel it in the air around me. So, with anticipation, I waited to hear what that handsome, sweet and caring man had to say.

2

"Betty Jean," he said, almost stunned that I was eaves dropping. "I was just…"

"I heard," I replied in the lowest voice I could, careful not to wake up the baby. Evan had put him back to sleep.

I went over and kissed Cody on his forehead then brushed his feather soft skin, "Lay'em back down. I'm sure he'll sleep for a little while longer. It won't be long b'fore he's ready to get up and eat though."

He did so and we left the room as quietly as we entered. Dean looked almost uneasy that I heard him talking about such things and when we reached the couch to sit down, he turned to me.

"I didn't mean to go assuming anything when I was talking to him in there. I was only relaying to him what I was thinkin' that's all."

Sitting down, I thought for a moment, trying to figure out what I wanted to ask him. I knew that most men were scared away by kids, but he didn't seem to be that way. In fact, he seemed drawn to me because of it. I honestly didn't know what to think of a man like him. I was attracted to him for that very reason, but not only for that reason. At the same time, it frightened me. Some folks could look at his attentiveness towards Cody as just plain ole trying to get to me, into my heart a little bit further, but I didn't want to think that way. Ma always told me you have to trust folks. She said that when you get to where you question everything, in your eyes, no one's telling the truth. I didn't want to turn out that way, even though I seemed so a few months earlier.

"Did you want kids…b'fore you met me I mean?" I asked carefully, almost afraid of the answer that might come.

"I've always thought about it."

"Thought about it in a good way or…"

"A good way!" he insisted, stopping me before I entered negative thinking in the least. "In fact, I used to date a girl four or five years ago who wanted children."

"And you didn't want any then?"

"Betty Jean, I was eighteen and still trying to make my mind up on whether or not I wanted to join the service. I didn't know what I wanted, but I knew I was too young for kids at that point in my life."

Being a sly bit nosy, "What was her name?"

"Oh no!" he said. "You're gonna start something that's gonna end us up in a fight."

"No…really. I'd like to know. It's in the past. I know she can't hurt me now…RIGHT!"

Letting out a huge breath, he answered my question. "Her name was Lisa."

"Lisa?" I said. "What happened with ya'll two?"

"She just got too dang serious. She called and called over and over again after we split, but I never returned a call. Then I left for the service…haven't seen'er since."

"Hmmm," I mumbled, thinking he might do the same to me if I got too serious.

"See there. I knew if I answered your question…"

Echoes From Heaven

"I'm just playing," I retorted quickly, just so he'd know it didn't bother me. "I guess I just wanted to know if me having a child bothers you or makes you feel like I'm forcing you into wanting to be a daddy."

Looking me square in the eye, his hands cradled my face for a moment, stroking and caressing sweetly. "Baby, I told you earlier how I feel about you."

"I don't recall," I said, turning my head sideways, wanting to hear it once more.

"I *said* I love you," he said, going along with my little game.

My playfulness showed right after those words came flying from his sexy, pouty lips. I couldn't help but smile on the outside like I was smiling on the inside. Then he began to shake his head.

"I just can't figure you out. I swear, you're unlike any other girl I ever went out with."

"And don't you forget it Mr. Bain."

"There you go with that last name stuff again," he said with a sly grin. "Alright Ms. Hendrix."

With that, he started tickling me profusely, making me forget all about that Lisa girl and set my thoughts on *him* and *me* instead. I darn near had tears pouring down from laughter until I pushed him off me and ran. I had made it into the kitchen and he caught me. He turned me facing him and lifted me up before I knew it.

"Evan…stop it!"

"Why?" he said, "Nobody's watchin'."

His hands crawled around my waist in the slowest way possible and my hands were resting on his wide, bulked up shoulders.

"What'cha think?" I asked, curious how he'd get out of that question.

I got nothing but a grin. That was exactly what I thought. His mind was exactly in the same place as mine was, only that I knew better to think such thoughts so soon.

"Maybe this'll help you remember," I said, leaning over, our lips fitting perfectly together.

Tasting his heated breath was so appealing, almost making me go crazy inside trying to remember the exact reason he and I needed to wait before getting any more intimate. It took a little searching, but I finally remembered. In one sense, it seemed logical, but in another, I wanted to forget about such caution and go with my feelings, my wants and my needs.

"You're teasing me," he replied, after our lips parted subtly.

"I'm sorry. Now help me down," I apologized, placing my arms around his neck.

He lifted me up then down again to where I was looking up at him once more.

"You know I want you Evan, but…"

"I understand baby. We need to wait. We got all the time in the world," he whispered. "I'm not goin' anywhere. That's a promise!"

"So you say," I said, walking away, again seeing his reaction.

Before I could get too far way, he grasped onto my arm and pulled me back to him hurriedly, making me realize that what he and I had was not something I needed to play games with. I needed to be upfront and honest like Ma always said.

"How's this for proof," kissing me with enough heated passion to set all the woods around us afire.

I did nothing but melt in the inferno of his powerful kiss. He pulled me so tightly against his hard, irresistible body, that I didn't want to move a muscle. I wanted to stay that way for as long as he would allow me too, but just the feel of him being that close, made me rethink my morals. It was broad daylight but I wanted nothing more than to take him into my room and make love to him more passionately than he would ever imagine in a million years. I wanted to show him every ounce of love and dedication that was welling up inside this wanting heart of mine. It was a feeling I just couldn't release easily…least wise not while he had me in such a position.

When the heat of the fire between us cooled down a hint, no words were spoken…no words had to be. Everything we needed to say was being spoken in the way we were looking deep down in to each other's souls. I was sure he saw my adoration for him, and I was seeing the same, as loving if not more.

"Hmmm," I sounded once more.

"I take that was a good hmmm, not a bad one."

"Definitely good!"

Swimming in the moment, not wanting it to pass, I put my arms around his neck and he just held me. I could feel his warm breath on my neck and it was tantalizing to say the least. I wanted to stay like that forever even though I knew it was totally impossible. So instead, as I always did, I put that moment in my mind as a memory for me to look back on over and over again, whenever I'd feel lonely. I knew if I could think of that exact moment in time, whatever was happening in my life, I'd have to smile.

After that we just talked. There wasn't a subject we didn't touch. From politics to religion, we covered it all. He was so easy to talk to and his attentiveness towards me was hard to believe. Not even Lonnie paid that much attention to what I said. He acted like he was listening to royalty with each word that sprung from my mouth. It was all so new to me. Of course I suppose I was the same with him. I didn't want to miss a single sentence. He intrigued me with his intellectual side, but at the same time, his tenderness was beyond any man I've seen. I could tell he was related to Dean. Dean was always so wonderful to my sister Lizzy.

I remember asking Lizzy once when she first met Dean if he had a brother…well, I didn't think if he had a cousin. I'm sure Lonnie would've had a run for his money if Evan had showed up around that time.

Several hours passed in a flash. It didn't seem like it, but before too long, Cody was up again. I was sure he was hungry so I got him up. We went into the kitchen and I sat him carefully in his highchair. His eagerness for dinner was all too clear and it didn't seem like I could get it in his mouth quick enough. His squirming around after each bite told me that. Evan sat there laughing at him all the while.

"He's got a healthy appetite don't he?" he said, wiping his mouth each time Cody's dribble some.

"Always had. I suppose he gets that from his uncle Douglas."

"Douglas can't be that bad…can he?" he asked, still helping me with Cody.

Turning to him I shook my head and grinned. "Let me put it to ya this way Evan. There ain't been a single meal in Ma and Pa's house that Douglas didn't try to start supper before grace was said. And there ain't been a single night us three kids didn't have to tell him to shut up just so we could get some rest."

"How old is he?"

"He'll be goin' on seventeen now I suppose, but he sure don't act like it."

"What about a girlfriend?" he asked, seeming to be totally interested in my family.

"There's Tricia. That's who he likes, and I suppose he's grown up some since she started showin' interest in him, but he still has a long way to go."

Soon enough Cody was spitting out more than he was eating.

"I guess that means he's full," Evan laughed.

"Guess so," I replied, cleaning Cody and his chair up.

Evan had his elbow up on the table and his chin was heavily resting on his hand. He looked like he just had a brainstorm, but I didn't ask a thing. I figured if he did, he'd share it with me.

"How about we all go to Dean and Lizzy's? I'm sure they'll be glad to know you came to your senses," he kidded.

"Me come to *my* senses?"

"You know I'm just jokin' baby. You wanna go?"

Agreeing without hesitation, knowing I didn't want to be stuck at the house all day long, I got Cody cleaned up and dressed to go. Evan was helping every step of the way as if he was used to such, and after a little bit, we were on our way. Evan buckled Cody in securely and started to get in on the driver's side.

"And what do you think you're doin'?" I asked, as he was getting in my car.

"Well," he retorted quickly. "There's no sense in a beautiful lady like yourself havin' to drive when she's got a man here who wants to chauffer you around."

"I guess I can't argue with that Mr. Bain."

Shaking his head because of my use of his last name again, we got in and left. It took a moment or two for the car to heat up from the cold which had built up in there, but soon enough it did. And when we pulled into Lizzy and Dean's drive, Lizzy had just stepped outside. The look on her face was one of pure joy. I could tell she wanted to jump up and down considering her plan to get us together finally worked.

Evan got the baby out while I went up to meet her standing at the top of the steps.

"When did all this happen?" she said almost hysterically.

"Shhh," I whispered. "I'll tell ya later. All I can say is that I was wrong. He's a great guy and I'm in…"

"Here we go code man," he said, coming up behind me, cutting off my sentence. Lizzy was in complete suspense and I figured I'd leave it that way…for a while anyway. She just looked at me as if she wanted me to finish what I had started, but like I said, I wanted to make her think for a while about it.

"Are we goin' in or are we gonna stand out here in the cold all day long?" he said, nudging me along.

Lizzy didn't say anything. She just went inside where Dean was sitting on the couch. He got up and greeted us in a very friendly way as usual.

"Hey cuz," he said. "So what's goin' on? You two together finally?"

Evan handed Cody off to Dean then put his arms around me. "Yep. I finally got her to see what a great guy I really am."

"Oh please!!" I said in a kidding voice, hugging him back.

"Well I'm glad," Dean replied. "It's about dang time. I swear, I didn't think you two would ever work this thing out."

Lizzy went and got Angel, her baby girl, from the nursery and came back down that gorgeous stairway.

"Ya'll hungry?" she said. "I been tryin' to talk Dean into cookin' all mornin' but he just plain wouldn't do it."

Dean just shook his head and went along with her remark. "Yeah, let's go eat. It's on me. There's this new place on the west end of town called "The Singing Café." There's folks that go just to show off their yodelin' skills. I hear it's not a bad place to eat."

With everyone in agreement, we split up in separate cars and we followed Dean and Lizzy to the place he was talking about. My stomach was making noises I kept trying to cover up, but it was impossible. Evan kept staring over and laughing at me each time it would growl again.

"Sounds like you got wild animal in there sweetie," he aggravated.

"Feels like there is, and I think he done ate up all my food. That's why I'm so darned hungry."

Laughing together, we pulled into the eatin' place. There was a big sign hanging up with musical signs on each end of it. It was an interesting place to say the least, so we got out as quickly as we could. It was far too cold to keep the baby out in it for too long. And we all made it inside about the same time.

"Whew," Lizzy said, taking the hood off her head and the baby's. "It's colder than a well digger's…"

"Darlin'!" Dean cut in.

"Behind," she said. "I was gonna say behind."

All four of us chuckled at her use of foul language. Lizzy never had been one to talk dirty. That's when the waitress came over.

"Ya'll just sit yourselves down anywhere. I'll try and be with ya shortly."

She was young, but cute. Her hair was long, blonde and kinda curly. It looked like she spent all day making her face look just perfect, because it did. Each hair was just so, and her bright eyes stood out, no doubt at all.

There was this tiny stage built up in the corner of the café with a microphone, speaker and a record player. Of course nobody was singing, but I was interested if anybody would.

"Why don't you get up there and bellow out a tune Betty Jean," Dean said, trying me, knowing I couldn't carry a tune in a bucket with a lid on it…never could.

Lizzy and I grabbed a few highchairs and got the kids situated and comfortable, then sat next to the men we were with.

Running over, that waitress was singing the whole way. When she reached us, she seemed clean out of breath.

"You sing?" I asked.

"Shoot yeah," she replied quickly. "Heck I been tryin' to break into the big time and be a famous singer, but it ain't happened yet. So for now, I'm stuck here waiting on folks."

There weren't many people in there, so we asked her to get up and sing one for us. We figured that since we were in "The Singing Café," we might as well get to hear somebody sing.

She looked around and then agreed. Putting down her pad and pencil on our table, she stepped up onto that small stage and started to sing with no music. Her voice was beautiful. She had a different sort of twang to her sound. It was different from any other singer I'd heard. And when she was finished, she stepped down.

A woman came running from the back room. "Tosha, you entertaining these nice people."

"Tryin' to mama," she said, looking somewhat embarrassed.

The woman came to our table and introduced herself. "My name's Debbie Nicholson. That's my daughter Tosha. I swear…that girl's been singin' since before she could walk."

Tosha stepped in and started taking our order. It was all she could to do to make her mama stop talking, but she did so.

It was hard to believe somebody here in our own hometown had so much talent. But then again, none of us knew about all the folks in town.

My stomach started rumbling even louder, Evan steadily laughing, so we decided to order their special. It was chicken fried steak, English Peas, creamed potatoes and salad. Shoot, just looking at the menu made my mouth water.

Dean and Lizzy kept staring at Evan and me. It was like they were watching something so very entertaining. Just because of that, Evan put his arm around me and pulled me as close to him as I could possibly get, then he leaned over and kissed me on the cheek.

Since I was never one to be that open with my feelings and about what was going on with me and my personal life, I was surprised about what came out of Evan's mouth next.

3

"You know I'm in love with your sister don't ya? " he said to Lizzy, clearly grabbing that from out of the clear blue sky.

Grinning from ear to ear, she replied happily, "I'm so happy for ya'll Evan. I knew you were perfect for each other the first time I met you. I told Betty Jean that too, but she was bein' so…"

Dean put his hand over her mouth suddenly as if to tell her to stop babbling. She didn't mind though. That smile she had when Evan first announced his feelings still remained evident as ever. Her dimples that seemed almost inexistent most of the time, were shining like the summer sun on a clear day. I could tell she was dying to keep on talking, but Dean kept staring at her making sure she didn't embarrass me too terribly.

"You got yourself a sweet woman Evan," Dean said, shaking his hand like it was custom to do so when you announce you love someone.

It didn't matter to me though. As long as he didn't mind anyone knowing, that also meant he was sincere in the words he was speaking. Shoot, I was beginning to wonder if Lizzy wasn't as excited or more so than I was about the situation. More than anything, I think she was just glad I finally decided to start living for today and stop dwelling on the past.

Suddenly I heard sirens. I cop car pulled up right in front of the café, with its lights brightly shining and causing everyone that had come in after us, to look and see what the trouble was.

The door flung open and there stood the sheriff. He saw Dean and came over to our table.

"How you and you new two newlyweds doin'?" he asked in a friendly voice.

"Just find sir," Dean said, shaking his hand, then pointing to Evan. "Evan this is Jimmy, our sheriff."

"Nice to meet you," Evan nodded.

"You come in here to get a bite?" Dean asked.

"Yes and no," he replied confusingly enough. "This is my wife's place, and I was gonna eat me some lunch, but I just came in to tell Debbie I got a call about a disturbance at that drive-in burger joint down the way. It's your brother I hate to say it Lizzy."

"You mean the famous Douglas Cole?" Evan laughed.

"Famous for gettin' into trouble," the sheriff answered, looking a bit agitated that he had to postpone his lunch for him.

Tosha had just come up with our food and put it all down in the proper places, and all I could do was shake my head. I thought Douglas had done gotten past that rebellion stage, but I guess not.

We scarfed up what we could, paid the bill and were right behind the sheriff as he responded to the call he had gotten. We had just about gotten to where I work when I saw Douglas running away. There were three or four boys chasing after him. I told Evan to turn and catch up with him, and did just so as quickly as he possibly could. Douglas reached the car and I opened the door to where he could hop in hurriedly. He was sweating up a storm and panting like one of them old hound dogs that go running around by Ma and Pa's, trying to stir up trouble. And I suppose he's more similar to them than I realized.

"What in God's name was you doin' little brother?" I scolded.

Evan jumped in without notice. "Now listen to what the boy's got to say now BJ. I'm sure he's got a good explanation for why them boys was chasing him. Maybe they was trying to rob him or somethin' like that."

"For what? He ain't got two dimes to rub together. What would they be tryin' to rob him for?"

"Yeah!" Douglas insisted. "They was robbers!"

"Oh come on Douglas," I blurted out, then turned to Evan. "And you...takin' up for the little trouble maker."

"Boys will be boys B.J. It's a fact."

Dean and Lizzy followed us out to Ma and Pa's and turned in behind us, pulling off to the side. And as I got out, I heard Douglas say "thanks man!" to Evan. It came close to infuriating me, but I let it go. I wanted to deal with the moment at hand, which was carrying Douglas inside and making sure Ma and Pa were aware of what he'd done, even though I wasn't quite sure what happened.

Douglas hopped out and I was right behind him. The way I looked at it, he might be an close to an adult age wise, but his mentality was that of a five year old...always had been.

Ma came out and Pa was right behind her. "What's goin' on Betty Jean?" Pa said, crossing his arms and putting on his mean face, the one I was always afraid of.

"Douglas started a ruckus in town," I replied. "The sheriff told us about it and we followed him. We caught Douglas runnin' from some ole boys up from the drive-in."

Turning to his wild-eyed son, he burst out, "You git yourself in your room and wait. I'll tear you up boy...gettin' the law after ya."

"But Pa…"

"No buts boy…you heard me."

Douglas made it about to the doorway, and then he turned back. "Don't none a ya'll wanna listen to me. I been tryin' to tell ya what happened. I wished I was gone from here. I might as well be."

He slammed the screen door and stomped inside.

"You mind sir?" Evan said, stepping towards the door.

"What are you doin'? " I asked, wondering what crazy idea he had going through that brain of his.

"I figure he'll talk to me better than he will family. It's worth a try…right?"

Shrugging my shoulders, Pa nodded in agreement and just a few moments later, he came back out with Douglas by his side.

"Now I ain't no psychiatrist or nothin' like that," Evan said respectfully, "But I think if somebody would just listen to him, you might learn a lot more than just jumping to conclusions."

"What are ya sayin' Evan?" Ma asked sweetly.

Evan glanced over at Douglas, "Tell'em what you told me."

My little brother stuttered a little, then started. "Well," he said. "I went down to get me a burger with Leo and David Lee, and that's when I saw'em."

"Saw who?" Pa asked, trying to keep his calm.

"Them boys messin' with Tricia," he replied. "Heck Pa…you always taught me to protect women folk, and that's what I was doin' Pa. I was just doin' like you taught me. And all I get for it, is get yelled at."

Pa lowered his head. I could tell he felt bad for getting onto him and not giving him the chance to explain. At the same time, I felt pretty bad myself. Evan kept staring at me as if I had turned into some type of demon with my brother. That's when I went to Douglas and put my hand on his shoulder.

"I'm sorry little brother," I whispered apologetically.

"I didn't hear ya sis," he replied, wanting everyone to hear me apologize...a rare occurrence in our family.

"I said I'm sorry!" even louder.

He grinned from ear to ear, but I could tell he was still waiting to hear the same from Pa. Although I wasn't sure Pa would admit being wrong, I could see it on his face regardless.

"Son," Pa said in a low voice. "I gotta say I'm proud you was tryin' to protect that girl you care about."

"Really!" Douglas replied, almost in shock to hear such words from his mouth.

"Yeah, well, I guess I was wrong."

They both nodded and grinned as if to say, "It's okay."

Evan stood there still and silent. I was proud of him for doing such a good deed. It was strange for someone Douglas hardly knew, to make us all think about the way we always treated him. For the most part, he deserved his punishment, but then again, he never was given much chance to explain. Pa usually just assumed he'd done what somebody said and took that to be that.

We started to leave when Ma came out to the car.

"Why don't you leave Cody with me and your Pa...just for the day? I'll keep little Angel too. Ya'll four can go off and do what you want," she said, motioning to Lizzy.

I figured I might enjoy some time alone with Evan since we had made everything official and Lizzy sure didn't mind the time alone with Dean. Pa took Cody and Ma cradled Angel. They hurried inside soon after.

Dean and Lizzy backed out and were on their way home I figured, but before we left, Evan turned facing me.

"What?" I questioned, noticing the way he was looking at me.

"He ain't a bad kid like you said."

Looking down, "I know…don't remind me. I feel bad enough as it is."

"Just try and ask questions from now on. Maybe that's why he rebelled to begin with…because nobody bothered to ask him questions."

"Maybe so," I replied. "But I know he set the woods on fire that one time."

He laughed, started up the car and started down the winding road to town.

"I wanna take you somewhere," he said in a flash, as if he had just gotten a grand idea.

"And where might that be?"

"It's a surprise!"

"Hmmm," I sounded.

"Is that a good hmmm, or a bad hmmm?"

"I'll answer that when we get to where you're takin' me."

When we got to town he turned then he turned again going towards Rich Mountain. And as we started to climb the huge mound, turn after turn, I noticed his hand began to crawl across the seat, finding a resting spot on my knee. That touch alone gave me a tingling feeling all over, and he could tell it by the way my body shivered the moment his hand came into contact with me.

"You cold?" he asked, grinning cleverly.

"I'm alright," I replied. "Just keep your eyes on the road. I ain't never been one to much like heights."

"Hmmm," he sounded.

"No…no Evan Bain. Don't you go foolin' 'round here on the mount. Shoot you're liable to wreck us down there for sure if ya do."

"Baby I'd never do that to you."

I was hoping he wasn't storyin', but deep down I figured he was thinking of tricking me in some sense.

As I remembered from my last trip up there, the view was nothing short of spectacular. I was still afraid to look too much, but with him, I didn't fear it near as bad. He seemed to calm my uncertainties and replace them with self-assurance that we'd be just fine. It was strange, but it was like he was the other part of me, the one God meant for me to be with. It was in the way he talked to me, the way he looked at me, and lastly, the way he showed his affection to me.

When we reached the top and turned around the last winding curve, he pulled into the parking lot. There stood the hotel big and beautiful overlooking the magnificent view of the many hills looking as though they overlapped one another. Once we had stopped, I wasn't nearly as afraid of heights.

"Come on," he said, taking my hand firmly and leading me down to a trail that started at the bottom of these wooden steps.

"Where we goin'?"

"You'll see." he insisted.

"But it's freezin' out here Evan."

"I'll keep you warm baby. You ain't gotta worry about that, B'sides, this won't take long."

"But..."

"Shhh, just humor me okay," he said, whispering in my ear then sweetly kissing my cheek.

"Alright Mr. Bain, but if I catch pneumonia from bein' out here like this, you're gonna be the one that's gonna take care a me."

"I wouldn't want nobody else to take care of you baby," he retorted thoughtfully, winning more and more points with each word spoken.

We walked a little ways, following this slightly narrow trail that led through the wood that was located at the side of the mountain. I was very careful to watch where I stepped for fear I'd slip and that would be the end of me.

"What'cha thinkin'? " he asked, considering I was being so very quiet.

"Oh, nothin' really. Just thinkin' how beautiful it is up here. It's a sight I gotta say."

"It's right up here baby…not too much further."

"What?"

"Patience…patience…patience my dear," he replied, squeezing my hand for reassurance. "I swear, you're more hard headed than I thought."

"I am not."

"Okay," he said. "You're not."

I knew he was only saying that to pacify me, but that was alright. I was glad he felt like he needed to make me happy.

"It's just around the corner."

I didn't even bother to ask what because I knew he'd say I was impatient again, so I just kept my mouth shut and waited to see what was so dad-blamed important for him to show me. Anyway, I hoped it wouldn't take too much longer because my fingers were about to freeze plum off my hands.

He stopped, put his hands over my eyes and placed me in front of him, walking me a few more feet.

"Come on Evan," I said. "Let me see what you're so dead set on me seein'."

"You sure you're ready?"

"I been ready since we started down this trail…now hurry up already."

He took his hands away and for that first few seconds I felt queasy. We were standing at the edge of what seemed to be a cliff. There was a tiny rail, but it didn't seem like it would keep anyone from falling off. Actually, it was no more than a few pieces of wood that made up what looked like railings.

There were grayish white rocks beneath our feet and Evan was holding me tightly. Suddenly my fear of heights came up on me in the most fierce way. I started trembling and the view down didn't help one single bit.

"Back up Evan," I stuttered, my voice shaky and short. "We're too close."

"I gotcha B.J. I won't let nothin' happen to you."

"I know you wouldn't intentionally, but I'd feel better if you just moved back a little."

He felt me shaking all over and started to do as I asked when the rocks under my feet made me lose my footing.

4

As if I were in the middle of a horrible nightmare, in slow motion, I began to fall. I still felt Evan's hands trying to hold onto me, but they were slipping the further I fell. Suddenly I stopped. I was dangling from the steep drop off with nothing to hold onto but one hand of Evan's. He was clinching tight to me, but my panic was purely unexplainable. I could just see myself falling the rest of the way down onto the huge, sharp rocks below like a rag doll just waiting to be mangled as I landed abruptly.

"E…Evan!" I stammered, tears beginning to pour rapidly down my terror stricken face. "p…please help me!"

I could hear his heavy breathing giving me the signal that he was just as terrified as I was, and his strength was the only thing keeping me where I was…still hanging.

"Baby, don't worry," he muttered, scrambling to pull me back up to him.

My biggest fear flashing in front of my face…leaving my son without his mom or his dad.

Inch by inch, he finally took a hold of me with both hands, careful not to slip himself. I knew if he wasn't careful, we would both be dead.

"Be careful Evan!"

"I'm just worried about gettin' you back up baby…just hold on. Just a little bit more."

With all of his efforts, the edge wasn't very stable and a slew of tiny rocks came plummeting down in my face the more he moved. All of the sudden I was so frightened, my entire body went limp and I lost all consciousness. I wasn't sure if I was going to live or die, but regardless, as I was taught from the time I was a little girl, my life was in the hands of God and nobody else.

When my eyes opened, I was in the arms of the man who was trying so extensively to save me. I felt bits of rock in my eye and I wanted to rub them, but he told me to be still. In just a moment, he found what was hindering my vision and discarded it.

"There," he said, stroking my hair slowly. "I told you not to worry."

That's when I stared out at the mountains and the extraordinary drop I almost used as my means for the end of my life.

"I was so scared Evan. I thought I was gonna leave everybody I love. I was afraid Cody was gonna be left without me."

Shaking his head, "I never woulda let that happen baby…never!"

"And I was scared I'd leave you too. I don't ever want anybody to feel the way I did when Lonnie died."

Slightly grinning, he replied sincerely, "Well…if you had fallen, I would have felt just like the guy in the story."

"What story?"

"The story about this place…about "Lover's Leap." I probably would've been so heartbroken that I'd a been right behind you baby."

"Don't be silly," I replied, disbelieving the words he had just said.

Looking down then into my eyes, he finished, "I've never felt this way about anyone before Betty Jean. And the way I see it, if I did live after you died, I'd only compare every other woman I'd meet, to you."

"Is that right?" I said, still trying to gain my composure and calm down.

"And let me tell you…nobody would even come close."

Wrapping my arms around him, I held on as tightly as I could. In his arms I felt more than safe, and at that moment, I knew he had saved me…not only from dying literally, but also from dying emotionally.

"Thank you," I whispered, expressing the emotion that was overwhelming my heart.

"For what?""

"For bein' who you are that's all…just for bein' who you are."

He scooted back further, making sure we weren't anywhere near close to the edge of the cliff, and he held me in his arms like a little baby as he stood up and carried me away from that place which I thought might be the last view I ever saw. Then he stopped.

"You are ready to go home aren't you?" he asked, trying to crack a joke.

"What do you think?"

"Just checkin'" he smiled, kissing my forehead and following down the trail all the way down to where we parked.

"I can walk," I said, clearing my throat, just about to the car.

"You sure? I don't mind carrying you at all. In fact," he said. "I kinda enjoy it."

"You do…do ya?"

"Without a doubt!"

Giving in to his charms, I let him cradle me in his strong arms the rest of the way to the car. When he started to put me down, I didn't remove my arms from around his neck. It seemed so natural to be that way.

"Now I can't carry you the rest of the way home baby. I would if it wasn't so far."

Peering at him as if he were my night in shining armor, I didn't say a word. There were a few people walking by, but I pretended there was no one around but he and I.

"What's that look for?"

"Just lookin' at the man I love…that's all."

Letting out a sign of relief, he gave me a short, sweet, sincere kiss.

"What was that for?" I asked, repeating his question to me.

"Just kissin' the woman I love…that's all."

I normally wasn't one to blush by no means, but I think he might've made me a little with that engaging remark.

Brushing his face with my small hands that were still a little shaky, "Let's go home please."

"Anything you want," he replied, still staring me in the eye. "You probably could use a nap."

"That sounds good to me."

We made our way to the car and he helped me in then shut the door after I was situated. The drive down the mountain was a lot slower than on the way up. I think he was just as shaky as I was considering we both came only inches from plunging down God knows how far. Truth be known, those few moments of fear, helped me to better sort out my priorities…even though I thought I already had them sorted out pretty good.

"You okay?" he asked, grasping my hand and squeezing it securely.

"I'm fine. I'm just glad you were there," I answered. "Just do me one favor will ya?"

"Anything."

"Don't take me back up there okay. It's beautiful and all, but…uh, well, I'd just a soon keep my feet on solid ground if ya know what I mean."

"You got it…no more mountain, or at least not 'Lover's Leap'."

The remainder of the drive was peaceful, or as peaceful as it could be after such an experience. We didn't even bother to go by Lizzy and Dean's. Instead, we just went back to my house. I was sure my sister wanted to be alone with her husband, and I was ready for a short nap to try and get over the accident on the mountain. If nothing else, I'd have a sexy man to snuggle up with while I did so.

He pulled up and parked just in front of the porch and jumped out, running around to my side before I could even reach for the handle.

"Goodness Evan…you're actin' like I'm crippled or somethin'."

"No baby, you just deserve to be treated like a lady and that's exactly what I'm trying to do," he replied with the perfect answer.

Taking my hand, he helped me up the steps and opened the front door for me.

"I could get used to this ya know."

"I hope so," he answered, going on in my room and turning back the covers. "Now, you take a nap and I'll be right back."

"Where you goin'?"

"It's a surprise. Now you lay your pretty little head down and relax. When you wake up I'll be here."

"But…"

"There you go again," he interrupted. "That stubborn part of you just won't stay in for too long will it?"

"Fine then," I said. "I'll take a nap, but I'll still be wonderin' what you're up to."

"Wonder all you want baby, but you'll find out *after* you get some rest."

I was snowed under by his excessive concern and earnest caring for me. It reminded me of how Lizzy was when she first met Dean. I recall her talking about how he made her feel like a princess, like no other woman could compare to her. Evan made me feel the same way. It was something I didn't think I'd ever find again, but then again, Ma always told us girls that love don't find you when you're lookin'…it's when you look away that it sneaks up on ya.

Although I was trying to keep from going to sleep because of my curiosity, it didn't help. My eyes drooped and drooped until I was no longer in the world of reality, but instead in a world of fantasy and dreams. My mind was floating in a place where things seemed impossible and the reality of real life was so very far away.

I found myself once again, dangling at the edge of the cliff. I looked down and it appeared to be nothing short of a bottomless pit, not end in sight. Holding on tightly, I looked up to where Evan was standing. His hand kept reaching for me, but the more he extended his arm, the further away he seemed. Little by little, one finger a time, I just couldn't hold on any longer. I kept pleading for him to reach me, but by then, I couldn't see him anymore.

Twisting and trying my best to keep my grip onto the edge just above me, my efforts were fruitless. Before I knew it, I began to fall. Gasping for air, I sat straight up in my bed, still trying to catch my breath. Then I got to thinking. One of my greatest fears was the one thing I had confronted and conquered, but that didn't make the experience any less terrifying.

I looked around and it was already dark. Even though the days were much shorter, I still couldn't believe I had slept for so long. I must've been asleep for hours, but I felt like I still needed to get a few more Z's.

Stretching my arms up to the ceiling, I heard my body start to creak and crack in ways I never remembered it doing before. It almost sounded like the way Ma's bones popped each time she'd take a step. If that were true, I knew I was getting old in too much of a hurry.

My eyes were glued shut from sleep that had formed while I was reliving the incident from earlier in the day and I wiped them clean, trying to focus. There was little or no light that I could see and my first thought drifted off to where Evan was. He had told me he'd be here when I woke, but I didn't see hide nor hair of him anywhere.

I flung the covers off me, what little I didn't already kick off, and I went to the small mirror I had hanging on the wall. It was one I got from my grandparents. It was round and worn, but the marks in it seemed to symbolize a special time in their life, all their hardships and accomplishments. It always gave me great pleasure because I was always looking at myself. I was bad about that. I always worried about how I looked regardless if anyone was around or not. My hair was all messed up and I had lines across my face from where I was lying on the pillow. I'm sure I looked totally ridiculous.

Sliding my small feet across the wooden floors that graced my small cabin, moving fast just didn't seem to be in me at the moment. I was still trying to find my way back to the real world and away from the land of sleep. That's when I noticed a hint of light coming from the other room. It wasn't much, but it was enough to guide me.

"Evan!" I hollered out, but no answer came. So I just followed the light to see where it would lead me.

Turning the corner into the living room, there stood Evan. Two red candles were lit, one on each end of the coffee table, and two plates of food. I couldn't stop staring at Evan though. He had changed clothes. He had on a starched white shirt that set off his complexion, blue jeans, and a pair of boots that made him look even taller than he already was.

"What's all this?" I asked, still rubbing my eyes a little.

"Dinner," he replied, spreading out his arms.

Not aware of it, I was grinning from ear to ear. Even though I didn't look like a princess, he darn sure was treating me that way.

"What's the occasion?"

"Us," he replied, short and sweet. "Besides, I thought you'd be starved by now."

"Where'd you pick it up at?"

"Pick it up?" he asked, with the strangest look.

"Yeah."

"Baby I cooked."

"Come on now Evan. You expect me to believe you cooked dinner. I didn't even hear you. And I'm a darn sound sleeper."

"Believe it or not," he said. "But I used to be a cook in the service, at least for a little while. I learned a lot of short cuts and I can make a feast for a crowd like you never seen before."

I was overcome by his abilities and his wanting to do something so nice for me. A man in the kitchen was a hard thing to imagine. Pa always used to say it was a woman's place to cook and a man's place to bring home the bacon. I suppose that's the way it went most of the time, but Evan was bound to change such thoughts.

"Just let me go change. I feel kinda...well, just not suitably dressed," I said, turning to go in my room to see what sexy thing I could find to impress him with.

Before I could even turn the corner, he had a hold of my arm and stopped me...not in a mean way...mind you, but in more of a sincere kind of way.

"What?" I inquired, curious why he thought it so desperate to stop me in my tracks.

"You look perfect baby...just perfect."

"But my hair...my clothes," I continued.

"There you go again," he muttered, shaking his head from side to side.

"Now what are you talkin' 'bout?"

"I'm gonna shake that stubbornness outa you one of these days B.J. That's for sure."

"Then I'll eat in these raggedy old clothes...if that's what you want."

Laughing, he led me to the couch, put a pillow down on the floor for me and one for him on the opposite side. The light the room was wonderfully romantic. It gave me a new view of his handsome face and his eyes shimmered even more as the light from those flickering candles created the most amazing flecks show up in his eyes.

Looking down at the plate in front of me, I was clearly amazed. I could tell he had gone through a lot of trouble just for me and I was more than flattered. Then he pulled out two wine glasses. Shoot the only glasses I'd ever drank from weren't glad at all, but hard plastic instead. I just didn't know what to think.

"Is that all?" I asked, smiling.

"Nope," he answered, lifting up a bottle of red wine. "A little something special for a special lady."

"I ain't ever drank wine before," I said surprised, as he poured a little in my tall glass slowly and seductively.

"Well, there's a first time for everything Betty Jean."

He lifted up his glass and I did the same. "What should we drink to?" he inquired, his eyes still peering at me.

Thinking for a few seconds, "How about this night? It won't ever come again."

"To tonight!" he said heartily, barely touching his glass with mine.

"To tonight."

A slight "ting" and we took sips from the elegant looking drinking glasses I was pleasured to use. The wine was in between bitter and sweet, but tasty just the same. And when we sat them down, Evan's hand slid underneath the table.

"What are you doin'?"

He didn't say a word, he just kept feeling around until I could tell by the look on his face that he had in his hand exactly what he was looking for.

"Here it is," he said, slowly pulling his hand out.

I started to look, when he suddenly put it behind his back

"Patience…patience Betty Jean."

Shaking my head, "I swear Evan, you give me fits. I don't ever know what you're up to."

"And I hope you never do. It's the mystery that keeps a relationship fresh and exciting," he grinned.

"Fresh and exciting huh?"

"Yeah, you know. Some folks…after they've been together for some time, routine sets in and nothing's different. I don't ever want that to happen."

"So what's behind your back?"

"Alright," he replied, laughing at my impatience, "If you insist, but don't be expecting me to give in to you all the time now."

"I'll remember that!" I said playfully, as I watched him pull his hand from behind his back, grinning all the while.

5

Waiting impatiently, in the midst of his large, manly hand, was a small package. It was oblong shaped and wrapped up in paper that was shiny and pearl white in color with a matching bow. The bow was tied ever so uniquely and as he placed it in my hand, I just held it for a moment, scared of what I might find when the paper was unraveled and the bow was removed.

"You were so anxious…now look at ya," Evan shook his head.

"Just enjoying the moment that's all."

"You'd enjoy it a lot more if you'd only open it. I swear…"

A smile jumped out with his remark, and with two fingers I grabbed one end of the bow, untying it slowly, savoring the anticipation. The paper was so elegant, I hated to rip into it like I used to on Christmas morning when I was a kid, but after a moment of dithering, I did just that. My patience ran out and my anxiousness overpowered my actions without warning.

When the paper was laid to the side. I took in a soothing breath and held the top, lifting it with ease. What I saw was surprising.

"Do you like it Betty Jean? Tell me the truth now. I don't want you actin' like you do when you don't," he said as I sat there staring at the gift I'd just opened.

Without a word, I lifted it out at a snail's pace, studying its beauty. In my hand, I held a silver chain with a smooth silver half of a heart dangling from it. Beneath the chain was a piece of paper. Still holding that jewel of a present in my hand, I unfolded the small piece of paper to see what it was. This is what it read:

> *This heart is just a symbol*
> *With half for you to wear.*
> *Showing that you have my heart,*
> *In love and in despair.*
> *Take this heart and wear it,*
> *Making me always next to you,*
> *And I'll have the other half with me*
> *Confirming this is true.*
> *This heart is just a symbol*
> *You won't ever be alone…*
> *With my heart around your neck*
> *I'm never ever gone.*
>
> EVAN

I folded the piece of paper back up and felt a single tear running ever so slowly down my right cheek. He was so different from anyone I'd ever met. There was something about him that kept me on my toes and that same thing always made me wonder what he was going to do next.

"Well!" he said, raising his voice, getting a little impatient himself. "say something."

"It's beautiful Evan, but you didn't have to."

"I wanted to," he replied, unbuttoning a few buttons on his shirt and revealing to me the chain he wore with the exact same heart, only the other half. "No matter where I am, I want you to know I'm next to you."

"They're only necklaces Evan."

"They're not only necklaces B.J. I wanted you to wear my heart next to yours, and yours is next to mine. Some folks might say I'm a corny romantic whose lost his mind, but I like to see myself as the kind of man all men should be."

"And what kinda man is that?"

"The kind that sees his woman as his other half, not his slave…the kind who knows there's a meaning to life and that meaning starts the minute we meet the perfect woman."

Shaking my head, "You got that from a book didn't ya Mr. Bain."

"Is that what you think?"

Pausing, "Sometimes I think you're too perfect for me…ya know?"

"No," he answered. "Truth be known, I'm the one who should be lucky by being here."

He stood up and walked around, sitting on the couch behind me. He took the chain from my hand as I held my hair up so he could clasp such an offering. When he was done, I released my hair and I felt Evan brushing it to one side. His warm breath on my neck was felt immediately, along with short kisses and sexy massaging from his wet tongue moving in a circular motion. I began to get chill bumps, but with my head still leaned to the side, I let him feast on the softness of my skin. Just the feel of such a display, made me want him even more. It was all I could do to keep myself from turning to him and taking him…one woman to one man, showing him all of the affection I had been holding inside of me with all the strength I had. But I knew it wasn't the time. I kept thinking with all my might about how special it was for Lizzy and Dean to wait, and I wanted to do the same thing. I was determined that this relationship would be different, special... better than the rest.

Trying to stop him from getting me any more stimulated, "Aren't you hungry?"

"Hmmm," he moaned, continuing his soft erotic kisses around my neck and shoulders, then whispering, "Are you?"

Pulling my shoulders up to my ears, making him stop those irresistible advances, he got quiet.

"Come on Evan. I wanna taste this delicious meal you fixed for me. B'sides, I don't recall a man ever cookin' for me before. I wanna enjoy it."

He let out a huge sign as if he were utterly disappointed that I spoiled such a wonderful moment, but I knew if I let things go much further, I wouldn't have been able to stop myself from doing what I really wanted to do...making love to him in the most passionate way. Soon enough though, his disappointed look turned to a smile. I knew he understood me and my wants.

Our glasses weren't even half full, so he poured a little more. We both took a bite of the meal on our plates. It almost melted in my mouth it was so delicious. Closing my eyes, I savored every ounce of flavor within it, letting it grace every taste bud, then swallowing, ending with a "mmmm."

"Good?" he asked.

"I didn't know you could cook like this. I'm impressed."

"Your Pa don't cook?" he inquired, taking bite after bite.

"My Pa? Heck no," I answered. "He always sits and waits for Ma to whip somethin' up and fix his plate for him. I guess that's the way that generation is. He always acted like it wasn't the man's place to cook…it was the woman's."

"Oh well," he shook his head. "No disrespect to your Pa or nothin' like that, but I think it's a give and take sort of thing. You know, if you do for her she'll do for you. It's not supposed to be all take or all give."

"I like your thinkin' Mr. Bain."

"Would you *please* stop calling me that?" he begged with the cutest look on his face.

"Why? I think it's kinda sexy."

Tilting his head a little sideways, I could tell he was thinking on that reply. "Well, then, by all means, it's Mr. Bain to you…B.J."

Laughing at him, I continued eating. He had made a wonderful combination of roast beef, scalloped potatoes, fresh black-eyed peas, and hot buttered rolls to top it off. I was used to pinto beans and cornbread most of the time, even though Ma would sometimes cook a big meal on special occasions. She said pinto beans were cheap enough and they had plenty of protein. As far as a really nice meal, especially one with such terrific company, it was a rarity.

"Another toast," he said, holding up his glass when we were about done eating.

"To what?"

"To the most beautiful woman I've ever met."

Holding up my glass, I said, "To Lisa."

I almost saw a hint of anger fly from his once pleasant expression, and I knew I best take back what ignorance that flung from my mouth.

"I was only kiddin' Evan. Please don't be mad."

"I'm not," he said, holding his hand out and grasping mine. "I just wish I'da never told you."

"Why? I want you to be honest with me."

"Let's try this one more time," he said, lifting up his glass again. "To the most beautiful woman I've ever met…to you Betty Jean."

That's when I held mine up as well, "To the most handsome and loving man I've ever met…to you Evan."

Once more, our glasses made that "ting" sound and smiles followed. A moment earlier I was afraid I said something to offend him. That was the last thing I wanted to do. But in that moment, I realized, he didn't anger easily…it was just the opposite. I could tell by the way he looked at me, all he wanted, was to satisfy me. He didn't want to hurt me.

Dinner was finished and I sat there with my hands resting on my stomach as if I had eaten far too much. Evan pretty much did the same thing, then he came and sat next to me on the floor, leaning up against the front of the couch.

"You just couldn't stay away now could ya?" I teased.

"Not a chance," he answered, lifting his arm up and letting it fall around me as if it belonged there and nowhere else.

"You're daddy musta been a sweet talker too."

"Why do you say that?"

"Well, they say boys follow behind what they learn from their daddy's, and if that's so, I might wanna meet him," I kidded.

Tickling me from both sides, his hands crawling all over my body, the laughter he was pulling out of me, was something I needed desperately. Just being around him made me smile, but as Ma always told me, "laughter is the best medicine."

After such horseplay, we got very still. Scooting as close to him as I could get, my head rested on his shoulder like it were a reflex action, finding the perfect spot. My hand kept holding onto the necklace gracefully placed around my neck, and just feeling of it made me realize what a wonderful thing I'd found in him.

Through the window, all I could see was darkness, but the sounds were very clear, just as they were many times before. The howling of the wind almost seemed eerie, but only when I was alone. The sounds of the few creatures that still dared to roam in the cold, overlapped one another, creating a melody unlike any other. It sounded like a song God had taught them to do in unison, as one creature…one species.

Still in his loving arms, my mind was swept back to another time… to when I was a little girl no more than seven or eight. I remembered sitting on the floor, the winter already taking hold, and my grandpa dang near dancing around to the sounds he was making on his old fiddle. The cheer in his face was one I knew I'd never forget, and the sound of the music, was etched in my inner most memories. He always said there wasn't much to do when old Mr. Winter showed his face, except for sing and dance. His hands were swift in the way he created such a country sort of orchestra, and all of us kids would clap our hands until we were too tired to clap any longer.

Coming back to the spot I was sitting…reality of the moment, the wind still howling and the animals still making their noises, I couldn't help but smile. I had nothing to frown about. In my arms was the most caring and loving man; I had a handsome, wonderful son, and nothing seemed out of place at that point in my life. I had known disappointment in the past, but my future didn't look that way. It looked brighter and more in tune with the way I wished things would be.

"What have you got turnin' in that mind of yours B.J.?" he asked squeezing me slightly.

"Just thinkin' of my grandpa, and how he used to make me smile."

"How'd he do that?"

Turning to him, "Bein' himself I suppose. He was always so carefree. You could tell it by the look on his face and the way he smiled. There was somethin' about him that always made me wonder if he was an angel sent to us to make our poor, country existence, happier…ya know?"

With a sign, "Yeah, I know what'cha mean. My grandma was that way," he said. "She'd be in the kitchen cookin' her heart out and the whole time, singing and humming as if she was the happiest person alive."

"It's somethin' ain't it? They probably had less than us, but it just didn't matter."

Being quiet for a moment, he answered, "I guess that oughta teach us a lesson."

"What lesson is that Evan?"

"Some folks think they got to have what they want to make them happy, but what they don't see, is that they'd be happy as long as they have what they need."

"Yeah," I muttered, burying my head even further into his chest.

"And you know what Betty Jean?"

"What?"

"There's a lot I dream of having and many things I want, but…"

"But what?"

"But I know what I need," he continued. "I need my family, my dignity, happiness, and I need someone to love."

"Me too."

"I don't need it anymore though…I already have it. It's been a tough road, but I finally got through to you. I finally got you to understand what I've been trying to tell you from the first time we met. You're special and unique…unlike anyone I've ever known."

"I feel the same way Evan. Even though I didn't want to admit how attracted I was to you at first, I knew it deep down. I struggled with it every time I was in the same room with you."

Stoking my hair and twisting a few strands here and there, we seemed to melt into the moment. It was one I didn't want to leave. Being there in that way, I felt him next to me, his scent was that of the most masculine of men, and his touch was as tender as any I'd known. With all of that, my mind did start to wonder. I wanted to ask him a question, but I didn't want to offend him once more. I was curious about his past. He knew all about mine and I saw it fit that I knew just the same.

Getting my courage up, I lifted my head and our eyes met, like two rays of light not turning away from one another.

"Evan…"

"Yeah," he responded attentively.

"I don't wanna make you mad again, but I have to ask you one question."

"I'm listening," he replied.

"How did you feel about Lisa? I mean…did you think there was a future or anything like that or was it just…"

"It was nothing," he interrupted. "I told you that. I was young and I didn't know what I wanted."

"But I'm asking you if you…"

"Loved her?" he said, ending my sentence.

"Yes! Did you love her?"

Surprisingly enough, with that question, he hesitated, taking his eyes away from me. Glancing towards the window then back to where I was patiently waiting for his reply.

6

His wavering made me wonder what was going through his heart and mind. I couldn't really tell from the look on his face. To be honest, it didn't have any sort of distinction, but this feeling inside of me, wasn't a good feeling at all.

Answering finally, "I used to care."

"You mean you used to love her?"

"I don't know B.J. I was young. I'm not so sure I knew what love was. I think that I thought I did, but now I know what true love really feels like," he softly spoke. "And please don't take this in a way to where you think I don't love you…because it don't have anything to do with you."

Lowering my head, I didn't really know what to think of the comments he'd just made. It was nice to know how he felt about me without a doubt, but at the same time, he seemed unsure about his feelings that might still be lingering inside of him about this woman in his past. There was something I wasn't catching in between his words…something that wasn't spoken, but still there.

The only think that kept racing in and out of my head, was the fear…the fear I might end up left alone just like her…like Lisa. He said it himself. He thought he loved her. Maybe, just the same, he thinks he loves me, but might figure out later on, he really doesn't. Even though I was always the one trying to teach my sister how to think positively, it was ironic how she and I had changed places in such a short time.

"Betty Jean," he muttered. "I'm not sure why we're even talkin' about this. You took my heart the moment I saw you."

"I feel the same way Evan, but I just don't want you to figure out later on that I ain't the one for you after I done fell hard."

His hands came up and rested on my face, gently stroking me with his masculine fingers. "Baby," he whispered. "That was then...but this is now. I know what I want. Back then, I was only wandering around in a daze. When I went into the service, I found myself. But when I met you, I found the other half of me."

Grinning and slightly shaking my head, "Why is it you always know just what to say?"

"I don't...I'm just sayin' what I'm feeling. And right now, I feel like the luckiest man alive. Please don't ruin it with talk of the past. You know as well as I do...if you let the past dictate the future, the future's not even worth living. I don't wanna dwell on what used to be. I'd rather think of what will be...and that's us...together."

With such poetic words, I started to feel guilty I even brought up such a conversation. For a little while, I turned the most romantic evening, into a battleground of defending the past instead of leaning on what the future held.

"I'm sorry Evan. I didn't mean to..."

Stopping my words from being uttered, he let our lips connect like two extremely strong magnets, almost impossible to pull apart. His hand went around my small waist and rubbed my back up and down as our tongues began to wrestle in such a deep and intensely passionate kiss. I felt all the tension from moments earlier dissipate and as my eyes were closed, fireworks were going off in my mind. Every sensation I was trying to avoid began to flutter throughout my entire body, and the feel of his touch was almost more than I could handle.

I could hear his breathing get heavier as he pressed up against me, and then, without a word, he stopped, lifted me up, and started walking to my room. One part of me kept yelling "NO," but the other, was more submissive than ever.

We made it to the foot of my bed and my heart was pounding in my chest so terribly, I thought it might just jump clean out of me before I knew it. I didn't fear anything, especially when he sat me down on the edge of the bed.

Still hearing the noises combined outside, he kneeled in front of me. His eyes were affixed on mine, and I was utterly speechless. The way he seemed to take me without question, was so very seductive that all I wanted to do was lie there and let him devour me like a love crazed man willing to do anything to show his affection.

It was dark in my room, but a hint of light still gleamed through my tiny window to my left. Once again, as before, the view of his veneer look, engulfed every part of me. I wanted him more and more each moment passing, and with his subtle advances, I sat in waiting of what might happen next.

Still dressed in slouchy clothes, it didn't seem to phase him a single bit. He looked at me as if I were dressed in some sort of slinky nighty… his hands climbing their way up from my calves to my thighs.

"Evan," I whispered lightly.

"I love you Betty Jean," he said back to me, shutting me up with one long, soft, sincere kiss, sending me back off into a land of wanting and ardor of his diligence to prove to me that I was the one he loved.

My hands began to crawl around him, making a trail up and down his back in the most alluring way. That, along with the closeness we seized, made the moment come to life in the most colorful way.

Leaning back from me for a short time, he took my hands. Unsure of what he was doing, I was aware soon after. He began to kiss each and every one of my fingertips, tasting them. Chills started running up and down and all through me like a strong lightning bold of excitement, wanting more and more. Those tiny kisses seemed to arouse me even more as I sat there anticipation the all too near future.

Then, without a word, his fingers tickled my waist a hint as he grasped a hold of the bottom of my shirt, slowly but surely, raising it, revealing to him more of me than he'd ever seen before. I wanted to stop him in a way, but I was so into the moment, all I wanted to do was follow his lead and let go of my inhibitions.

Lifting my shirt over my head, his expression grew even more seductive, his eyes showing me a picture show of what was playing inside his heart. It was erotic, sweet, sincere and more loving than I ever imagined.

Kneeling back down, his arms went around me, slightly making me lean backwards. With my head resting back, that's when I felt his lips intensely touch the bottom of my stomach, touching every inch. His tongue began to twirl around and round tasting my flesh, but I didn't stop him, instead, I allowed such an action. I enjoyed the feeling it gave me.

His lips moved further up, touching every place he felt the need to stop at and linger, enticing me the entire time. Then those manly hands behind me unhooked my bra, letting it fall down, then tossed it aside.

For the first time I was showing him a side of me he'd never seen before…the side that wanted him. At first I thought I'd feel uncomfortable doing such, but it was just the opposite. I was more relaxed than I ever thought I would be. His touch was sincere and honest…just like I dreamed, and his kiss was so very tender.

Lying back on the bed completely and scooting up, he joined me… covering me, starting from my waist up. Again giving small kisses, he made his way to my chest where my breasts were showing gallantly.

His hand moved up and began touching them, lightly caressing my nipple, following that with the presence of his tongue going around and around it. I had almost forgotten such a sensation, and I couldn't help but arch my back in wanting more. I wanted so much more.

His little nibbles of love got me so stimulated, I no longer wanted to wait. I wanted to indulge in the distinct pleasures of making love to a man who loved me for who I was and nothing more. I wanted to swim in the waters of passion and find myself wet from the satisfaction of being with such an incredible, loving and sexy man.

I was so into the moment, when I heard a loud noise from outside. I thought I might have been mistaken, but if I was hearing right, it sounded like Pa's truck clamoring as it was turned off.

"Quick!" I stammered, trying to get the clothes on I had shed.

Doing so, I tried to make myself look presentable and innocent as I made my way into the living room to wait for a knock on the door. Evan wasn't far behind me, and when they finally did knock, I got up as calmly as I could and opened the door.

"Here's your little one dear," Ma said. "Your Pa and I were gonna run to town and I thought it'd be much easier without havin' to tote Cody around."

"Thanks Ma," I said, hoping that what I was doing before they showed up, didn't show on my face.

"What's wrong dear? You look a little flushed. Get some rest ya hear. You might be comin' down with that old bug goin' around," she continued.

"I will Ma…I promise."

She handed Cody to me and pecked me on the cheek. Pa was waiting in the truck and he just waved. Grinning, I waved back until they were out of sight. It was funny. I was grown and had a place of my own, but I still didn't want Pa to catch me doin' such things with a man. I guess reason bein', I knew it wasn't right, least wise not until marriage. That's what Ma always said was the right order in things.

"Hey sweetie," I uttered in baby talk. "How's my handsome boy tonight?"

The smile on his face was like seeing a rainbow after a horrible rain. And just holding him was a great feeling. Even though Evan and I were interrupted in the middle of such a heated moment, getting my baby home was worth it. I could tell he had missed me all day and with one long tight hug, I carried him into the living room where Evan sat patiently.

"There he is," Evan said, springing up from his seat to take him from me.

"You don't have to pretend you like the idea of bein' with someone who already has a child Evan…really."

"Baby, I'm not. I love you and he's a part of you. Why wouldn't I love him too?"

"Just makin' sure you ain't just tryin' to get to me a little more by bein' sweet to Cody."

Stepping to me, still holding the baby, his other arm went around me. "I think we make a good-lookin' family…don't you?"

In hopes that he was being honest and true, I replied "Yeah, I think we do. And who knows, maybe we'll extend this family one day."

A sly grin appeared suddenly, "It sure would be fun tryin' wouldn't it?"

Nudging him, "Evan Bain!"

"Just bein' honest baby…just bein' honest."

We sat down with Cody and turned on that television Dean so generously gave to me, and watched a few shows. It didn't take too awful long for Cody to decide he wanted to find his land of slumber and his eyes closed, his head resting on Evan's chest.

"I think I might need to put him in bed…ya think?"

"It looks like it," I replied. "He must be worn plum out. I suppose Pa did nothing but play with him all day."

"Yeah, you're Pa seems to be that type with these kids," he replied. "I'll be right back."

He stood up slowly, careful not to wake up my little man, and he went into the room where Cody's crib was. Staring at the T.V. I wasn't really paying attention to what I was watching. More than anything, I was thinking. I was wondering what would've happened if Ma and Pa hadn't showed up when they did. In a way, it appeared to be a sign by God almighty…a sign to let us know it's not time yet. I wasn't sure, but all I knew was that if they hadn't come when they did, there was no telling what would've happened.

"He's fast asleep baby," Evan said, entering the room again.

"Thanks."

"Uh oh," he sounded.

"What?" I asked, holding my hands out.

"Somethin's on your mind."

Crossing my arms, "Now how in the world can you tell that?"

Tilting his head to the side and shrugging his shoulder a hair, he replied, "I know you!"

"You *think* you know me."

"I know you B.J. You were thinkin' about what might've happened if your Ma and Pa didn't come by with little Cody. And you were thinkin' if it wasn't a good sign."

Amazed, but not wanting to let him know he was right, "Nope...you're totally wrong."

"I am? Then what? What was you thinkin'?"

"I was...uh, well, I..."

"I told you," he laughed as if he had me pegged.

"Maybe you're right, but how'd you know?"

"I already told you baby. I know you. I can tell by your expression, the way your eyebrows tilt and your forehead wrinkles when you're in deep thought; I can tell by the way you get this serious look when you're thinkin' of us...like you're unsure of what's happenin'."

"You're somethin' else. That's all I can say. I just wish I could read you like that."

"You can."

"How?" I asked curiously.

"Okay," he answered. "Tell me what I was thinking before your parents showed up."

"That's easy."

"It is? I was thinkin' about how it might damage our relationship to go much further so soon. I was also thinkin' about how much I respect you and how I'd never wanna do anything to disrespect someone I love."

"Oh," I muttered, once again amazed at him.

"You didn't guess that did ya Betty Jean?"

"I gotta say...I didn't, but I thought..."

Interrupting, "You thought I wanted to have sex."

"Well yeah."

Shaking his head, he kissed me on my forehead, "Baby, you and I will NEVER have sex. If we do anything, we'll make love. You have sex with someone you don't care about, but you make love to someone who holds your heart in their hand."

"Have you ever just has sex?"

"Ohhh no! I'm not answering that question," he burst out, knowing if he had answered it, I probably would have gone nuts on him.

"Never mind. I think most people have, but that doesn't matter. It's in the past."

"That's what I like to hear. I guess you're not as hard headed as I thought Mrs. Hendrix," he replied, hugging me sweetly, stroking my hair as he did so.

In his arms, I whispered very lightly, *"I'm not hard headed."*

Laughing at me, his aggravating side took over and his fingers started tickling me in places that drove me absolutely crazy. All I could do was run from him. Around the couch and table I dashed, staying more than arms length away from him. The more he tried to catch me, the quicker I became.

"You *know* I can catch ya," he stated positively.

"Sure you can," with sarcasm I continued to dodge his playful advances to me until I was plum tuckered out from running from him.

His energy never seem to cease, so I finally stopped. He snatched me up and twirled me around as if to say "you're it," as we used to do when we were kids.

"I swear Evan…you're worse than a kid," I said laughing.

"The way I look at it," he replied. "The day I stop actin' like a kid, is the day I grow old. And I don't ever plan on getting old, at least not in my mind."

"Then I suppose you'll be young forever sweetie."

The candles had burned down to where there was about half left, and the wax had ran down the side, making streaks of red. Our plates were still sitting on the table, so I figured it best I get things cleaned up.

"Nope!" he demanded. "I cooked…I'll clean."

"No!" insisting he let me. "You did enough Evan…besides, there were a few more dishes in there I needed to do."

"Only if you let me help."

"I'll say it again Mr. Bain…you're somethin' else."

Strangely enough, he and I got to work and cleaned up what little mess had been made, wiped our hands, and started back into the living room to sit down when I noticed what was going on outside. Snow was coming down pretty heavily. It was a lovely sight in one sense, but in another, terrifying. I remembered several winters when we were all stuck inside with little food because we couldn't get to town. Ma used to try and calm us by telling us we had plenty and not to worry, but I was the oldest and knew better.

"Looks like you might be stuck here for the night Evan," I stuttered.

"Would that be so bad?"

"Not bad," I replied. "Tempting is a better word."

"We're adults B.J. Besides, even if I wanted to leave, it wouldn't be safe, especially the way it's coming down out there right now."

"Yeah, well, I wouldn't want you to," I replied. "To be honest, I didn't really want ya goin' anyway."

"And I didn't want to."

Pushing away from him seriously, "We need to get somethin' straight though."

"What's that?"

"You can sleep with me, but you have to behave yourself."

"Behave myself?"

"You know what I'm sayin' Evan. I'm not one to resist such a temptation, and good Lord, are you a temptation," I finished.

"That's nice to know," he grinned.

Shoving him because of his silly remark, "I'm gonna make some hot chocolate. It's getting' chilly in here. And will you do me a favor?"

"Anything."

"Make sure the baby's covered up good. I'd hate for him to catch his death a cold."

I went into the kitchen and he went to do as I asked. His agreeability was almost astounding to me. Looking back to when we first met, he and I didn't even remotely agree on anything, but I suppose things change. He sure did anyway. I know I changed, especially having to do with my attitude.

Stirring up the hot chocolate and sipping it to make sure it was just perfect, I steadily and slowly left the kitchen, trying not to spill it on me. But as I reached the hallway, I noticed the candles were out.

"Evan!" I said as loud as I could without waking Cody.

Stepping out in front of me from the bedroom, he took both cups from me and sat them down on the table just to the right of him against the wall. My eyes were glued on him. He had taken off his shirt showing his perfectly muscular and cut physique. The only thing he had on, was a pair of black colored boxer shorts.

I stood there like a frozen statue, staring at him as if I had never seen a man before in my life, or at least not in that way, and that's when he took my hand, kissing it slowly. His charm was overflowing into every pore of my skin and even though I tried to fight it off, it didn't matter. The spell he put on me, was working successfully.

"You ready for bed?" he uttered in a slow deep voice, steering me in the direction of the room where I'd slept many nights alone.

7

Trying to gain my composure, holding back everything my mind was thinking, I followed him. His hand held mine affectionately, stroking it as we walked down the short walk to our bunk for the night. I could tell he was trying to see how far I would go, but I was willing to hold my ground and do as I believed before, even though the enticement of earlier in the evening was almost too much for me to take. Then, I wanted to set aside all my morals, but after thought, I knew the interruption was well needed.

As we entered my room, he already had the covers laid back perfectly. My pillow looked fluffed, as much as it could be, and the scent in the room was mannish, a scent coming from only one person…him.

With the wind still weeping outside and the trees that were bear were still slightly swaying, I was almost embarrassed to do as I normally did before I went to bed. Normally I would take off everything and slip on a long T-shirt, one soft to my skin. But for some reason, even after earlier events, my shyness showed through…a shyness I didn't know existed until that moment.

"Turn your head," I requested in a nice way.

"Anything for you baby," he replied, automatically turning to where he could get no glimpse of what I had to offer even though he'd seen part of me earlier in the day.

After undressing and putting on something comfortable, a long, soft white T-shirt, I climbed under the covers and situated myself, primping a bit and making sure my hair didn't look quite as bad as before.

"Okay, you can turn back around."

Still standing there looking downright too sexy for words to even describe, my eyes were on him and nothing else. His chest was big and strong, leading down to the tiny ripples in his stomach that were more appealing than I could've ever imagined. As before, my wants kept trying to override what I knew was right and wrong, but through the little will power inside of me, I held back, keeping in sight what was most important…taking things slow and easy. I didn't want to rush into anything with this man who I knew would more than likely be the one I wanted to spend the rest of my days with. I didn't want to mess up such a great thing with a few moments of unadulterated passion.

I could hear his feet sliding across my dusty hardwood floor as he slowly made his way to the other side of the bed. The entire time, he did nothing but stare at me. For a moment I felt a little uneasy, but I knew it was only a look of love…just the way I was looking at him. And I was sure he was thinking the same as me. That was the one thing that eased my mind enough to know that we could make it through the night without utter sexual contact.

He pulled back the covers and found a spot next to me in that small bed, inching over as if he were fooling me.

Yawning, "I'm so tired Evan. It's been a long day," I said, kissing him quickly and rolling over with my back to him, still fighting off the sex demon running rampant in my mind like a wild man.

"I'm tired too," he replied sleepily, masking what was truly on his mind.

He too turned in my direction and I felt his body blend with mine as he arched his massiveness next to me to where we fit together like two puzzle pieces, destined to be put together. Just feeling him against me, his manhood was evident, pressing against the very part of me that wanted him so very much. His hands roamed up and down my leg and hip, massaging and caressing in a way that made my heart beat faster and faster with each stroke, making it even harder to go along with my rational thoughts. He had a way about him that was completely and utterly irresistible. I just had to find a way to focus on something other than the man lying ever so close to me.

Whispering to me, "It feels so good to be here like this with you."

"It does feel nice," I replied, trying not to get too graphic.

"There was a time I didn't think you'd ever talk to me again."

"Well, you cured that in a hurry," I replied. "Now…let's get some sleep. There's no tellin' when Cody's gonna decide to wake us up."

"He's a good-lookin' fella. You know that don't ya?"

"You didn't have to tell *me* that. I knew that the first time I held him."

"Night baby," he said sweetly, leaning up to kiss my cheek.

"Night," I replied, pulling his arm around me even further, creating one body between the two of us.

In such a comfortable position, I felt so secure with him. His arms were like a shield from all of the hurt and pain I'd been through in the past and his love was the bond he and I finally decided to share.

Many thoughts rambling in my head made me tired, and before too long, I was fast asleep…being cradled in the arms of a man who loved me. My dreams were peaceful and full of nothing but good thoughts. But before I knew it, I heard Cody crying. I looked at the clock and it was a hair passed six. His whimpers of wanting something, rang clear.

Carefully prying Evan's arm from me, I was slow in getting up, cautious not to wake him. The undisturbed look about him, was attractive, but innocent, and I knew I could've sat there and watched him until his eyes opened to greet the day.

Cody's cries got louder and when I stood, I felt him grab a hold of my hand.

"Where you goin'?" he asked wearily.

"I'll be back," I whispered. "I'll get Cody back to sleep and I'll be back."

Rubbing his eyes that were full of sleep, he nodded in agreement and hugged the pillow next to him, again finding a spot where he was comfortable.

Picking Cody up, he immediately stopped he bellowing. Ma told me he was purely spoiled, but I refused to believe such, and before I went into the kitchen to feed him, I glanced back into my room once more. Evan was lying there half covered, his naked chest apparent to my wanting eyes. He looked like one of them models you see in those magazines, rugged and strong…the kind you stare at until you're sure a guy like that wouldn't be interested in you. But I was wrong…he was interested.

Starting to whine again, my little one was giving me a clear signal that he was hungry. I didn't hesitate any longer and into the kitchen I went, hurrying to fix him a bottle and feed him. I knew he'd go right back to sleep afterwards, for a little while anyway, and I'd have a chance to do something nice for Evan.

He ate right up, sucking the bottle dry before I knew it, and his eyes closed bit by bit as he did so, drifting off into the land of sleep he was in before he so suddenly woke me. Holding him in a tender, motherly way,

I tip-toed back to where his bed was and laid him back down, covering his tiny little body to ensure he didn't get cold.

I didn't hesitate to go back into my room. Evan look purely exhausted even though I knew he didn't do much to get that way, and I sat down on the bed, resting my hand on him, and leaning down.

"Mornin'," I whispered.

With a slight tired grin, "Mornin' baby. What time is it?"

"Early."

A short chuckle, "That tells me a lot."

"Why you wantin' to know? You got some place to go?"

Suddenly, his big strong hands grabbed me and pulled me down next to him. "The only place I wanna be…is right here. That's a promise."

"Just checkin'," I said playfully, grinning the whole time.

While he shook his head at me, I got an idea. He had treated me the night before, I thought it only fair I do the same for him.

"You sit tight and rest," I muttered, starting to get up. "I'm makin' you breakfast."

"That sounds nice baby, but wait a bit."

"Why?" I asked. "so you can keep on makin' me go crazy with all your little touches and kisses. Nope!"

As I was leaving the room, I heard him say, "Hard-headed!"

Leaning back in for just a second, I replied "You darn right."

His laughter was evident as I started into the kitchen to make a good morning feast. I didn't have a whole lot to work with, but enough just the same. I wanted to show him I was willing to do just as much for him. I was always told it was a fifty-fifty thing in a relationship and I wanted to make things right.

I put on my "kiss the cook" apron and began. I started off by cutting up potatoes. Ma used to make the most delicious fried breakfast potatoes, and I was gonna do the same. Next I made a batch of homemade biscuits like my grandma taught me how to make. I was only hoping they turned out like my grandma's when I was finished. I didn't have much in meat, but I did have a little ham steak. I got out two plates and poured two big glasses of cold milk. When the eggs and everything else was ready I fixed both plates and sat them on the table just so. Evan still hadn't gotten up, so after I grabbed the silverware, I turned to go get him, only to be surprised by that very man standing in front of me.

"Be careful now," he laughed, you might poke me if you're not careful.

"Well, I oughta. You're scared the dickens outa me."

"I'm sorry baby," he mumbled, giving me a sweet morning kiss.

"What was that for?"

"Your apron says to kiss the cook."

Grinning, "Not that I minded or anything."

"How 'bout one more then?"

Not giving an answer verbally, I did in another way, pressing my lips against his suddenly. His hands ran through my hair that wasn't the least bit perfectly fixed, but he didn't seem to mind in the least.

Stopping suddenly, "Breakfast is getting cold."

"But I'm not," he said seductively.

Swatting him away, "See what I mean Evan. You're just tryin' to see how long it'll take for me to give in to you. Well, I can tell ya right now…"

Slowing down my talk, "it probably won't be long, but stop your pushin'. Good Heaven's you're somethin'."

Leading him over to the table, we both sat down and started.

"I'm starved baby. This looks great!"

"Thanks. It's not as fancy as what you did last night, but it's food."

"Like I said baby…it looks great," he said, leaning over and barely gracing my cheek with his full and gorgeous lips.

He made me feel as if I were so very important in everything he did, no matter how little it was. That was the one thing that always rang true in in actions. I wanted to do the same for him. I knew I was nothing but an ole country girl, but I still had a few things in my mind I could do for him that would take him off guard…or at least I hoped they would.

"Uh oh," he said. "You've got that look again."

"What look?"

"You know what look."

"I don't have a clue what you're talkin' about Mr. Bain," I replied, slightly smiling at his remark.

It seemed he could read me like a book. The only problem was that I could read him nearly as well. Sometimes he seemed so very open, but other times, it was like trying to crack a safe with a lost combination.

Finishing up, he quickly got up and grabbled the plates like I had done the night before.

"What do you think you're doin'?"

"I'm gonna clean up while you get yourself and Cody dressed."

"Where we goin'?"

"To the market. Looks like you're a little low in the kitchen."

"Yeah, but…"

"No butts," he interrupted. "We're going to the market and that's that."

Not wanting to argue, I went and got dressed, fixed my hair and painted my face. Not long after, Cody began to move around, opening those beautiful blue eyes of his. He looked refreshed and ready to go, so I got him ready in a flash as well as the bag with all his things.

Evan came out from the kitchen wiping his hands, brushed by me and went to spiffy up. Him being a man, it didn't take him but two shakes to do so.

He took Cody and the bag from my hand and went outside.

"You must think I can't do nothin'," I said, wondering why he did everything for me.

"No," he answered. "It's just being respectful baby. I've seen plenty of men who don't care to do nothin' for their women, but I *am not* one of those men."

He got Cody buckled in tightly and placed a small blanket over him to keep him warm. He seemed amazing to me. His actions were unlike any man's, except for Dean maybe, but they were related so that explained it.

Driving to town, he made each curve carefully since there was still snow here and there. In some places it had already melted, but there were still patches that could've caused a terrible accident if you weren't paying attention good enough. I think he knew how that one accident affected me and he was making sure we got to where we were going slowly and safely. He seemed to have everything down pat. He knew what to say, how to act, and exactly what to do to make me feel like nothing short of a queen.

"Here we are," he said, pulling into the market.

I suppose most folks were afraid of getting iced and snowed in, especially those who lived out a bit like I did, so there was people everywhere. I was beginning to wonder if there'd even be a dozen eggs left in there the way those folks were taking bags out of that store.

"Come on code man," Evan said enthused unlocking my son and picking him up, lifting him clean into the air.

"Be careful now," I stated quickly, afraid he'd drop him.

"You're mama's a worry wart...ya know that Cody?"

Funny enough, it almost sounded like my tiny son was agreeing with him by the sounds he was making, and all I could do was shake my head from the way them two were bonding together in such a hurry. It was nice to know he would have a father figure to look up to. That was one thing I worried about soon after the death of my husband. I didn't want him having someone like Douglas to look up to. Lord help me if that had been the case.

We got in the store and there were folks scrambling around like they were never gonna have another chance to buy food again, and all Evan and I could do, was laugh at them all.

"Get what'cha need," he declared, making sure I wouldn't give him an argument for wanting to help.

"Maybe just a few things," I said. "I don't need much."

"I *said*...get what you need!"

Amidst all the people, I stopped, stepped up to him almost in slow motion and leaned up to him, kissing both him and my handsome little boy he held firmly in his arms.

"What would I do without you...without either of you?"

He let one of his hands fall free and it stopped at my face, caressing it sweetly, "You won't ever have to find out baby."

He gave me my son and went from aisle to aisle, filling the buggy full of everything from different meats, to potatoes, vegetables, baby food, coffee, and sweets for deserts.

"I'm not used to so much Evan...really!"

"Get used to it," he said. "I'm not rich like my dear cousin Dean, but I got quite a bit saved. I'll get a job and we'll be fine."

"We'll?"

"Did I stutter baby?" he answered quickly.

"No but…"

About that time, Evan's attention turned. There was a woman standing at the front of the store. She was about my height, petite and had short blonde hair. His face changed from pleasant and loving to angry and shocked. He just stood there staring at her. He seemed to be in another world. She did the same. She looked at him as if she'd found someone she had been looking for. I didn't know what to think about what was happening. His entire mood was transformed into something I'd never seen before. His hands were fidgety and the smile he always seemed to wear, was no longer, instead, it was an expression never seen by my eyes.

"I'll be right back," he said, still not taking his eyes from her.

Holding my baby in my arms tightly, embracing him, a million fears did a contagion through me. I had never seen him act in such a way that made me confused and unaware of what was going through his mind.

For a moment I watched them. At first it was calm, but then, all of the sudden, he through his hands up in the air and he began to raise his voice to her.

"You're a liar!" he said, turning to come back to me. "Let's go Betty Jean!"

"What's wrong? Who was that?"

"I *said* let's go!" he demanded, paying for the items in the buggy and hurrying out of the store as if he were running from someone.

8

I didn't want to admit to it, but the green eyed monster had set his sights on me. My jealousy level had erupted to an extremely high plain and I was being eaten up inside with questions I wanted to ask. I felt like I had the right to know what just happened. In a moment, the tone between he and I changed and I had no clue why.

Even though he demanded we leave in the manner in which he spoke, I did so, just to find out why he was acting so erratic. His eyes almost appeared to have fire flying from them, and when we got in the car and left, his driving wasn't nearly as slow. For the first time, he was scaring me. I could just see us slipping on a slick spot in the road and possibly hurting Cody.

"I don't know who that was back there, but slow down….NOW!"

With that said, it looked like he was coming back to reality. His speeding ceased, but he still didn't say a word. All he did, was stare directly in front of him, not once glancing my way. I knew then something was terribly wrong. I kept debating in my mind what to say or how to say it, but without the knowledge of why he was acting so strangely, I was confused.

All the way home, he didn't say a word. He just sat there in another world. I could only guess at who that woman was and what she could've said to upset him so much. But I knew the only way I was going to find out, was ask. That would be the tricky part.

Evan pulled into my yard and got Cody out just as he would have normally, but still with the same angry expression painted across his once happy face. Something gave me the impression I didn't need to ask too many questions, but it was killing me inside. The air was beginning to get colder just as the night before, but it was cold enough by the way he was acting. He turned a once warm and toasty feeling into ice almost instantly.

Getting Cody settled inside, he still kept fidgeting, still not saying anything. He always told me he could tell when something was on my mind, and I guess I could do the same with him. I knew there was something he was struggling with and I was bound to find out exactly what it was.

I laid out a pallet on the floor so Cody could play and I went over to the couch.

"Sit down," I almost demanded, looking at him still standing in the entranceway.

"I can't," he replied. "I need to go."

"What! What is it?" Who was that woman?"

"I can't talk about this now."

Stopping him before he made it to the door, I grabbed his arm. It wasn't like I could keep him from leaving, but I was doing my hardest to do so. When he turned and looked at me, his eyes were showing something heart wrenching.

"Please tell me!" I pleaded, clinging to him.

"Nothing's changed with us Betty Jean. That's all I can say. I love you and that won't change, but there's something I have to do."

"I don't understand. You mean you're gonna leave me here to wonder about what's so terrible you can't tell me. I thought we could talk to each other about anything."

"Not this…not now," he muttered, his head lowered as if he were ashamed of something.

"If you gotta go…go!"

His hand on the door knob, he turned back to me, peering at me with those eyes that always compelled me to listen to him. He didn't say anything for a second, but then he acted like he wanted to spill everything out into the open.

"Betty Jean," he said in a whispering voice. "when I know how to explain this to you, I will. But you have to trust me. Please trust me. I wouldn't do anything to hurt you…not intentionally anyway. Just believe me when I tell you there's something I have to do and when the time's right, I'll tell you everything. I promise!"

I wanted to believe him, but it was so very hard. From what I saw, it looked like what he had to take care of, wasn't a minor thing at all, but complicated instead. My thoughts went crazy. First I thought that was his wife he never told me about, but then I shrugged such a silly notion. I was beginning to think such crazy things that I surprised myself. In any case, I knew I had to let him go. I couldn't hold him there if he didn't want to say.

"I'll be back," he said, placing his hands on my shoulders and kissing my forehead.

"What if I said I was jealous?"

Slightly shaking his head, "There's nobody you need to be jealous of."

Trying to shake off the image of he and that other woman staring at one another, I was quiet after his short remark. I didn't want to think the worst, but at times, it seemed to be my trademark.

"Do you trust me?" he asked sincerely, still holding onto me slightly.

Hesitating, "I want to Evan."

"I wouldn't lie to you, and I wouldn't hurt you or Cody."

"I really wanna believe you, but…"

"But what?" he pleaded.

"I don't wanna lose anybody else that I love. I just don't think I could take it. It was hard enough losing my husband, but now you have my heart and…"

"And I won't break it. Please just let me go and I'll be back to explain."

Taking a deep breath and expelling it, I did something that was hard for me to do.

"Go then. I'll be here waiting."

Leaning down slowly, he gently gave me a kiss, trying to give me reassurance that things would be okay, but I still had my doubts.

Shortly after, he got in his truck and was gone. As soon as he turned out of my driveway, I heard him speed away like a bat out of hell. I didn't know where he was trying to get in such a hurry, but I wanted to find out.

I kept thinking what I had just told him…that I'd be there waiting, but I never was one to be the patient type. The truth be known, I got my impatience from Pa. He was probably the most impatient person I knew, next to me that is, and I knew what I had to do.

Cody was happily playing in the living room and although I hated to get him out in such weather, I bundled him up and I went straight to Ma and Pa's. Douglas was sitting on the front porch with a toboggan, gloves and heavy coat to protect him from such a chilling wind, when I got there. Me and Cody went right passed him and found shelter inside where Ma was cooking.

"Well, isn't this a surprise," she said, then turning to Cody. "How's my grandson today?"

"Ma," I said quietly. "You mind watchin' Cody just for a little while?"

"I gotta finish supper, but I'm sure your brother Luther'll do it till I get free," she replied. "What's the matter dear?"

"I don't know."

Looking perplexed, I told her what happened. She was just as confused as I was. The look on her face showed bewilderment of Evan's actions.

"You do what you gotta do dear, but be careful," she said sweetly.

"I'm just scared Ma."

Coming to me, she took my hand. "The only thing you're scared of is losin' somebody you love. What you gotta ask yourself is, do you think he loves you. If he does, you got nothin' to worry about."

"But that woman Ma!"

"Darlin'," she continued. "That woman could be a misunderstanding just like the other one was. You had yourself convinced that was he girlfriend when it wasn't anyone but his own sister. Give'em a chance Betty Jean. Don't jump to conclusions so quick."

"Okay Ma, I won't. I'll be back in a bit," I said, agreeing with her and leaving.

Backing out, I tried my best to do as Ma said. I knew she was right. Most of the time she was, but in a far spot of my mind, I had a terrible feeling. I didn't think it was something that wasn't fixable, but I was sure it was something that would be a tremendous problem for us in the future.

It reminded me of a poem Luther wrote once. It was one that dealt with life. When I first read it, something about it didn't make sense, but at that moment, it made perfect sense. It was called "Life".

Tammy D. Thompson

Waking every morning,
Not knowing what's in store.
The one's I trust surround me
Showing love and so much more.
When a hardship shows it's ugly face
That's when trust comes alive.
That's when you stand together,
As through that hardship…strive.
Going to bed each and every night,
Your dreams take you away,
But never replacing a single thing,
That happened during the day.
For life is filled with many things,
Some you wish to disappear,
But you can get through anything
If you hold close those that are dear.
In every life there's sorrow.
In every life there are smiles,
But what makes all the difference,
Is when you go that extra mile.
So cherish those who love you,
And let them cherish what you give.
For that is what life's all about.
What you take and what you give.
Never doubt unless there's reason.
Never lie no time at all,
And when you follow all of this,
Through every day you will stand tall.
For each day is nothing short
Of a gift from God above.
So live it as if it's your last,
And do nothing but to love.

It made sense to me. I understand that when something seems to be wrong I shouldn't jump to conclusions, but in a heart that's already been tortured enough, it seemed to be a defense mechanism built inside of me.

Pulling into town, I noticed Lizzy's car parked at the market. I wanted to see if she knew anything that was going on, so I parked right next to her. She was walking out with a bag of groceries as I got out and I met her at the car.

"Hey sis," she said energetically. "Where's Evan? I figured you two were hittin' it off pretty well since we didn't see hide nor hair of him last night."

"He stayed with me."

"I figured that," she replied. "So why the depressed look? I figured you'd be jumpin' for joy like I was when I found Dean."

"Somethin's goin' on Lizzy, but I ain't sure just what."

I told her just what I told Ma. She looked puzzled too, but the first thing she did was start reasoning. In her maturing, she had started doing that instead of putting the cart before the horse.

"It's probably nothin' to worry about sis," she said assuringly. "Now, why don't you follow me home and visit for a bit. We'll talk about it there. Besides, it's too darn cold out here to be standin' around. I'm liable to…"

"Catch your death a cold…I know. Alright," I said, a little sarcasm shooting from my mouth. "I'll meet you there."

Rushing to get back in the car, the whistling wind was brisk and very cold, showing me that winter had surely found it's way fully to us. The sky was overcast and it looked as if we might get more snow. I didn't mind it so much, but I loved it when I was a kid. Lizzy and I used to gang up on Douglas and bomb him over and over again with big snowballs. He always ran crying to Ma, but she always thought Douglas probably started it, so she didn't do much to stop us.

My mind slowly coming back after a moment of the past trampling in the midst of my memory, I backed out and got right in behind Lizzy. She was going at a snail's pace, inching down the road. If I didn't know any better, I would've thought she had a flat tire or something, but it was just because of her cautiousness on the road. She never was one to take the least bit of a chance to wreck. And as slow as she was going, if she had hit someone, there wouldn't even be a scratch to show for it.

She turned off the side road and head towards her house. It was a little up the road and the ice was very evident. There were patches all over the place. If you were to hit just the wrong spot, you'd go spinning in circles, so I was very careful.

Few cars were left on that particular highway because of that, and when we were just about in front of Lizzy's driveway, I noticed something.

Dean's vehicle was there, but also Evan's and a strange car I'd never seen. It was light blue and small. It had Missouri plates and I was concerned more then than ever. I was doing just as I was told not to do…jump to conclusions, but that's all I knew at that moment.

Lizzy was already out of her car when I pulled up and when I stepped out, I heard yelling from inside the house. Evan's voice was apparent, but the other voice, I didn't recognize. The closer I got, the more I could understand. Lizzy just looked at me like she always did when my life was taking a bad turn. It was one that was almost saying "I'm sorry."

"You sure you wanna go in sis?"

"I'm positive Lizzy. There' somethin' goin' on and I'm determined to find out," I said. "Was anybody here when you left."

"No," she answered. "Just Dean and Angel. Angel was asleep upstairs."

"Well then," I stated nervously. "Let's go see who we got in there."

"But wait Betty Jean."

"Why?"

"He said he'd explain," she said, trying to keep me from entering her house.

"Yeah, and now's the perfect time sis. I can't think of a better time or place."

Opening the front door, I heard a woman's voice say something that cut me to the bone. She was raising her voice to Evan, and at that moment, my heart stopped.

9

"You can't turn away from me Evan. I'm sick, but what about Jade?" she pleaded.

"You're gonna ruin my life! You're a liar and I don't believe a word of what you're saying. It's not mine." Evan yelled.

Then a woman's voice replied, "It's a SHE"

"I told you a long time ago Lisa, I don't want any kids," he shouted. "You never did understand that."

And as I turned the corner...it was her again, the one from the market. Evan's head glanced in my direction and he almost turned completely white. He was standing there looking as if he'd seen a ghost. All conversation stopped and the room was totally silent. But in my heart, I could still hear those words echoing over and over again. It was all clear to me, but I was smart enough to read between the lines.

"Betty Jean," Evan said, running over to me in a sorrowful way. "I can explain."

Not saying a word, I could do nothing but stand there, shake my head from side to side, and try to fight the tears that wanted to come pouring down like an out of control summer rain. I didn't know what to say, what to do, or which direction to turn. Lizzy was right beside me with the same expression as me, but I was sure her heart wasn't nearly as torn.

"So this is Betty Jean," the woman said, walking up to me and holding out her hand. "I'm Lisa...Lisa Hennessy."

"I know who you are," I said coldly, not returning the favor of a handshake.

"Tell me Evan!"

Turning from me, he took a few steps and it appeared he was thinking of exactly the right words to say, if there were any, then he glanced back.

"Betty Jean, I swear I didn't know. It's been years since I've seen her...I told you that."

"And..."

"She claims I'm the father to her daughter Jade. She's almost four years old," he tried to explain.

"Is it true?" I asked her, a few tears finding their way down my cheeks.

"Yes it is," she said, pulling out a picture. "This is my daughter... our daughter. And it's true that he never knew, but he always made it clear how he felt about kids."

"Why now?" he asked, in a tone just shy of furious. "Why didn't you tell me then?"

"I didn't know where you were."

"You didn't tell my parents or anyone who could find me either did you?"

"No, but I thought..."

"You thought you'd pin this on me years later."

"NO!" she yelled. "I'm sick Evan. You know my mom died when I was a little girl and I don't have anyone else to turn to really. My three sisters have enough to handle, especially Wanda. She's got three kids and can't take on no more."

"I don't understand," he shrieked out. "What do you expect me to do?"

"Take her…love her."

He walked over to me and tried to shake me out of being in such shock. "I love you…you know that."

All I could do was shake my head. I knew he did, but something inside of me made me hold back. I wanted to embrace him to where he felt like he could confide in me, but I just couldn't. I didn't have it in me. The strength wasn't there.

"Evan," she pleaded once more. "I don't have much money and the doctor bills are takin' all I got. She deserves to live with somebody that can take care of her. From what the doctors say, there ain't much they can do. And I don't want her left alone to be put in an orphanage somewhere. I love 'er too much for that."

"How do I know she's mine?"

Reaching in her pocket, she pulled out a picture, handing it to him very slowly. My nerves were jumping and the intenseness of the moment was too much for me. I saw him look at what she handed him and his eyes were affixed on it. He just kept staring at it as if he were looking at a mirrored image of himself.

"Her eyes," he said.

"They're yours," Lisa continued.

"I can't…I just can't."

"But you have to!"

Strangely, I almost felt sorry for her. I could see the hurt in her eyes, and the way she talked to him was almost in a begging manner. Even though I wasn't sure if she was telling the truth, I couldn't see how anyone would lie about such a thing. I didn't know her, but for some reason, I believed her.

My face was covered with streaks from where tears had made a trail, and I stepped to Evan, "What if she is yours Evan?"

"I don't know," he said, then yelling. "I don't KNOW!"

Running out of the house, his rage engulfed the entire room, leaving me and Lisa almost standing side by side and the picture of her daughter was lying in the floor. Evan had dropped it just before he flew out the front door.

She looked at me with saddening eyes, "I didn't mean to barge into your life and ruin anything, but I love my daughter and I'd do anything for her."

I wanted to sympathize with her, but I was torn. I too was a mother and if it came down to it, would do anything for my son, but in this situation, I loved Evan too. It was as though everything he and I started was being disrupted by something so very unexpected that neither of us knew how to react or what to do about it.

"Talk to him please," she beseeched. "I'm bringing Jade to meet her daddy in a day or two. I know where you live also. I followed him there, but I didn't see it fit to knock at your house. I felt better coming here. I've known Dean for a long time."

She left in a hurry and all I could do was go in the living room in front of the fire and deliberate over what I needed to do. I felt betrayed even though I truly had no reason to feel that way, and the future started looking a lot different than I had seen it the past few days.

"Betty Jean," Dean said, coming over and sitting next to me. "She's tellin' the truth ya know. She contacted me several years back about trying to find Evan, but I didn't know how to get in touch with him until after he came back from the service. After he did, I had forgotten she ever called. I'm sorry."

"It's not your fault, and it's not the baby's fault. She's just a little girl. She ain't got a clue what struggle this is gonna cause. To be honest, I ain't quite sure what it's gonna cause. All I know is that Evan had a chance to tell me earlier before he ever came here, and he didn't."

"He was afraid," Dean replied, putting his hand on my shoulder.

"Afraid? Of *me*?"

"Afraid he'd lose you if all this was true. He wanted to find out it was true before he said anything," he continued.

"Well, now I know."

"The question is…how you gonna deal with it."

Sighing, "I ain't got a clue Dean…really."

"All I can say is, if you push him away because of this, you'll lose him."

"And if I don't…"

"You'll have a daughter," he answered sweetly, trying to console me and make things look clearer.

"She's NOT my daughter."

Dean could do nothing but look at me in a way he never did before. It was as if he was ashamed of what I just said. In a way, so was I. I knew if he and I ever got married, she would be my daughter in a sense. And if her mother does die, I would be the only mother figure she'd have, but it still didn't seem right.

"Why can't things just work out like they're supposed to?" I cried, leaning on his shoulder.

"Who knows how things are supposed to work out? Only God knows. Ask him and you just might get your answer Betty Jean. In fact, I know you'll get your answer if you ask him."

I got up and looked outside to see if I could see Evan anywhere. His truck was gone and every inch of me started to worry. I knew the way he drove when he was angry and I didn't want anything happening to him. If I knew anything at that point, it was that I still loved him with all my heart…with everything I had in me.

"Where do you think he went to?" I asked, hoping Dean would have an idea.

Shaking his head, "I don't know sis…I really don't know. But if you wanna find him that badly, you'll find'im…that's a promise."

Lizzy was still standing over in the entranceway still as a statue. It was strange to have her not saying a word, but then again, I'm sure she didn't know what to say. Ma always taught us that if we didn't have anything good to say, don't say nothin' atoll, and I suppose that's why she didn't speak a word.

"I've gotta find him Dean," I said, walking towards the door.

"Sis," Lizzy spoke out. "I'm sorry, but things'll work out."

"I know Lizzy, but right now, I gotta find Evan. I have to tell him I love him."

"You'd be surprised at what wonders that will do," Dean said, pulling Lizzy to him tenderly.

I didn't waste a moment getting to the car. I wasn't sure where to look or where he might have gone first, but I knew I was going to search until I found him. Something told me to go near my house. As much as we walked around up there, I was sure he had a spot he preferred more than any other. And even though it was cold, with everything that was happening, it probably didn't seem as cold as before.

I dropped by Ma's and let her know what was happening and she gave me an extra jacket just to make sure I was warm enough. Pa offered to help look, but I wanted to find him on my own. The way I acted to him was uncalled for and probably unforgivable, but I wanted to try and preserve what was left of our trust. And as I drove, I thought of a saying I'd seen once. It said, "The greatest gift of all, is the gift of love and trust…all others fall by the waist side…lesser and unimportant."

My philosophical mind was overflowing with what if's and why's that I was driving myself crazy. And after a while, I decided just to go back to the house. I thought there might be a chance he was there waiting for me to show up so we could talk...or at least I hoped so anyway.

I turned the last curve and his truck was sitting just in front of my porch. A smile automatically appeared on my previously saddened face, and I hopped out in the hopes he'd come running out to meet me. Sadly enough, that didn't happen. I went inside and looked all around. Evan was nowhere to be found.

"Evan!" I bellowed out. "Where are you!"

No answer made my worrisome side swell to the point to where I was shaking and just as fidgety as he was when Lisa told him the news.

I went outside and walked around the house...still no sign of the man I was trying with all my efforts to find. The sun was shining directly over my head, but the cold was still just as unnerving as before, forcing me to lace my fingers to keep them from shaking.

"EVAN!" I yelled even louder. "I LOVE YOU!"

After a while, distress set in. It seemed like I had scoured every inch of my place, but then I remembered how we all went walking up around the side of the mountain. Beyond my better judgment, I set out, climbing rocks that had sharp edges and yelling out his name.

Suddenly, I heard something strange. It sounded like echoes from heaven, being repeated over and over again.

"Why me?" I heard, as it bounced off of rock after rock until it was faintly heard by my ears.

"EVAN, where are you!"

Every few minutes, I would hear an echo of someone's voice. In my dreams it would sound like it was coming from heaven, but I knew better. I was sure it was Evan further up screaming out all of his woes into the clean air above. It might sound kind of crazy, but there had been a few times I wanted to do the same thing. Honestly, I had done that a few time, just not as far up as he was.

Climbing a while, I finally crossed over a steep area and looked on the other side.

10

I could see Evan kneeling down. It looked like he was praying. I wasn't sure what he'd be praying for, but I wanted to be by his side as he did so. His thoughts were obviously not on where he was, but instead, where he'd been. The way he stared straight ahead of him, made me wonder if he wasn't beginning to regret he and I ever getting together. I had acted so horribly to him about the situation and I felt more than awful about it.

With crackling below my feet, I went to him slowly. He didn't even turn his head my way. For some reason, I was sure he knew it was me. It was like that from the beginning. No matter how much I tried to deny that I was feeling something, I believe he knew better all the while.

I rested my hand on his shoulder, moving it slowly up and down, caressing his bulging, muscular arms as I did so. Still he never turned to me. That's when I started to get a very uneasy feeling. I feared losing him, but I knew if I did so, it would only be because of my selfish, spoiled attitude I'd shown so much of in recent days.

Using a light, whispering voice, "Evan." For a moment he didn't reply, but then I was relieved just as quickly. He turned and looked up at me, his eyes dancing as their compelling color seemed to jump out at me, hypnotizing my heart once more.

"I'm sorry I ran off like that Betty Jean...I just..."

"You don't have to explain Evan," I replied, my love for him overflowing the entire time. "I figured you was just upset. I figured you just didn't know what to do."

"I don't!" his tone changing to frustration. "I don't know a thing about bein' a father."

"Well," I said, getting ready to quote my Pa for the one hundred and fiftieth time. "Like Pa always said. Any man can be a father, but it takes a special person to be a daddy."

"A daddy," he muttered just below his breath.

Finding a spot next to him, our arms intertwined and tried to keep the cold away. "I've seen you with Cody," I grinned. "Now if that ain't actin' like a daddy...I don't know what is."

"That's different Betty Jean."

"How's it different? You're gonna be his daddy just like you're gonna have to be that little girl's."

"What if she don't like me?"

Shaking my head then resting it on his shoulder, "How can anyone in their right mind not like you Mr. Bain?"

His body shifted. Parallel to mine, one of his hands rested on my face and the other commenced to stroking my silky straight hair. It was almost like he loved it when I called him that. Then he leaned over. At first I thought he was going to kiss me, but when he got close enough, he rested his head on my chest, wrapping both arms around me. The way he was acting, I felt like his mother, almost cradling him in his time of need. He appeared like a hurt child looking for comfort.

"Evan, you ain't got a thing to worry 'bout."

Raising up, looking me directly in the eye, "You really think so?"

"Shoot, what more trouble can a little girl be than Douglas was...I'll declare. If I could handle Douglas, I'm sure Jade'll be a breeze."

His frown of uncertainty, soon changed to a hint of laughter. It was funny, but every time I mentioned Douglas and his crazy ways, it was always very amusing. Somehow Douglas's screw ups came to be more of a thought get-a-way for us. We could dang near forget about our own problems just for a little while if we could only think back at what stunts my younger brother had pulled on us and people he didn't even know. I swear, I always wondered how Ma ever made it as long as did.

"You and your brother..." he said. A few strands of his hair had fallen down in his face because of the winds swiftly shuttering by, and I reached over to brush them aside.

"What can I say Evan...my lil' brother always gave us somethin' to talk about."

"Like what?"

Letting my mind wander back, I could help but laugh hysterically. "I remember several times when he crawled under the house and started a fire. And let me tell you, Ma and Pa were fit to be tied. I swore each time he did somethin' that Pa'd teach him a lesson, but I don't reckon he's learned a lesson yet."

"You gotta be kiddin'."

"Not atoll," I replied, a tear rolling down my slender cheek just from the thought of it. "If Pa told him once, he told him a thousand times to stop playing with fire. But Douglas had this fascination with a flame. He'd set anything afire."

"He sounds like a real sweetheart of a brother," laughing with me.

"Yeah, well, I suppose he's gettin' better. He's got this girl that likes him and the way he acts, I figure he likes her just the same, but you just can't ever tell about Douglas."

Pulling me to him, the cold still sweeping by hurriedly, "I know what it's like to be ripped away from your old ways 'cause of a woman."

"Do ya now?"

"No doubt baby…no doubt," kissing my forehead, cheek, chin and lastly, barely gracing my lips with his own full, luscious, irresistible lips that tempted me constantly. "I knew it that day I opened the door at Dean and Lizzy's place."

"You knew what?"

His eyes focusing on me intensely, I knew he didn't have to answer such a question. Just the look on his face, was answer enough. For that one moment, it seemed all the dilemmas around us were gone and the only two that mattered were he and I. But I knew all too well, that would change soon enough.

"I guess I should a played more hard to get."

"Oh, you were hard to get, but more than that, hard to figure out," he said sarcastically.

"I was just bein' me Evan. And I figured if anybody liked me, they'd have to like me just the way I am."

"How 'bout somebody lovin' you just the way you are?" he teased.

Half grinning, feeling my freezing skin turn a shade of red, "I knew you was okay Evan."

"I just don't know what to do Betty Jean. I feel like I've been thrown in a situation I just ain't ready for." His eyes looked down then back up again, his long, dark eye-lashes fluttering in a sexy manner.

"You'll figure it all out, I promise," I said. I wasn't sure if my words of encouragement would help, but I did catch a glimpse of a smile from him, trying to peek out.

"Now let's go!" I demanded in a playful way. "My poor toes are 'bout to fall off they're so cold."

With no hesitation, he blanketed me all the way home. Not much was said as we traveled down the path that led through the thicket to that small little cabin in the woods that sheltered me each and every night. He held me close, but all I heard was his breathing…in and out. I watched as the smoke from each exhale was shown through the chilling air around us. It was a silent sign that winter was in full force and I knew it would be a while before we'd feel the warmth of a summer's day.

"What's on your mind?" he asked as we reached the house and he opened the door for me like a perfect gentleman.

"The summer."

"The summer? What about it?"

Beginning to warm up, I went over to the couch, sat down, and pulled my knees up to my chest, wrapping my arms around them. "The cold of winter never could compare to the summer days 'round here."

"Tell me," he said, trying to pluck the thoughts right out of my brain.

"From the time I was a kid, even though we all had our chores to do, after we were done, the day was filled with romping around, the sun shining down the whole time," I replied. "Lizzy and me would wade barefoot in puddles of mud, hoping Douglas would come by so we could splatter some on him."

"Sounds to me like ya'll didn't give him much choice than to be mean."

"You don't understand Evan. If we didn't he'd be waitin' 'round the corner with somethin' to throw at us. Shoot, he hit me right in the head with a rock once then ran off like Leo or David Lee done it."

He didn't say anything, but instead, his chuckle was obvious and clear. I could tell my story was amusing him.

"Just a downright, country, red-neck sort a family huh B.J.?"

Lacing my fingers and staring at him profusely, "I wouldn't say we was rednecks...not really."

"There's nothin' wrong with that...I mean, you gotta have a little bit a red-neck in ya if you live around here."

I released my fingers and slid one hand down beside the couch where I had leaned a small pillow up. Then without any warning to Evan, I grasped it tightly and flung it over towards him like a torpedo in a war zone. His eyes got as big as saucers, but seconds later, the fight was on. He picked one up from beside him and I hopped up from my comfortable position to run from him. He got close to me a few times, but I kept just a hint out of arm's reach from him.

It seemed like we had only been home a short while, but before I knew it, all of the horseplay and aggravating, took over the better part of the day. Before I knew it, the sun that had shown itself all day, was falling suddenly. Evan was tired, but I was starting to hear a rumble coming from my belly which hadn't been fed all day long. It sounded like there was an animal lose in my small home, but all of the sudden, Evan's expression changed.

"You hungry?" I asked, stepping toward the kitchen. Following my question, I got no reply, Evan was just standing there holding a picture of Cody and looking more spaced out than ever.

"Evan!"

"Huh, yeah...yeah!" he exclaimed, acting as though he heard every word I said.

"What'd I just ask you?"

"I...I'm not sure," he replied. "I was a million miles away."

"I'm gonna fix somethin' to eat." Aggravated, I set my mind on nothing more than soothing my hunger, putting everything else aside.

I spent a while whipping up dinner, but as soon as it was ready, I fixed two plates and called for him to eat. Then again, I called for him.

Exasperated, I huffed a little and went into the living room. Evan was facing the window and his arms were crossed loosely. The sounds of winter were screaming outside as the wind started to pick up even more. I could see it in the sway of the bare branches on the trees, and the leaves were swirling around and around like a tornado in the Fall. I didn't know what to say to him. After such a peaceful evening talking and trying to get away from the reality of what was happening, he had slipped back into the same state of mind he was in when I found him earlier in the day…dazed and confused.

"Now it's my turn to ask," I whispered, walking up behind him, my right hand resting on the bottom of his back, looping my fingers around a loop in his jeans.

"Ask me what?"

"What's on your mind?" I said, presenting the same question to him as he had done earlier.

Shaking his head slowly, he turned to me. He cradled my face in the palms of his hands, almost staring straight through me. For once he wasn't looking at me…he was seeing something else when his eyes gazed in my direction. "I need to go," he said. His hands fell to his side and with that he headed for the door.

"But wait!"

Cutting his eyes back, "I can't…not tonight. I got so much on my mind baby. It has nothing to do with you. I just need to put my priorities in order before I do anything else.

Lividly, I stopped him, "And I'm not at the top of that list anymore… am I?"

"You're jumping to conclusions Betty Jean."

"Am I? Tell me something then!" I demanded.

"Anything."

"How could you let this happen Evan?"

His mouth dropped wide open as if he were offended by my remark. "What!"

"You heard me. We had everything planned out. I just knew that you, me and Cody were gonna live a happy life together."

"We can still have a baby."

"How? The most important woman in your life from now on, won't be me…it'll be Jade."

"That's not fair!" raising his voice.

"Fair! I'm not being fair?" I exclaimed, releasing every ounce of feeling from my intimidation, out. "I know I'm probably being selfish…but she's not my daughter. She might not even be yours for that matter."

"Lisa wouldn't lie B.J."

"Oh, I see," I continued. "At my sister's house you called her a liar, but *now* you say she won't lie."

"I just don't think…"

"NO!" I interrupted. "I don't think I know who you are anymore Evan. You're not the man I met."

"No, I'm not!" he replied angrily, throwing his arms up in the air…his expression showing pure frustration. "*Now* I'm a father. *Now* I have responsibilities to somebody other than just myself."

I was speechless. All of the words to lash out at him, just wouldn't come, and I stood there staring at him. I knew if I could've frozen that moment in time, I would've seen nothing but two people who seemed like strangers. The open heart he always had before appeared to be closing more and more by the minute, and that shimmer in those hypnotizing eyes of his, was no longer there. All of the spirit he once had, seemed dead and gone…much the same as mine after I found out about such a secret.

"Maybe you just need to go," I muttered, my eyes looking down.

Hearing his sigh, I knew he felt as bad as I did. "I don't wanna leave things like this Betty Jean…I don't."

"I'm fine Evan. I suppose we're just gonna have to learn to deal with things in a little better way, but for tonight.…"

"I know," he said softly. "I'll go."

His masculine hand started turning the door knob, when he stopped. I didn't want him to leave, but I knew it was probably best. I very seldom let my temper get the best of me, but for some strange reason, it prevailed tremendously when we started discussing what was going on. I wasn't sure if it was because I felt threatened by such a little girl, or if it was because I simply didn't want to share him with anybody.

This time he didn't bother to turn to me, but he spoke just the same.

"Have supper with me tomorrow night," he said, but not in a insistent way. His voice was soft and he stood there awaiting an answer.

"After work?"

"I'll pick you up," he replied, leaving to go outside.

I stood there until I heard him on the last step of the stairs to my porch. That's when I decided I couldn't let him leave that way. I rushed out. He had already gotten in and started to crank up his truck. It crackled and backfired somewhat, but still not as bad as Pa's, and I hurried around to the side he was on so I could say a proper good-bye. I didn't want him to think anything bad was going on with us. I knew he had enough to deal with as it was.

"What is it Betty Jean?" staring straight ahead, warming up the truck.

"I love you," I replied humbly, hoping he'd turn and smile.

The smile didn't come, but a little grin was sufficient. "I love you too," he countered. "I'll see you tomorrow."

That was the first time I remembered him leaving without giving me a kiss. His demeanor was hurt filled and perplexed. Although I'd known him to always be one to hold his head up high, I didn't see that side of him anymore. The part I did see though, was the part that I'm sure he wanted to keep hidden, his insecure and indecisive side. He didn't act as if he knew which way to turn, much less what kind of decision he needed to make.

His tail lights faded off into the distance and I stood out there in the cold, numb. That night, after eating supper and getting Cody home, I couldn't help but walk around like a zombie, unaware of what I was doing and time was pointless.

I couldn't stand what this big secret was doing to he and I. He was dumbfounded by the news, and I was in pure shock. Just when I had things mapped out for us, something had to come along and mess up such perfect plans. I knew the moment I heard Lisa's name for the first time, there would be trouble. Something deep down inside of me began to twist and turn until my woman's intuition kicked in full force, almost seeing the future before it actually showed itself.

The night went by slowly. Tossing and turning, dream after dream, all ending up badly, I woke feeling the bed next to me. He was in my thoughts so much, I prayed he'd be there when my eyes opened to greet the new day. To my dismay, as the morning sun arose, I arose with it…alone. Something told me as I began to get ready for work, things would be okay, but I had doubts about that. In fact, I was even starting to have doubts about mine and Evan's future.

Ma kept Cody and I went on to work, dragging throughout the day, watching the clock each time five minutes would pass. It made for a long day, but when five o'clock rolled around, I took off my apron and took one last look at my hair.

"You're man's here," Kim said, winking in a crazy way. "Lookin' fine if I do say so myself…no offense."

"I'll be right out," I answered, grinning at her behavior. It was always nice to know I had her to make me laugh when I needed it, even though sometimes there wasn't anything that could make me smile but him.

When I pushed the door open, he stood there leaning up against one of the poles directly in front of where he parked his truck. He was dressed in dark jeans and boots. His hair was slicked back like James Dean and the smile he was carrying was enough to wash away all of the doubts I held plentiful in my mind after he left the night before. A tiny voice in my head was saying," *It's gonna be alright,*" but I knew it was just the beginning on a journey for both of us. It was going to be a journey that involved trust, honesty and above all…love.

"You ready?" he asked, offering his hand to me. "I been wantin' to see you all day."

"I'm ready…and I've missed you too," I replied, smiling a smile to match his perfectly.

Without another word spoken, he helped me in the truck. His manly scent filled the air all around me. It was so appealing that it was all I could do to keep from having him to take me to the house and letting him ravage his wife to be in the most passionate way.

We pulled into "Sally's Diner," and parked. The raggedy engine of his sputtered to a halt and we both sat there. His hand crawled on my leg like a reptile and it finally landed on my knee. He squeezed it lightly then leaned over kissing me lightly on the cheek.

"I'm sorry about last night," he said apologetically.

"No! I'm sorry. I was the one that…"

"I said I was sorry first."

"But…"

"Okay…okay," he said, stopping that silly little, juvenile game we were playing. "We're both sorry. Now let's go in and get somethin' to eat. I'm starved."

"Me too."

I scooted out, shut the door, and took his hand, gripping it tightly, making sure he didn't go anywhere, but stay with me. That's when we heard another car door shut behind us as we had almost made it to the entrance of the diner. Evan slowed his walk suddenly. It was like he got this strange feeling something was happening…something he wasn't quite ready for.

The air grew thick all of the sudden, and Evan's hand began to sweat. The cold outside didn't effect him a bit, but the intenseness of something else was absorbing into him to the extent that he was almost shaking.

That's when we heard someone speak.

11

"Evan," the voice spoke, just loud enough for him to hear. "Would you like to meet your daughter?"

Those words made Evan's entire body freeze in the spot he was standing. His hand was still clinging to mine, but in a different way. I got the feeling his nerves were jumping on his insides. I could tell he didn't know what to do. People passed by us, but it didn't phase him a bit. Finally, he released me, and began to turn around slowly.

The look on his face was one of a combination of things. I saw a splash of fear with a pinch of anticipation. I wasn't sure how to make out what was going on in his mind, but as I turned with him, I saw her standing there. She was holding onto the little girl's hand firmly and looking at Evan. It was obvious she was waiting on a reaction, but initially, she didn't get much of one. With me linking myself to him with my arm, we took a few steps in their direction. I could hear his breathing get more intense and I knew if I could feel his heart beating, it would be pounding ever so fast.

I couldn't help but look at the tiny little girl standing there looking up at us so innocently. She was very small with golden hair that was done in curly Q's. And she had the most breathtaking, carefree eyes

I'd ever seen in my life. She was bundled up in a coat that matched her clothes and shoes, and the bow that twirled down in the midst of all those curls, made her look like she should've been on television. Adorable didn't even come close to describing her.

"Evan," Lisa said. "How are you?"

He didn't answer her right away. To be honest, I'm not sure if he even heard her. His sights were set on nothing but the little girl that stood just knee high to him. That's when his expression changed from confused, to profound joy. I saw the smile I fell in love with, but for the first time, another girl was putting it on his face…his daughter.

In that moment, I felt inferior to a child and unwanted by the man who stood by my side. I felt like I didn't even need to be there. What I was seeing, was a mom, a dad and a little girl who needed them both. But in reality, that wasn't what was there. Still, that's the way my eyes were seeing the scene in front of me.

Evan finally spoke, stuttering "F…fine," he said. "How are you?"

She nodded as if to say "Okay," and the stares were powerful. Not just the stares from him to his daughter, but the way Lisa looked at Evan almost made me want to scream with the most jealously I ever felt. She kept batting her eyes at him like she was only in the first stages of trying to get him back, but I for one, was going to keep anything like that from happening.

Lisa kneeled down to her daughter and played with a few of the curls that hung down gracefully beside her beautiful face. I could see the expression on Lisa's face was also a mixture of many emotions, but I tried not to feel sorry for her. The way I saw it, she had three years to tell him, but she waited until then to do so.

"Jade honey," she whispered softly, "I want you to meet someone… someone very nice sweetie."

Jade peered at her with those big sincere eyes, but didn't say a word. She looked almost as frozen as Evan did earlier. Her eyebrows squinted together and those pouty lips of hers poked out a hint as if to say "Who mommy?"

"Jade," she said, pointing up at Evan standing tall and handsome. "This is your daddy."

"My daddy?" she whispered, almost questioning what her mom had just told her.

"Yes honey...your daddy," she replied. "He's been wanting to meet you for a long time now."

The ache in Lisa's heart was evident by the single tear I saw progressing down her face ever so slowly. I could tell it was killing her to do this, but if what she had told Evan was true, I think she it was something she knew she had to do.

Jade took a few tiny steps away from her and came closer to Evan and I. He began to fidget excessively, showing outwardly his nervousness. I squeezed his arm to show my support, but he still acted like he didn't have anything to say. I think he was speechless because he didn't know what the right thing to say was.

Finally, she reached us and her eyes went up until she was staring directly at Evan. Again, he froze. His body stiffened up and his eyes were affixed on the precious little thing before him. I could tell he was memorizing everything about her. I was sure he was trying to see if she had his nose or mouth. But deep down, I was sure she'd have his smile. God must've given her his smile.

"Are you my daddy?" she asked sweetly, her eyes turning sad as she spoke.

I wasn't sure if they were looking that way because she had dreamed of having a daddy or if it was just the intense moment.

Suddenly, his stiffened body went half-way limp, giving in to his emotions in every sense. His eyes filled with tears and as he wiped a few of them away, that man I'd known to be big and strong, was transformed into a bundle of emotions getting ready to explode. I could tell he was being faced with a moment he would never see again…the first view of his child. To me, that was the most precious time in my life. I just wondered exactly how he would've described such a moment.

He kneeled down to her to where they were eye to eye and they appeared to be in awe of each other. They were studying each other's expressions and look. Finally, Evan took the first step to grasping his responsibilities. He reached out to her, gently taking her small hand in his large masculine one, and smiling at her lovingly.

"Yes Jade," he said, still wiping tears. "I'm your daddy."

"Daddy," she whispered again. "Can I give you a hug?"

Surprised, but happy, Evan gave her an answer, but not with words. He picked her up quickly. Her arms went around him as if it were second nature, and just seeing that, made me want to cry myself. Jade rested her head on his shoulder and gripped tightly onto him, sure not to fall. It was a unique moment for me. Evan twirled her around and around and they both began to laugh.

"Daddy!" she said, even louder this time, her curls swinging around as precious as you please.

"Yes baby…yes," he said, his tears pouring down like a river, leaving streak after streak down his good-looking façade.

Lisa wasn't saying a word. She was leaning against her car with the most gratifying look. She and I both were seeing him give his daughter an embrace for the very first time and even though I wasn't truly a part of what was happening, my heart strings were being pulled in every direction. I was filled with an overflowing feeling of love just watching them. It didn't seem he like he wanted to let her go. He just held her to him as if he were making up for some of the time he had missed when she was little. Of course I knew it would take a lot more than just one hug to do that, but it was a start.

Lisa finally walked over to them and from a distance it would probably appear they were a family, but my one fear was that they just might be. In the back of my mind I was afraid he'd decide he wanted her, or at least until she was no longer around. It was silly I know, but still, like Lizzy, my imagination started going crazy in my mixed up head.

When Evan finally released his little girl, he turned to me. "This is B.J." he said. "I'm gonna marry her."

"B.J.," she said, repeating what he had said.

"You sure are pretty Jade," I added, brushing her hand slightly.

She didn't say a word to me. Honestly, I wasn't sure if she even knew what marriage was or even if she knew that mommies and daddies were supposed to be together. All she knew was that she had just met the man who should've been in her life up until that point.

Lisa took her and put her in the car, only to come back again.

"We need to talk," she said in that voice that was unmistakable. "I'm not well Evan. And I wanna make sure Jade's taken care of."

"Come on Lisa," he said. "Is all of this just a trick."

I watched a tear stream down her face as she answered him right back. "It's no trick Evan. I've been fighting this for a while now, but I just don't have any strength left to fight."

"What's wrong with you?" he asked in a very caring voice.

"They're not sure, but the doctor says he thinks it's some kind of rare disease."

"Can't they do something?"

Shaking her head regretfully, "They say no."

"But what about your family. Won't they..."

"Forget it!" she said, raising her voice. "I knew you wouldn't want her. You're her daddy, and you don't want her."

"No wait!" he hollered before she made it to the car. "I didn't say that."

When she turned back to him, the frustration that showed only a moment earlier, was gone and it was replaced with the relief that he did want his daughter. If what she was saying was true, I felt sorry for her, but if she was playing a trick on us, I was sure my vengeful side would come crashing through without warning.

"I've got Dean's number," she said. "I'll be in touch."

"But when can I see her again," he said, almost pleading.

"Evan, you can see her anytime, but it is an hour's drive from here or maybe even a little more. I live in the same place just this side of Fort Smith," she replied, then she took out a pen and piece of paper. "Here's my number."

She placed the tiny piece of paper in his hand and he stuck it in his pocket as if it didn't matter. Although he acted that way, I knew better. I could see it in his eyes. The way he watched the car as they drove off, I knew he was a changed man from that day forward. His dreams would be filled with visions of his daughter. And his nightmares would probably consist of his losing her. In any case, the first thing I had to do, was learn how to live with what God had just thrown in our path.

"Come on," he said. "let's eat."

Stopping him, "You okay Evan?"

"I'm fine."

With a peck on the cheek, we went inside. There was a new waitress there I hadn't seen before. Her name tag said "Wanda." She was average height and had long flowing brown hair. It wasn't long after we sat down, that she came over to take our order.

"What can I do for ya'll tonight?" she asked friendly enough.

"I'll have the pork loin with fried potatoes, pinto beans and a piece of your pecan pie," I said, my mouth watering the entire time I was talking.

She turned to Evan quickly and just said "the same."

There was a juke box playing in the corner, but I could barely hear it. After a while I could make it out. That sexy, wiggling rocker Elvis was singing and it almost made me want to get up and dance.

"How about a dance good-lookin'?" I said, moving my body around.

He just grinned, and stared out the window. It looked like he was watching cars pass, but I knew that wasn't what was on his mind.

"You thinkin' 'bout her?"

"I don't see how I couldn't," he nodded. "She's beautiful Betty Jean."

"Just like her daddy," I replied, placing my hand on his and rubbing it gently.

"How could she not tell me until now?"

"I don't know but…"

"How could she keep such a secret from me?" he continued, cutting into my reply without any thought.

After that, I couldn't get a word in edgewise. He was talking, but I'm not sure if it was to me. More than anything, I think he was talking to himself, questioning himself about his past and what faced him…his future.

With her hair swaying from side to side, Wanda came back with both dinners in hand. She didn't smile a whole lot, but she wasn't rude either. I got the feeling it was simply the way she was.

"Wanda Jo," a man yelled from the back. "Order up!"

"Thank ya," she nodded. "Come back ya'll."

We agreed and I was about to say something to Evan when the front door flew open and three kids ran in. There were two girls and a boy. One of the girl's might've been about twelve and the other girl wasn't much younger, but the boy was bound to be eight or nine. Wanda hurried out from behind the counter and commenced to yelling at the oldest girl, almost as if she was in charge of the other two. They all sat down and lowered their heads because of the tongue lashing they'd gotten. But the youngest girl, lifted her head up and smiled as Wanda walked off.

She came back over to our table moments later and asked if we needed anything else.

"We're fine…thanks," I said, then stopping her before she could walk off. "Wanda!"

"Yep," she answered quickly.

"Those your kids?" I asked curiously, Evan staring at me as if it were none of my business.

"Sure are!" she retorted, glancing over to them at the same time. "And I tell ya…sometimes I wonder if I'm even gonna make it."

"You married?" continuing my interrogation, but in a friendly manner.

"Nope," she muttered, looking away. "My husband killed himself when my Mandy was just a baby."

"I'm sorry."

"Awe, ain't no sense in bein' sorry. Sometimes it's hard to keep bread on the table, but we make it. We always have and I suppose we always will," she replied, her head lifted high as if she wasn't going to let it bother her.

"You got guts," Evan said. "I mean…you know…raisin' those kids by yourself."

"Guts ain't got nothin' to do with it. Ya see. You do what you gotta do, and that was one thing I had to do. I got three sisters, but my mama died when I was a little girl."

"What about your Pa?"

"My daddy ain't good for nothin' if you ask me. I'd just as soon not have a daddy than have him."

"Wanda Jo!" the voice rang again from the rear of the café.

"Gotta run. Nice talkin' to ya'll," she said, hurrying off.

When she walked off, Evan's eyes turned blank. He wasn't looking at me, but instead, his eyes were focused passed me.

"Evan, talk to me!" I insisted. "We ain't gonna resolve nothin' like this. And to be honest, I feel like I'm only in the way of what you need to be doin'."

He sat there with his fork in hand twirling his food around and around, playing with it more than he was eating, and I watched him. As each moment passed, he was further and further away in his mind. His body was with me, but his thoughts were somewhere I was unaware of. I could see it in the way his eyes danced around, not focusing on anything in particular.

"Take me back to my car!" I demanded. "I can't take this anymore. I thought I could, but I can't. I feel like I'm rippin' your feelings into and I don't wanna cause anymore pain or confusion than you already got dancin' in your head."

"I just gotta figure out a few things Betty Jean."

"I know, and now here's your chance," I replied, raising my eyebrows, signaling he would have all the time he needed to make a decision one way or another.

"I don't wanna lose you Betty Jean. You mean the world to me," he stated sweetly.

Placing my palms on his rugged face that hadn't been shaved a several days, "I'm here. I'll always be here."

He drove me back to my car and we sat there for a few moments listening to the sounds that the wind often made, echoing through the hills as if it were coming from Heaven, and before I could think, I leaned over and rested my head on his shoulder. The scent I could always smell even when he wasn't around, was as invigorating as it always was, close and irresistible.

"When you can make sense of everything," I said. "Let me know. And like I said…I'll be here for ya…always."

Kissing my forehead, his dimple showed brilliantly, erasing any bad thoughts I had and replacing them with the hope that everything would be okay. At least that's the way I wanted to think.

I got out and watched him leave, turning towards my sister's house. But before he was out of sight, his head turned to me and he waved. I felt a little empty, but at the same time, I knew some time apart would be good for both of us. I didn't want him to feel pressured into anything, but I also didn't want to lose one of the best things that ever happened to me.

Kim walked up before I could get in my car and gave me that look.

"What?" I asked, knowing she'd give me a long, drown out version of her question.

"What is it with you two?" she answered. "I swear, for ya'll to be so dang much alike, I'm beginnin' to wonder if you're gonna make it atoll."

"You know Kim, after Lonnie died, I thought my life was over. I felt like I'd never be happy again. And even though I had Cody to love, something still seemed to be missing. Then I met Evan."

She stood there attentively and listened as I rambled on.

"He was kind, sweet, funny, and as straight forward as I've ever met."

"Then what's the problem?" she asked, curiosity filling her wild eyes.

"There wasn't a problem...least wise not until a few days ago."

I told her the whole story and she could do nothing but stand there with her mouth so wide open, if there had been mosquitoes out, she'd a had'em for dinner. It seemed so unbelievable to her. To be honest, it seemed pretty much the same to me too, but I tried to act different.

Continuing, "I was scared to fall in love with him even though I knew I would regardless how I acted to him. But somehow, I threw out my fear and didn't follow my mind...I followed my heart. What an idiot!"

"I don't think so Betty Jean. Look at it this way," she replied supportively. "He's a handsome man who loves you, but also he wants to take responsibility of his child he didn't know about until days ago. He's a good man just for that. Admit it."

"I know you're right, but I ain't so dang sure I'm ready to go forward and be a part of that little girl's life if she'd gonna take part of my time with Evan."

She looked at me a little on the mean side.

"Now what?"

"How selfish can you get," she said, putting her hands on her hips. "This baby's gonna lose her mama and you're worried about havin' to share your time with Evan with her."

Lowering my head, I felt more than a little ashamed. I was ashamed to the extent that I felt like going and apologizing to Evan right then and there.

"You're right," I replied, seeing the light, but still somewhat in the tunnel of darkness that separated me from where I was and true reality.

"I gotta go," she said. "Let me know what happens…and remember, it ain't her fault. She's just a baby."

The next few days went by and I didn't hear a word from Evan. He didn't even show up at my job to tantalize me. I was more than surprised. I knew he was going to show up at some time or another, but again…I was wrong. Kim and I continuously talked and the more we did, the more I realized that I was being immature and terribly selfish about the whole thing.

Then after work one day, I went by Ma's to pick up my handsome son, but she wanted him to stay the night. She said Pa was having a ball having him around, so I drug home, tired and ready to just hit the bed as soon as I got there. But when I pulled up in front of my poor looking cabin, Evan's truck was boldly parked to the left of the porch. With him, I didn't know what to expect, but regardless, I was tired and needed to get inside. My feet ached and my body felt like it had been run over by one of them eighteen wheelers.

With a clomp…clomp from my steps, I turned the knob and slowly opened the door to the entranceway to my humble quarters, only to find Evan standing just a few feet away from me. He had on a neat sweater with a pair of khaki pants. He was normally in jeans, but in my view he was handsome just the same.

"What are…"

"Shhh," he sounded, handing me an envelope.

Anxious to see what was in there, my fingers fidgeted so much, I seemed clumsy even getting it out. When I did so and opened the card that was enclosed, the words touched my soul.

I read each line slowly, so as to take in the meaning he put behind it. This is what it said.

12

I've grasped beauty in my hands.
I've kissed an angel with hidden wings.
I have fallen for someone
That through her words, she sings.
I've longed for happiness,
But always fell short in all.
But now I have decided,
Not to fight the fall.
So I'm asking such a beauty,
And looking an angel in the eyes,
Longing for the answer
To a question sure to surprise.
So for the question,
All you have to do is use your nose,
Use your senses swiftly,
As you carefully smell this rose.
EVAN

When I read the last line, I looked up and he was holding a long stemmed red rose out to me. His glistening eyes and sexy lips took in every part of me that once wanted to argue with him and turned it into the simplicity of my true feelings bursting through every vein of my body like a rainbow of bright colors.

"Evan…what's all this?" I asked softly, blown away by the way he was expressing himself to me.

"Here," he uttered in that deep sexy tone, melting me all over again. "It's for you."

My hand met his and I was holding the stunning, red brilliance that only God could've made. Evan kept staring at me as the color of his eyes were magnified by the moonlight brightly coming from the window to my left.

"Smell of it," he said. "You might be surprised. It's different than any rose you've had before."

"It's beautiful Evan," I replied, putting my nose up to it and taking in a whiff of such a compelling scent from nature. And that's when I looked down at it.

My sights were set on the magnificent thing before me, but it wasn't the rose I was so entranced by, it was from what was lying in the middle of it. There was a gold ring with a small diamond in the shape of a circle in it. It glistened like the waves on the lake in the summer when the sunlight would catch the water just right. I picked it up, careful not to drop it.

My speech was impaired briefly, and I was almost afraid to put it on for fear I might be dreaming.

"Pinch me," I said, comically, hoping it was all happening just as it seemed.

"What?" shaking his head.

"I just wanna make sure I ain't dreamin'."

Stepping to me, he took the ring from me and placed it amiably on my left hand. Then he curled my fingers up a hair and started to kiss each and every one, nibbling on them as if they were candy. His touch was magnificent, sending more emotion through me the longer he teased, then his eyes peered into mine. I was spellbound the instant

I saw the ring, but as moments passed, I went deeper and deeper into a sleep I never wanted to wake from.

"Betty Jean Cole," he said, dropping to one knee. "I love you and I want you to..."

"Hold on," I murmured, rushing to my room and fixing myself, hair and make-up a like. I was sure he thought I had gone plumb crazy, but I wanted to look decent when or if he was going to ask what I thought he was going to. Then I ran back to where he was. "Okay Evan. Now I look proper."

"I'll just get to the point Betty Jean," he said, coming right out with it. "I love you and I don't wanna spend another day away from you. It's plain and simple. I want Cody to be my son and I want you to be..."

"To be?" I said, trying to get him to keep on with what was on his mind.

He stood up, almost in an aggravating sense, "Awe...never mind."

"Never mind!" I retorted, unsure of what he was trying to pull. "Evan Bain, you get you're tail back here b'fore I whoop it."

He started laughing and turned back. His dimples were more evident than ever and this time when he took my hand, I took in a deep breath and let out a sigh.

"Do I have to say it?" he questioned, as if I were supposed to know for sure what he was going to say next.

"Why yeah!" I insisted, still standing there waiting for those magical words to come flying from his irresistible lips.

"Oh alright," he replied, still grinning from his little practical joke he tried to play on me. "Will you be my...I can't do it"

"Why?" I asked, anticipation growing inside of me the entire time he was playing such games with my heart.

"I'm afraid a what you're gonna say."

"Yes...yes...yes," I answered, before he could even ask the question properly.

"You will?"

"I will what?"

"Be my wife?" he said, his eyebrows raised, waiting on the answer.

"That's what I wanted to hear," I replied. "And yes...I will."

Letting him swing me around and around, in that little area next to my living room, I felt the air grace my face as I went around, clinging to him all the while. I could tell his excitement, but mine was just as immense. Just knowing he wanted me that much, was something for me to hang onto. I'd done that "for better or for worse...till death do us part," thing before, but this time I wanted it to last forever. And I had a feeling, things wouldn't be anything like they were when Lonnie and I were married. To be honest, he and I weren't together long enough to even get the act of being married down yet. We were still getting used to each other's faults, not that I had many. And there was Evan, standing in front of me like an answer to all of my weary prayers. He seemed to put the life back into my heart that didn't seem to have one until he showed up. He added laughter where sadness used to be, and his touch took away every ounce of loneliness I ever felt. In his voice, I could almost hear God's voice echoing down from heaven, trying to tell me that life does go on and to never give up on being truly happy. That's what I saw just by looking at him.

Standing there with that shiny piece of jewelry on my hand, my eyes were affixed on it as he and I were melted together, hanging on for dear life. That's when I pictured our wedding day. I could see him in a handsome looking suit with his gorgeous eyes glowing from happiness. And there I was, in the midst of my own mind, decked out in the fanciest of all dresses, with sprays of lace flowing down like the water at that beautiful fall not far away. Those thoughts warmed me heart and soul, covering up any doubts I ever had about him. Then my thoughts turned to something else.

"I'll marry you on one condition," I said, pulling away from him just enough to where I could see into those crystal ball eyes of his.

"And what would that be?" he asked, inquisitiveness filling him.

"I wanna wait till Cody can walk down the aisle as a ring bearer. That'd make it perfect."

He paused for a few moments. I could tell his thoughts were doing summersaults about the timing, but then he replied sweetly.

"If that's what it takes to have you…I'll wait."

"Who knows," I said. "Cody might be so smart that he starts walkin' real soon."

"Well, he *is* startin' to pull up on things."

"See," I replied optimistically. "It won't be long, besides, the best things come to those who wait."

Grinning peculiarly, "I sure hope so."

"Just shut up and kiss me," I demanded, not waiting even a second before I pressed my wanting lips to his.

That night was perfect. He and I fell asleep on the couch cuddled up together like two pieces of a puzzle that fit just right, never breaking away, but getting even closer. And as much as I was tempted by his masculinity, I contained all of the raging hormones that were aching for him to show me his passion…his love…and all he had to give.

Then, as dawn approached, a hint of the most beautiful light fell through the window, landing on his face just so. His hair was all a mess and his head was cocked sideways, still clinging to me with all his might. So I laid there with my eyes open just looking at him. There was a tenderness about the way he looked at that moment, that was beyond any kind I'd seen. Every little bit, the corner of his mouth would raise, saying to me that he was dreaming of something that made him want to smile. I only hoped it was about me.

Each deep breath in and out from him was felt on my skin, caressing it, nourishing it fully. Then finally, a few moans and groans were apparent, and his eyes that were filled with sleep, opened and then closed back immediately.

"It's bright this mornin' baby," he whispered, his voice cracking from not being fully awake yet.

I didn't reply. What I did do, was rest my head on his chest, fitting it every so slightly under his chin to where I was extremely comfortable. His tiny sighs of sleepiness, made me sigh right along with him. The feeling of being much at ease, was one I never wanted to be without.

"You workin' today?" he asked, kissing my forehead, then stroking my hair that was probably going in every direction.

"Not today. I gotta open tomorrow though,"

"Hmmm," he hummed out.

"Why," I replied, lifting my head to where we were eye to eye. "What'd ya have in mind?"

"I thought we might go to Dean's and see if they wanna run around for a while."

"Dean ain't workin' today?"

"He said he took a few days off to spend with Lizzy and the baby."

Crinkling my nose, "If he took off to spend time with my sister, I sure don't wanna be one to keep 'em from doin' it."

Feeling his fingers begin to tickle me, I pleaded for him to stop. Finally we rolled off the couch onto the floor until he was hovering over me. His body was pressed against mine and my blood started pumping faster and faster as my heart pounded in my chest.

"You best be careful 'bout what you get started now Evan."

"Is that right?" he whispered, lightly kissing my neck, earlobe then cheek, working his way to my waiting lips. "Now what am I gettin' started?"

"You best stop it...I mean it," I stammered, not saying it in any way that might make him think I was serious. Truth be known, I was enjoying every touch, every kiss, and every ounce of attention he was showering me with. I was just lying there in another world, letting myself get absorbed by his tenderness, charm and sexual appeal.

Suddenly, he hopped up, grabbed my hands and pulled me to where I was on my feet. Instead of continuing his seduction in the most sensual way possible, he put his teasing to a halt.

"I see how you're gonna be," I muttered, walking off from him.

"Come on Betty Jean...let's go to your sister's. We could pick Cody up and all of us could go somewhere...you know, spend some time together."

"Evan, you're with Dean all the time."

"It's different now. I wanna celebrate," he insisted.

"Celebrate what?" I questioned, momentarily forgetting the events of the night before.

The look he gave was one I'd never forget. His eyes began to droop like that ole sad looking hound dog at Ma and Pa's, and his hands fell to his side as if to say, "You mean you don't remember?"

"I was only kiddin' Evan," I continued, trying to take back what I had said that seemed to hurt him terribly. "Let's go over there. I'm sure they'll be glad to hear the news, but first we gotta go by Ma and Pa's and tell them. Ma surely would never forgive me if I didn't tell her first."

That grim look quickly turned to a smile and he waited for me to dress. I kept hearing him outside the doorway as if he wanted to come in on me, but I didn't have a doubt that he had more class than that. Finally, I was ready to go and break the news to my family that I was going to marry for the second, hopefully last, time. I knew Ma would be extremely pleased, but I wasn't sure 'bout Pa. He was always strange that way. Even though I was grown, I could tell he still looked at me like his little girl.

Evan helped me with my Jacket and off we went. For some strange reason, I wasn't the least bit nervous. I was sure everyone knew it was coming sooner or later, but even if they thought it'd be later, what was the difference. The fact was, I needed someone to love and Cody needed a man to fill the place his daddy had left empty. To me, it was perfect timing. I knew he loved me and I loved him, even if there were a few unresolved problems to work out. I had no doubt we would make it.

Pulling up to my old house, Pa was sitting on the front porch with his old, greasy work coat on, whittling up a storm. He had a serious look about him, but not in a mad way, just to where I could tell his mind was thinkin' about somethin'.

"How ya'll kids doin'?" he said, looking up from that chiseled piece of wood he held firmly in his left hand.

"Good sir," Evan replied, nodding out of respect.

"Where's Cody?" I asked. It seemed every time he stayed over there, I'd miss him so much that when I did go get him, I'd hug him like I'd been gone for ages.

"Awe, he's in there with your Ma. She's probably spoilin' him like always," he answered. "I swear, that boy ain't gonna wanna do nothin' for himself if he stays over here too much."

"He's still a baby Pa."

"Yeah, well, I gotta feelin' your Ma's gonna be that way with these grandkids till they're grown...God help'em."

Laughing at him we asked if he'd come in 'cause we had something to talk to them about. He got this familiar look across his slightly wrinkled face. Then he got up and went inside to where Ma was sitting on the couch talking to my sweet little boy. Cody was looking at her like she'd lost her mind, but that didn't stop her from babbling all sorts of baby talk.

"Mrs. Cole," Evan said, nodding to her as well, then turning to Pa. "Mr. Cole, we got somethin' to tell ya."

"When ya'll gettin' hitched?" Pa asked with his head turned sideways and wearing a slight grin as if he knew what we were going to say all the while.

"How'd you..." Evan started.

"I can see the signs boy," he answered, shaking his head a hint. "The way you look at my daughter here, I figured you'd either marry 'er or go on about your business not long after. You didn't go on about your business, so that only left one option."

Evan looked shocked that my Pa was so insightful, but I have to admit, I was a little shocked myself. He didn't throw a fit of any sort, and after a minute, he stood up and came over just to shake Evan's hand. Firmly, they gave each other a gesture that said a million things without saying a word, then Ma brought my baby over.

"Looks like you're gonna be playin' daddy to this handsome little boy," she said sweetly, glancing down at Cody as she said it.

"No ma'am," he replied, making all of us look at him in an ill way. "I don't wanna play his daddy...I wanna be his daddy."

Those short frowns he made appear quickly, disappeared in a hurry after such a charming remark, and Ma handed Cody to him carefully.

"Well then," she said. "Here you go daddy."

"I like the sound a that...now more than ever," he uttered in a low voice, his strong arms around my baby, holding him as if he were his father.

In a way it saddened me knowing Cody would never really know his real father, but I also knew I'd never forget enough to where I wouldn't be able to tell him. It was only fair for him to know the truth, but even more fair for him to have a man to take the place of the father he lost before he was ever born.

Lost in the moment, it was crushed abruptly by a clattering noise outside on the front porch. Pa flung open the door and there stood Ollie Ray. He was a boy that used to try and come a courtin' me. He was about my height, had brownish hair, and always made us all laugh. He knew I was never interested in him except for bein' his friend, but he never did give up much.

"Ollie," I said, pointing to Evan that stood beside me. "This is Evan Bain…my fiancé'."

"I'll be dang," he replied, snapping his finger in front of him. "You mean I'm too late Betty Jean?"

"Afraid so Ollie, but we still got our memories," I muttered as sweetly as I could, knowing he still carried a torch for me.

"Memories for sure," he laughed. "I remember that time I was comin' over to see if you wanted to go to the movies, but your Ma come out on the front porch with that double barrel shot gun and pointed it right at me."

"I was not," Ma jumped in. "I was shootin' an ole black bird off that fence by the garden."

"Maybe so Mrs. Cole, but I decided right then and there, it just wasn't safe to be comin' 'round askin' Betty Jean out."

We all laughed, and I kept thinking back to all the crazy things he used to do. If nothing else, he was about the most entertaining boy I was ever around. In fact, he was a great friend to me for years, even when I wasn't the greatest friend to him.

"How's Mary Jane?" I asked, referring to his girlfriend that everyone knew he'd marry eventually.

"Just as crazy as ever…just kiddin'," he chuckled. "Heck if she can put up with me, I suppose she's got a be a little on the crazy side. Shoot, she takes in every stray animal that comes around. I figure before too long, she's gonna have her own zoo."

"She's a sweetheart Ollie. Now don't go talkin' 'bout her like that."

"I ain't talkin' bad…just tellin' the truth that's all," he said. "Now I need to be gettin' to work."

"That's all you ever do is work, I hear," Pa mumbled. "But that's a good quality son…don't ever lose it."

"Don't worry Mr. Cole, I figure I'll be workin' for a long time… unless I get rich first," laughing again, then leaving, just as energetic as he always was. He hopped in that truck of his and he was gone.

"I swear," Pa tittered. "That boy came by askin' you out so many times I lost count."

Evan looked at me in a jealous, but kidding manner. "He *did*, did he?"

Nudging him, "Stop it! I can't help if I was irresistible. You know, I do have this certain amount of charm that all the boys were attracted to."

That's when Pa got that same look Evan had previously. "Not you *too* Pa!"

All me and Ma could do, was laugh. Those two acted like they'd been around one another all their life the way their expressions were the same. And it was funny to me, that they were both so protective over me. In any case, it was nice to be cared about.

Ma gave me Cody's things and we left. The sky was clear as the sun was bright, and few clouds showed their way into our view. It was cold, but other than that, it was a very spectacular day. Maybe I felt that way because of everything that was happening, but it didn't matter to me why…al I knew was that everything was going my way.

As we reached my sister's house, we noticed they were coming out and locking the door. Evan went ahead and pulled in and got out. I cracked my door open so I could hear where they were going, then Lizzy came over.

"Hey sis," she grinned. "I heard the good news. But I'm not gonna say I told you so. I ain't. I refuse to gloat."

"You can say it sis. You was right from the start. He's 'bout the most sweetest, caring man I think I ever did see and I have to thank you for gettin' us together."

"Don't thank me," she said, leaning over and hugging me to say congratulations. "You're the one who decided to come outa that shell you was livin' in. Now look how good you got it."

"Yeah, well, I only hope it stays that way."

With her hands propping up on her hips, "No more talk like that Betty Jean. What'd I tell you 'bout that. Don't be worryin' bout problems before they come. If ya do, it sure does make life pretty darn miserable."

Agreeing with her, we all talked about going somewhere together. Both of the babies were wide awake and in rare form, babbling and trying to act like they were really saying something to one another. It was hard to keep from laughing at them.

"Let's go to that new antique shop that just opened a month or so ago. I hear it's got some beautiful stuff in there," Lizzy blurted out, her eyes lighting up just from coming up with such an idea.

Dean shrugged his shoulders then nodded, "Why not darlin'? And after that, I'll take you all out to this real fancy shmancy restaurant. It's a good ways off, almost to Fort Smith, but we got all day."

The suggestion sounded wonderful. I was geared up to spend the day with the most special people in my life, and it felt good to be able to smile a true smile again. Lizzy looked happier than I'd ever seen her, even happier than the day she married Dean, and that showed me that true love does weather any storm. I only hoped it would be the same for me and Evan.

After traveling a couple of miles, we pulled up in front of this building that was painted snow white with a burgundy awning covering the front. The sign above it read: "Danyett's Unique Antiques," and it was written in Gold lettering on a dark colored background. In the window were many different types of things. From clocks to coins and everything in between. Then with no more hesitation, we got the babies out and carefully tottered inside. The men stepped aside as my sister and I went in first, and they followed after.

As soon as I was inside, something caught my eye and made me think back to when I was very young. Almost too young to remember fully, but I remembered still. And I reached out to hold the object before me.

13

On a dusty, half-stained shelf just within my reach, sat a fiddle made of dark wood with streaks of lighter color blending in to give it a most unique look. There wasn't a string missing, and the pearl white on the small rectangle knobs that changed the key, made it look practically brand new. Almost automatically, the woman I had turned into, suddenly transformed into the little girl I used to be. I closed my eyes as I held that wonderful instrument in my hands, and I could see one night in particular just like it was happening all over again.

My grandpa was standing in the corner and playing his fiddle away while us kids danced around and around, laughing the whole time. The look on his face was one that consumed us all, spreading joy into each of our hearts as he played tune after tune, never seeming to run out of energy.

The wrinkles on his face were profusely evident and the limp in his walk told me constantly that he was old and probably didn't have a lot longer with us, but when he was playing that fiddle, his youth materialized all over again. It was like he had stepped into a time machine and traveled back to a time when he was nimble and full of wild aspirations to do whatever he set his mind to. The twinkle in those baby blues of his when he was standing there playing, pretty much told a story without him ever having to say a word. To be honest, I always thought he was some kind of angel. He always appeared when I needed him, and with just one hug from that spectacular man, swept away every worry I had before hand.

"You play?" Evan asked, one of his hands slide around my waist and he sweetly kissed the back of my neck.

"Not *me*," I replied, still seeing my grandpa's face in my mind as I continued to hold such an item.

He looked at me kind of funny, but after telling him a short story about what was on my mind, he smiled and squeezed me to him for just a moment, as Cody was sandwiched between us. His tenderness was something almost unbelievable, but at the same time, his masculinity was abundant.

"What'cha lookin' at sis?" Lizzy said, romping over with all the energy in the world. Dean still had Angel. He was across the room, but all of us could still hear him talking to her like they were having the most interesting conversation.

"Just this," I replied, handing it to her.

"Grandpa!" she muttered, clinging to it. "I miss 'im, don't you?"

"Sure do," I replied, grinning at the thought of him. "He was unforgettable."

"You can say that again. You remember when he used to let us put our feet on top of his so he could teach us how to dance."

Laughing, "Yeah, and he'd 'bout pull his back out from bendin' over just to hang on to us."

"Sounds like he was a great man," Evan said, finding a spot in the conversation.

"A one of a kind…that he was," I replied, placing the fiddle back on the shelf I got it from.

Still listening to Dean and his funny baby talk, a woman walked out from behind the curtain that was draped over the doorway leading to the back room. She was smart looking with her narrow, attractive glasses that sat resting at the center of her nose. Her dark wavy hair was shiny as the sprays of light dancing across the lake in summer time, and she looked about Ma's age.

With a contagious smile, she walked up with a pep in each step she took.

"What can I do for ya'll?" she asked, weaving her fingers together and letting her arms fall in front of her.

"Oh, we're just lookin' ma'am. But you do got some nice stuff in here," I answered, trying to be as kind and friendly as she was being.

"Yes…yes," she continued. "I've spent a lot of years collecting some of these things. Some have sentimental value, but I've learned, you can only keep so much. After a while, all you got is clutter and I hate clutter."

"Yes ma'am," I replied, listening to her attentively. "I'm Betty Jean. This is my fiancé' Evan, my son Cody, and my sister Lizzy Thomas."

"Well, it sure is nice to have such young folks in here interested in what I have in this little ole shop of mine," she continued. "And who might that young man be over there."

Lizzy answered that one, still hearing Dean carrying on with Angel, "That's my husband Dean and my daughter Angel," she said. "He's… well…a little…"

"Sweet from what I can tell," she smiled. "By the way, I'm Danyett Holbrook. I own this little nook of a store. It's a fixer upper if I can ever get time to do it."

Her voice was as sweet as the whispering wind at sunrise, and the impression I got of her, was one of self-assurance and total confidence in herself and her career. She held her head up high and you could tell she didn't let much get to her. Without many words spoken, I could sense she was the type of woman who was living for today and hoped for tomorrow.

She walked over to Dean and held out her finger to Angel. Of course, angel wrapped her tiny hand around it immediately and acted like she was never going to let go.

"What a sweetie!" she emphasized. "I just love babies, especially those as adorable as these two you got."

Lizzy and I both said "thank you" and continued shuffling our feet as we slowly went around and glanced at every little tiny thing in there. Up until a year or so earlier, I didn't have much use in doing such things, but as time went on, my likes and dislikes changed. Ma said that happens to a woman more than it does a man. She said that men start out one way and end up just the same way, mostly stubborn and hard-headed. I thought it somewhat comical until I started dating. Then I found out she was exactly right. I quickly found out that men were a strange species, and yet, a species I wanted to get to know better.

"I'll be right over here if ya'll need me," she said in a friendly voice, politely walking off to give us a chance to browse some more.

"See anything you like darlin'?" Dean said, coming up behind Lizzy unexpectedly.

"EVERYTHING!" she uttered, her dimples showing as she did so.

"Alright then," he exclaimed. "We'll take everything."

Shaking her head at him, Angel started to whimper and stuck her hands out for her mama to hold her. She was rotten that way. I suppose most babies are though. There's always something about the bond between a baby and his mama…a bond nobody can break.

"Come on sweetheart," Lizzy said, talking in a more high pitched voice as she took her precious child from her most loving husband. To me, sometimes their life seemed too perfect, but then again, it wasn't. After all they'd been through, I knew they both deserved to be happy and in a perfect sort of way. And that was exactly what I saw when I looked at them. I saw a man and a woman peering at one another as if no one else existed in the universe. I saw a husband and wife who were meant to be together, holding a child who was probably one of the luckiest children born to this earth. It gave me a sense of peace and the warmest feeling inside just knowing I was around such people.

Although it didn't seem so, we spent quite some time in there. She had so many things to see. Some things were old and some were new, but all in all, she had a little bit of something from several generations… from mine all the way back to my great grandpa's time. Lizzy and I figured after a while that we could get lost in there with no question, but then my stomach started rumbling so terribly, if I hadn't known better, I'd a thought there was an angry wolf outside just waiting to nab us when we left.

I suppose everyone was getting 'bout near as hungry as me, but as we reached the door, the store owner came back up to us. She had put a silk flower in her dark curvy hair, and in her hand, were two more.

"You two are so pretty," she said kindly. "Here's something that'll enhance your beauty even more."

Danyett put a flower in each one of our hands and before we could say a word, Evan took mine and Dean took Lizzy's. They reached their hands up and placed the flower's just so in our hair. It was like they had orchestrated the entire thing. I couldn't tell by the look on Danyett's face, but no matter, in such a simple action, I felt beautiful all over again.

"You kids have a great day," she said, then laughed a little. "Listen at me calling ya'll kids. You got kids of your own."

Angel was resting her head on Lizzy's shoulder when my sister laughed with her, "Sometimes ma'am, I wish I could be a kid again… just for a day."

Letting out a huge sigh, I could tell Mrs. Holbrook was thinking about something important, maybe even the past. Her eyes seemed to dance around as she looked through us, instead of at us.

"Time goes too fast," she spoke glancing away. "One minute you're just a child, and the next thing you know…you're old, just old."

With all of that talk, I felt sorry for her, but she didn't see herself the way I saw her. I thought she was very pretty. Her wrinkles were minimal, very few showing, and those glasses she wore, gave her the most appealing look, smart and mature. Of course, I was sure no word from me would change her thoughts.

"Well ma'am," I said. "You have a nice day. Dean's buyin' lunch so we're gonna go before it sounds like I got a pack a wolves howlin' inside a me."

"You go dear and ya'll have a nice lunch. Come back when you get a chance," she replied, both sides of her mouth raising to show her pleasure in us coming to her store.

"We will," we all answered, waving and leaving.

Knowing we had a good bit of a drive to where Dean wanted to go, I just sat back and enjoyed the scenery. The trees on the side of the road were bare and every little bit you could hear a bird far off echoing his sounds across the sky. Ma told me once that was a mating call, but I wasn't sure about that. Then we passed a little town I didn't remember seeing before. It was called "Needmore."

"Needmore Arkansas!" I laughed. "Who ever heard of such a town."

"Yeah," Dean added. "Most folks would say there's enough a Arkansas as there is."

"Sure enough," Lizzy laughed.

Of course, by the time I blinked a couple of times, we were well passed that little town that I never knew existed, or didn't pay attention to it. It was funny though. I wondered how different towns were named, and at that moment, I wished I'd a known who was crazy enough to name a town something so silly. Mena didn't sound silly and neither did Fort Smith, but "Needmore," was a little much.

Dean let the radio play the entire way, and every time an Elvis song would come on, I just wanted to shimmy in my seat. Evan looked at me as if I'd lost what little mind I had left, but I didn't care. I saw Elvis as bein' 'bout near the sexiest man I ever did see, next to Evan. And his music was something that kept me hopin' and a jumpin'. I had heard most of the older folks talking bad about the way he danced around on stage, moving his leg and hips around like he had ants in his pants, but to me, I think that's why most girls went nuts about him. That's why I did anyway.

"Well, we're here," Dean said, finally pulling into the concreted parking lot in front of this very nice restaurant that we'd gone to a good long time before. I remembered it because of the way Pa and Douglas acted. I have to admit. It wasn't their cup of tea. Pa was used to eatin' in his khaki work pants and shirts, and Douglas...well, he was just plain used to eatin' any ole way.

We piled out of the car and paced, one step after another, into this eatin' joint I wasn't all used to myself. I was sure Dean was because of his background, but none the less, I was going to act as classy as any one else in the place. I was dressed up somewhat, and my hair looked just perfect as usual. Lizzy, on the other hand, had hers pulled up in a bun. She looked like a younger version of Ma, but that was okay. They were both pretty in a plain sense. I, on the other hand, liked to make myself up to look like one of them movie stars.

A man in a very exquisite suit, seated us at a table that had tall, slim crystal glasses that stood behind a napkin that was folded so it stood straight up right. There were two forks, two spoons, two knives and some strange looking utensil I don't recall ever laying my eyes on.

"Why so many eatin' tools," I said, probably as unladylike as I could, but I just couldn't help it.

Dean laughed, "The big fork is for the salad...the small fork is..."

"Never mind," I retorted, as confused as a chicken in a maze full a wolves. "I'll just use whatever I grab first."

"It's proper to use the right fork with the right meal," Lizzy said, as if she knew all about such things.

"Come on sis. You act like you're accustom to eatin' like this."

"Not really, but I know how."

"How about we just order," Evan cut in, trying to head off a feud before it got started good. And Lord knows she and I could argue. We got along mostly as kids, but sometimes, we'd go at it like we didn't even like each other.

Dean took the liberty of ordering for us. He knew what was good on the menu. Besides that, he was paying and I figured I best let him pick what price he wanted to pay for dinner. I glanced at the menu, but them prices were far out of my range. To be honest, with the cost of just one meal, I could have bought enough food for three or four days.

After a while, we talked and waited for the food to arrive. I kept clicking my fingernails on the table until Evan put his hand over mine.

"Nervous," he asked, trying to figure out why I was doing something that annoyed him so terribly.

"No, why?"

He just stared at me as if I was getting on his nerves. There were a few habits I had he hadn't seen, but I figured there was plenty of time for him to get to know me better.

"You better get used to me and all my bad habits. You're gonna be livin' with'em for a long time," I smirked.

"I got habits too ya know," he insisted, as if he was trying to get in the last word.

"Such as?"

"I'm not tellin'. You'll have to find out as we go along."

"Hmm," I replied, grinning at him the same as he was to me. I was sure he was only trying to spook me from tying the knot with him.

We all muddled through our meal in between talking about anything and everything. Dean was spurting out story after story and Lizzy sat there gazing at him like she was seeing him for the first time. It amazed me at how happy they were. It was always hugging and kissing with them, and it used to bother me until I found Evan. Before I found him, I was missing that kind of a relationship. Then one day, that all changed.

The food came and it was delicious. We all ate like we hadn't eaten in weeks. Then, wiping our mouths and taking one last sip of tea, Dean flung a few dollars on the table for the tip and we were on our way. It was another good drive home, and I was tired from eating so much. It always happened that way. Every time I'd eat a little too much, I felt like a big fat whale and the bed was what I wanted to find until that feeling went away. At that moment, I could've slept for hours, or at least it seemed so. I rested my head on Evan's shoulder and before I knew it, I woke myself up snoring.

Lizzy, Dean and Evan started laughing as I wiped the dribble from the corner of my mouth.

"What?" I demanded.

"You were snorin'" Evan insisted.

"I DO NOT snore!"

They continued laughing, but then I realized, I might've snored a little.

"You was snorin' so loud sis, I thought you was gonna suck in the top off the car."

Squinting my eyes at her in an angry, but kidding way, I stuck my tongue out at her like I used to do when we were little.

"We're home," Dean announced, pulling up slowly, but carefully. "Let me grab the mail."

He jumped out and headed for the mailbox, while Lizzy and me got the babies out of the car. Evan was still snickering about me snoring, but I ignored him completely. I was sure he wasn't going to like a lot of my day to day habits, but then again, it didn't matter. He had to deal with them.

We followed Lizzy inside and Dean was behind us sifting through the junk mail and the mail that he needed to read.

"Evan?" he said in a questioning voice. "There's one in here for you."

He held out the letter with a questioning look on his face.

"Who's it from?" I asked, but he didn't answer. All he could do was stare at Evan as they exchanged the letter that as being held ever so carefully in Dean's hand.

Evan looked at the return address and go the strangest look on his face. The color in his face went to pale and he held it with both hands as if he was afraid to open it.

"Evan!" I said, shaking him so he'd answer me.

Lizzy was in another world. She had both babies in the living room. They were playing on the floor, then she looked up to see what the silence was all about.

With one swift tear, Evan pulled the tan colored piece of paper out of the envelope. As he unfolded it and began to read, the expression on his face changed even more.

14

We all awaited what Evan would say next, but he steadily read the note line by line. With every word, his eyes began to water so much that a few tears found their way down his handsome cheek. At that time, I was more than anxious to find out what he was reading and who it was from. If it was something to upset him, I wanted to be the one by his side for comfort.

"Evan," I said, my hand resting on his shoulder. "What is it baby?"

His answer was silence as he lowered to slightly crinkled up piece of paper, folded it back neatly and slid it back in the envelope he held firmly in his hand. Turning away from us, step after step, he made his way to the window that looked out from the dining room. He did nothing but stare out leaving the stains of those few tears to dry on his face.

I started to go to him when Dean put his hand up.

"Let me," he requested, slowly pacing towards his cousin who stood as still as a statue.

It was all I could do to wait and see what had upset him so, but I knew if anyone could get it out of him…it was Dean. There was something about the way he talked to people, the way his presence was one of kindness everywhere he went. That was the only reason I let him go instead of myself. I got the feeling he and Evan were very close as children and still remained the same as adults.

Listening closely, I heard Dean whisper, "What is it cuz? What's happenin'?"

Still Evan didn't speak. All he seemed to be able to do, was lift up the letter and hand it to Evan then turn back to the window directly in front of him. After taking a deep breath, Dean unfolded the letter and started reading.

"Oh my God!" he said surprisingly. "I can't believe it!"

At this point Lizzy and I were beside ourselves and stood there edgily. We both knew something was dreadfully wrong, but as we looked at the two men we loved so dearly, they didn't offer anymore information right off.

I couldn't wait any longer. I strolled up to Dean and instead of asking him what the letter said, I took it from his slightly trembling hands. The words I was reading took me by complete surprise and shock. My mouth dropped at such a letter:

Dear Evan,
I hate to be the one to tell you this news, especially in a letter, but it couldn't be helped. I am writing to let you know that Lisa died last night. She hasn't felt good for sometime, but I truly believe she was only holding on so long because of Jade. She loved her so much. She had one request. She wanted Jade to be with you. She was very clear about that. The way she saw things, Jade needed to be with one of her parents. And since she knew she didn't have much time left, that was the reason she came to see you. I know this will be an adjustment, but she is your daughter and is a wonderful little girl. Please call me and

we can make arrangements for you to get her to where it is better for Jade.

The funeral is on Wednesday at the Holder Funeral Home. I know she would've wanted you there. But most of all, you need to be there for your daughter. Talk to you soon, and again, I'm sorry to do it this way.

Sincerely,
Joe

"Joe?" I said a hint aloud, trying to figure out who he was.

"It's her daddy," Evan answered from where he stood, still very quiet. "They were really close."

For the first time I could remember in a long time, I was utterly speechless. I didn't know whether I should say I was sorry or just stand there and try to hold him close to me, hoping he'd calm down some. The way he was acting had me puzzled about his true feelings for this girl he claimed he never wanted anything serious with. Of course, that wasn't the time to bicker about anything of the sort, but it still kept creeping in and out of my thoughts as I stood there trying hard to think of something suitable to say to this man who appeared to be hurting a great deal.

His head soon lowered and his hands fell limp to his side. For one moment, it looked as if his heart was breaking. I wanted to think it was breaking for his precious daughter, but somehow it didn't seem that way.

"You okay?" I asked in a low voice, resting my hands on his waist and my forehead on the back of his shoulder. "I'm here…you know that right?"

"I know," he muttered, still looking down as if I wasn't there at all.

I couldn't help but look back at Lizzy. She was tending to both of the kids. They had started getting somewhat fussy and she was trying to keep the noise down because of the news which plummeted down on us without any warning at all.

"She was tellin' the truth," he said beneath his breath. "She was tellin' the truth."

"You couldn't have known Evan. There's no way. For all you knew, she was just trying to get you back."

"But she wasn't Betty Jean. She did it for Jade…my daughter."

Again, no words crossed my lips. Lisa had gone from being a manipulator to a saint in just a moment and the look across his hurt face, was one of pure and total regret. I could tell he was thinking of things he should've said to her instead of fighting. In his eyes I saw the pity for his daughter because he knew she would never be the same without the one who gave her life. I saw a sadness that looked very familiar. I was sure I had that same look the day I found out Lonnie had died. No one could console me then, and I was sure it was going to be the same for him…at least for a little while.

"You goin' to the funeral?" I asked questionably, but realized I had made a horrid mistake by doing so.

He turned and the expression he showed wasn't one I wanted to see. It was a look of disbelief that I dared even asking such a question. And I felt myself cowing down the longer his stare seemed to burn a hole right through me.

"Yes I'm going," he said sharply, the whipping back around with his back to me.

I felt an inch tall. I didn't mean to insinuate he wouldn't go to her funeral, but it just kind of jumped out of my mouth before I thought about what I was saying. That happed to me a lot. Only this time, it wasn't the right time for me to blurt out something without thinking it through thoroughly.

"I wanna go too," I said, trying to redeem myself.

"You sure?"

"I'm positive. I wanna be there with you…to hold your hand and wipe your tears."

That angry face he had shown me only moments before, turned to a slight grin as he turned completely facing me.

"I'm sorry baby," he whispered, his hands running up and down my arm as he spoke. "I guess this just came as such a shock, I almost forgot about the woman who loves me most."

"I do love you Evan, and I don't wanna be nowhere but next to ya."

"Even after we have to take Jade in?" he inquired, as if he thought I would just walk away from him because of it.

"Baby, she's beautiful."

"That's not what I asked," he continued.

"I've always wanted a daughter," I smiled, putting my hands up to his face as if it were resting in my palms.

"Really?" he said, trying to get a little more assurance from me.

"Really? Besides, that way, it'll be two against one."

"Two against one?

"Yeah," I proclaimed. "Two girls against you."

"You're forgettin' 'bout little Code man in there."

"No I didn't, but he's too young to give an opinion."

It did my heart good to see him smile a little. Our arms embraced one another in the most tender way, but I could still feel his heart pounding from what he just found out. I was sure he still had some feelings for Lisa, but I just hoped it wasn't enough to get between what he and I had started so wonderfully.

We talked for a while, all for of us, but soon enough it got late. The tone had changed so much since early in the day and it was hard to keep from falling into a deep depression just knowing how young she was and also how most folks think they'll live forever. I didn't want to be like her and die before my child had a chance to get to know me. It was the most horrible thought, so I quickly chased such things out of my brain to make room for more pleasant thoughts.

"I'm just gonna stick around here tonight. Is that okay?"

"That's fine. My couch is kinda lumpy anyway," I replied, hoping I'd make him feel at ease.

Even though the cold was evident in the midst of it, just glancing out, it only looked peaceful and serene. The moon looked so gigantic, I felt like if I were to reach out, I surely touch it. The sky was clear as a bell and there were stars covering the blackness above, lighting it up with a brilliance beyond any other.

"I'll see ya'll tomorrow," I said, hugging Lizzy and Dean. Evan took the baby and bundled him up nice and warm, holding Cody next to him the whole way to the car. I got in and waiting for him to buckle my sweet little man in his car seat. Afterwards, he came around and got in on the rider's side of the car.

"I'm sorry about ruining our first day as an engaged couple," he said sweetly, placing his hand on mine and rubbing it gently.

"You ain't got nothin' to be sorry for. You can't help what happened. B'sides, we got plenty of time to spend together."

Lowering his head, "Or at least we *think* we do."

Getting the jest of what he was saying, I didn't want to reply. I knew he was right. I was always taught to live for today because tomorrow is never a guarantee, and I knew it was true. I wanted to live each and every day as if there was no other to follow. My Ma never went a day without saying "I love you," and Pa, well, we knew how he felt. I could always see it in his sky blue eyes when he'd look at us before praying at suppertime.

After a moment of silence after his last remark, Evan peered at me. "What'cha thinkin' baby?"

Sighing heavily, "I don't wanna waste a minute Evan. Gettin' married to you is somethin' I don't wanna wait for."

"Yeah, I guess today gave us a refresher course on how to live…day by day. And I do agree. I don't want to wait for you to be my wife."

Meeting each other in the middle, our lips embraced, but this time instead of releasing passion, it was truth, honesty and just the feeling that we wanted to be together for the rest of our days.

Saying goodnight was tough. I didn't want to be away from him not a moment longer than I had to, but I also knew it wasn't the proper thing to do, having a man who wasn't your husband stay with you. Weighing right and wrong, I didn't see either. I only saw what was real and true.

"I love you," he said as he got out of the car and ran back inside where it was warm from where Dean had started a fire. I could just hear the crackling of the wood and smell the scent it expelled throughout the whole house. To me, that was a soothing and comforting thought.

Although it was getting late, I decided to drop by Ma and Pa's and tell them what had happened. I was sure Ma would agree to watch the baby while I went to the funeral with Evan. And when I pull in, Douglas was sitting on the edge of the porch, bundled up heavily, looking up at the mountain that always hovered over us like it was God himself.

"Hey little brother," I murmured, almost sneaking up behind him.

"Betty Jean!" he hollered. "You liked to scared the dickens outa me."

"Sorry. I came to see Ma and Pa."

"Ma's in there getting' ready for bed and Pa's watchin' one a them crazy westerns on that picture tube he stays glued to at night."

Before I could get to the door, I thought of something, then I turned back around.

"How are you and Tricia doin'?"

Almost blushing momentarily, he answered "fine I suppose, but I tell ya Betty Jean, I don't think I'll ever figure out women."

"Like what Douglas?"

"Well," he said, that familiar smirk painted across his wild looking face. "She's always sayin' one thing then doin' another. If I say left, she says right. I swear sis, if I ever figure that species out, I'm gonna write a book and get to be the richest man in the world."

"Don't hold your breath Douglas. We ain't never gonna let any man figure out how we work."

He acted like he wanted to say something but he stopped before a single word could make its' way out properly.

"What is it?" grinning.

"Well sis...I kissed her."

"You did?"

"Yeah," he said seriously. "You think I oughta ask her to marry me now?"

He must've known I needed a good laugh because it was all I could do to keep from wetting in my pants. The funny thing, was that he was completely serious. He lowered his eyebrows at me and gave a look like he was getting ready to growl and attack before I knew it.

"Marry you?" I questioned. "You don't ask somebody to marry you just 'cause you kiss'em. If that was the case little brother, I'd a done been married thirty times."

"Forget it then," he said, stomping passed me. "I'm gonna ask her anyway. If she says no, then I'll wait till I kiss another girl. I suppose one day, one of 'em will say 'yes'."

"I suppose," I replied following behind him, still snickering from his ridiculous comment about marriage.

When I stepped in, the smell in the room was obvious. Ma had been burning incense and it was wonderful. It smelled like cinnamon. I always loved that scent. It reminded me of my grandma's homemade cinnamon rolls, buttered to the hilt and tons of icing to give it just the right taste...sweet and delicious.

I told Ma what happened and I saw her eyes sadden because of the little girl losing her Ma. Her heart went out to the entire family even though she didn't know them. She was that way. With the tenderest of hearts, I never recall a time when she didn't help somebody in need even when we were scraping to get by. Something inside of her made her want to give.

I asked her once "why?" Her answer was simple. She said she looked at it from a heavenly view. If there was a man, dirty, torn clothes and no shoes, she would do what she could for him because she truly believed he could possibly be God testing her faith in him and generosity towards others. If you ask me...she always passed the test with flying colors. There was never a time she didn't reach out her hand to someone in need, but unfairly enough, when we were in need, no one remotely held their hand out to us. It didn't seem just, but then again, no one said life was perfect.

After talking for a while, I stole my son from Pa's lap and started for the door.

"Betty Jean," Ma said sweetly. "Won't you stay here tonight? We got the wood stove burnin' and besides, we miss ya darlin'."

Thinking for a second, it hit me that I really didn't want to spend that particular night by myself, so I agreed. She ran in her room and got me a gown, took the baby, and off she went. It tickled me how energetic she became when Cody was around, but for some reason, he did something for her that no medicine ever could. He gave her the will to keep moving and not to get old before it was time.

"Douglas!" Pa rang out. "Git in here."

"Yeah Pa," he said, tuckered out from running.

"Give your sister her old bed back and you sleep where you used to."

"With Luther?" he whined, shimmying from side to side, shuffling his feet, mad that I was disrupting his nightly routine.

Pa didn't answer, but he might as well have. The unique blue eyes of his shot in the direction of my little brother so quickly, I had to jump out of the path of fire between the two. I thought, "Here we go again."

Douglas didn't say another word…aloud anyway. He mumbled all the way down the hallway to my old room and pulled the curtain to.

"I don't wanna impose Ma!" I insisted, but hoping she still wanted me to stay.

"Nonsense girl," she answered. "You know how that brother of yours is. He'd find somethin' else to argue about if it wasn't this…so don't worry about it."

Luther was sitting in the corner with his notepad and pencil just a writing away. He never even looked up from it. It was like his concentration was so strong, not even a scuffle between Pa and Douglas could pull him out. But I was sure he heard everything I told Ma and every word after.

"Come on Theron," Ma said, cradling Cody in such a loving way. "We got a little one to get to sleep. And you know how he loves his papa to rock'im."

The previous snarl, soon turned to an entertaining grin, as he got closer to my little one. And just like Dean was doing with Angel, Pa was talking funny, baby talk. I was sure if some of the men from the fields had seen such, they wouldn't have believed it. But it was our little secret. There was no sense in letting everyone know that side of him...only the special people.

Ma and Pa went into their room and took Cody with them. I, on the other hand, found a spot on my old bed, changed clothes, and crawled in, wedging into the exact perfect spot for me to spend the rest of the night. I could still hear Douglas over to my right mumbling in a griping manner, but I paid no mind to such crazy talk. I was tired and after I saw Luther come in and place his notepad on the table in between the two beds, I was off into another world.

My mind started drifting so far away that I wasn't quite sure where I was. As the little girl in "The Wizard of Oz" would say, "I'm not in Kansas anymore...Arkansas *that is*. Instead I had entered a dream I wanted to get out of.

15

From a distance I could see Lisa's face with a cloud of smoke surrounding her shadowy façade. In every direction there was nothing. It seemed like an endless tunnel every time I turned to find a way out. That's when I heard her voice. It was like a ghost speaking to me from the depths of where ever it was she had gone to. With each word, it echoed as if it were coming from heaven, but frantically, I tried to escape the sound.

"Take care of my baby," she spoke, plain and clear.

I seemed to turn around and around to the point to where I was dizzy from the confusion of what was happening, then I just stood still. The words being uttered from Lisa disappeared all of the sudden, leaving me standing in a deafening silent blackness that didn't appear to lead to anywhere significant. My mind kept going back to the moment I heard she had died, and with that, I was even more confused.

There was a light suddenly showing from a good distance away, so I started towards it, gasping from running so fiercely. To my surprise, the sight I saw when I looked up, was sincerely heartbreaking. Jade, with her hands reaching out and a single tear dripping down her sweet little face, she called out. "Mama…mama!"

Feeling her pain effortlessly, again my feet started moving again, trampling through what was left of the dark and trying my best to reach this little girl who had been left without warning. But as I reached her and our fingers touched…I woke. My body was covered with sweat from all of the emotions that had done a contagion through me from the time I went to sleep until the moment I was brought back to reality.

Pa and Douglas were going at it, but tuning them out was one thing I learned to do years earlier. Ma was always the referee and the rest of us were just innocent bystanders.

Lying in that small bed that I'd slept in for many years, I was still, quiet and did nothing but think. Just the thought of having to take the place of that little girl's mama, made chills run through me. I wasn't even sure if it was something I could do…and do it right. The question I posed to myself was "what is right?" I had no answer to that question and I couldn't help but rack my brain trying to give myself an answer to such a difficult question.

"Betty Jean!" Ma yelled out. "Breakfast is ready darlin'."

I didn't answer, but she knew it wouldn't take me long to get to the table. I pulled my legs around and placed my bare feet on the cold hard wood floors beneath me. Still, I wasn't thinking of the cold at all. I was only thinking about what I had to do next.

Bushed and still longing for a few more hours of sleep, I drug to the table. Ma was her spirited, merry self, but Pa looked a bit agitated.

"What's wrong Pa?" I yawned, as I looked over at him holding Cody.

"I swear Betty Jean. This boy didn't wanna do nothin' but get up and play last night. He don't ever do that over here."

"He musta known I wasn't far."

"That's gotta be it. He squirmed around like one a them big ole earth worms out there in the dirt until one or both of us got up with him," he continued.

"Why didn't you just wake me Pa?"

"Awe, you looked like you was restin' too good. We didn't wanna bother ya none."

"You should've," I whispered.

"What was that?" he questioned, still grasping onto my little one with his large, callused hands. Cody looked ever so happy to be in such a spot and his smile emulated that without a doubt. Pa, on the other hand, appeared plum exhausted. His eyes were drooping to where I thought he might just fall asleep right then and there.

"Here Pa, let me take 'im."

"I got this little rascal," he replied, shaking his head. "Besides, he likes bein' in his papa's lap."

Pa tickled him and made him let out his very inspiring giggle. That was one thing that made me sure everything would be just fine.

That's when I got to thinking. I needed a funeral dress, but all I had were casual clothes. I knew Ma didn't have one. The last one she wore was about twenty-five pounds ago, but it was still too large for me. I'd always been a bone as Pa said a hundred times, but all the boys seemed to like it, so I never indulged in food like my little brother Douglas.

We ate breakfast and I bathed quickly, then dressed to go to town. Ma agreed to keep Cody while I went to find a dress. I couldn't afford much, but I knew the perfect place. It was a clothing outlet of used clothes. There were many times I found very cute things in there for little of nothing.

With a hug and a kiss, Ma said good-bye. Cody's little gleaming eyes stayed on me until I was out the door. No matter what was going on in my life, he kept that hint of a smile regardless.

Getting to town, I got to where I was going and began to rummage around in the racks and racks of things they had marked down. There was one dress that stood out more than any. It was my size, but it was also perfect for such an occasion. It wasn't decorated with any kind of frill and the color was dull and just right for a funeral. I didn't want to stand out in the least. As far as the shoes, I had more shoes than I knew what to do with. In fact, Ma always said I had enough shoes to open up my own store.

The middle aged woman behind the counter started to ring up the dress then stopped.

"It's awfully dark young lady," she said, slowly putting a clear plastic bag over it.

"I'm goin' to a funeral ma'am."

"Oh," she replied. "Call me Donna. My husbands a local musician here in town. You may have seen him around...Gary Holden?"

"I don't recall."

"Well, he used to sing nothin' but country, but he does a little bit of everything now. In fact, he got our son in the music business. He's a drummer, and a darn good one I must say."

Smiling, "I don't suppose you're biased one tiny bit are ya?"

"Not at all," she grinned, taking my money and returning what was left in change.

The lady was not fat, but not skinny, with long graying hair. Her eyes were as blue as the clear sky on a beautiful summer's day and her voice was sweet as the smell of honeysuckles. There was something about her that told me she was unique.

"Does your son live here?" I asked.

"No, he used to though. He comes back from time to time. He's playing with some band and traveling around."

With enough small talk, I wrapped my fingers around the hanger the dress hung from and lapped the rest of it over my left arm. Turning, I heard a bell that signaled someone was coming in the store. To my surprise, it was Lizzy. She had her hair down for a change, and Angel wasn't with her.

"Hey sis," I said, going up and hugging her. "What are you doin' here?"

Whispering, "Tryin' to save some money. Shoot Dean spends it like it ain't ever gonna run out and I just don't know about that."

"But don't you have a funeral dress?"

"I got plenty of dresses, but none fittin' for a funeral."

Turning back to the woman behind the counter, "This is my sister Lizzy."

"Well, two lovely young ladies you are. What can I do for you?"

She told her, but in the middle of her trying to find something she remotely liked, we talked.

"How's Evan?"

Hesitating, grimace filled her expression. I wasn't sure how to take it, but I waited still for a reply.

"I think he's just confused about how to start this new life...you know, raisin' a little girl."

"But I'm there too."

"I know sis, but you need to be patient even though I know it ain't one of your good points."

Feeling compelled to find him, I told her I needed to go. I didn't want to wait to tell him how much I loved him and that I would always be there for him. It wasn't long before I had to be at work, but at least I wanted to try and see him if only for a moment.

Disappointed after driving around and not seeing hide nor hair of him, work was waiting on me. I saw Cammy and Kim clocking in as I walked up. Cammy looked so very tired, but Kim illuminated impressive energy. I only wished I had the same.

I didn't ignore them, but I honestly wasn't in the talking mood. Cammy had her hair all curled up and looking as though she was waiting on someone special to show, while Kim, on the other hand, was just being herself...crazy and full of life.

Waiting on customer after customer, I was utterly in another world. I couldn't get my mind off of Jade. I didn't know what kind of a step-mom I'd be, or even if I wanted to be one. I sure didn't want to take the place of the mom who loved her so much. Everything seemed so twisted inside my head, I wasn't sure if I'd ever unravel it in time to find what little bit of sanity I had left. After dealing with Lonnie's death, I was almost positive that before all of this was over, I would surely lose my mind.

"Order up," they hollered out, handing me a tray to take out to number 21. Step after step, I didn't even pay attention to who I was serving until I heard the voice. I glanced up as I hooked the tray on the window. To my surprise, it was Lonnie's uncle Donnie in this white Oldsmobile with shiny wheels and paint so pretty you could dang near see your reflection. It had been a long time since I'd seen him. He came to Lonnie's funeral but left early. I always assumed it was because it hurt too much to be there. From what my husband had told me when we first met, Donnie was just like a dad to him. I knew it was hard for him to take as well as everyone else to accept that he was gone.

"Hey girl!" he said enthusiastically. "Where you been hidin' yourself?"

"Ain't been hidin'...been workin'."

The look he gave me was an unusual one. I knew I was acting strangely, but it was something I couldn't help. My mind wasn't even right there, it was somewhere else in solitude trying to figure out what I had to do next.

Donnie gave me that silly little smirk he was famous for. Lonnie and I used to laugh at him. He was always the funniest out of all of Lonnie's relatives. I remembered once, he dressed up like Dracula on Halloween and Betty dressed in this long white flowing gown. He laid her on this table and it appeared she had blood dripping down her mouth. I swear, all the kids that came to their house, was scared plum to death. The eerie music he played outside his house as the children came up, didn't help none either. I was sure they thought they had gone to the house of some psycho. All I could do was laugh at it. He always did crazy stuff like that. Maybe that's why I took to him quicker than to anyone else in Lonnie's family.

"I'm gettin' married," I informed him. "don't know when, but I 'magine soon."

"You ain't…you know…are ya?"

"No uncle Donnie, I ain't with child. I got one already and he looks just like his daddy."

His smirk changed to a slight frown, "That's good to know Betty Jean. I'm sure Lonnie'd be glad a that."

"He knows," I replied smiling. "I'm positive he knows."

"I just got married myself," he grinned big as an opossum. "Pretty little gal I'm head over heals in love with. There's only one question on my mind though."

"What's that?"

"What woman would put up with my crazy ways? You know us Holdburgs. We got a crazy streak in all of us."

"Except for Lonnie *that is*."

"Oh, Betty Jean, Lonnie had his crazy side too, but he was too busy tryin' to impress you to let it out."

Winking at him, "Well I really need to run. I'm sure they'll be ready to fire me if I don't go in soon. But it was nice seein' ya uncle Donnie. Come see me sometime. I'm sure you'd have fun with little Cody."

"I'll do it Betty Jean. And tell your Ma and Pa I said 'hi'."

Nodding, I gave him his food and said a short good-bye. I figured orders were backing up the length of time I stayed out there talking to him. Even though he didn't live but about five miles out of town, I didn't see him much, or any really. I was glad he came by. He always did have a way of lifting my spirits, sometimes even when he wasn't speaking. He had a cheerful way about him that everyone loved. From his crazy jokes to his wonderful smile, he spread joy where ever he went.

The hours drug by, each minute seeming an hour in itself, but before long, it was time for me to clock out and call it a night. It was cold and the worn out coat I wore was do to be replaced anytime now. I had worn it for more years than I wanted to count, and when I left, I knew exactly where I needed to go. I hadn't seen Evan since the night before and I was worried about his state of mind. My own state of mind was confused, and I was positive his was even worse.

When I pulled in to my sisters, she was getting groceries out of the car. With a bag in one hand and her keys in the other, I came up behind her and opened the door. He smile was like always, penetrating, but nothing seemed to be able to penetrate the perplexity of the situation I was in.

"Is Evan here?" I asked curiously, hoping she'd point in the right direction.

"He ain't been here all day sis. He left this mornin' and went into Fort Smith."

"Oh," lowering my head, not having much else for a response.

"I'm sure he'll be back soon though."

With fidgety fingers, I waited. I helped her put up the groceries and I visited with Angel for a little while, but still no sign of Evan. Every car that I heard pass, I was sure it was him, but that wasn't the case. An hour or better went by when I realized he wasn't coming.

My head still heavy, "I better be gettin' to Ma's. Shoot they've had my baby more than I have lately. Before too long he'll be callin' her mama instead a me."

"Nonsense," she replied. "You've just had a lot on your mind sis."

"Yeah, well, I suppose. I'll see ya tomorrow."

"Why don't you come by here and we'll go to the funeral together. There ain't no sense in takin' separate cars," she said comforting.

"See ya tomorrow."

Lizzy could see my pain just by my tone of voice, but at the same time, she knew there was nothing she could do to ease it. Time would be the only thing to heal my wounds and everyone else's for that matter. Time was the only thing to make a difference. I hated that. Ma used to tell me that every time we lost a relative, or when I was going through a tough time. I hated the thought that the only thing that would make things better, was to wait. Patience was not one of my virtues. I was always the type to want everything "NOW." I suppose I got that from Pa.

Cody was asleep when I went to get him, so I bundled him up carefully and tip-toed out to the car, sure not to wake him. At home he fell right back off to sleep as if he was never moved, and his peaceful look made me want to just sit there and stare at him. The adorable way he looked reminded me what I was on this earth to do. He reminded me without saying a word, who I was. I was his mama, the one who wanted nothing more than to take care of him and teach him right from wrong. The only problem was, I needed to teach myself that first. All of the selfish thoughts running rampant in my bewildered mind, were almost turning me into someone I really wasn't at all. Being selfish wasn't me. If anything, I would give away everything I had to make other's happy. I wasn't sure what was happening to me.

After watching Cody breathe in and out for a while, releasing my frustration by doing so, I changed into some flannel pajamas. It was the only thing I figured would shield me from such a chill in the air.

Bundled up under a blanket and leaning back on a pillow in the corner of the couch, I rested my head back and let my thoughts take a form of their own. That's when I heard a knock at the door. Flinging the covers off me, I slipped on my house shoes and glided my feet across my hard wood floor until I reached the door. The sounds on the other side were minimal, but I knew someone was there wanting in.

Slowly turning the knob, I inched open the entranceway into my humble abode, only to be surprised at what I saw on the other side.

16

Evan was dressed in a pair of polyester slacks, a white dress shirt with narrow stripes, a look that was new for me to see on him, and next to him, was this tiny version of the man I loved. Jade was knee high to him and standing still as a statue with gloom as her sidekick. With her head lowered, her soft curls dangled caressing her round cheeks, bouncing with even the slightest movement from her. She was wearing an off white dress with socks to match and a bow in her lovely hair that made it look even more adorable than ever. But her behavior was far from adorable. It was like she was in another world, another place.

Evan held her hand, but she didn't seem to be holding his. It appeared more like she was only pacifying him by not fighting what she really wanted to do. Although she hadn't spoken, I knew she wanted to turn and run back to those she was used to. To be honest, at first thought, I saw it as a little odd they would let her off with him during such a trying time for her, but then again, he was the one Lisa wanted her to be with. I figured she would have to get to know him at some time or another.

"Come in," I said, extending my hand out from me and pointing into the living room where I had it nice and cozy.

"Thanks Betty Jean," Evan replied, still holding Jade's hand sweetly.

They went ahead of me and strolled a few feet into the next room and this little girl that was suddenly in our lives, began to look around. That blank look she had at first glance, turned to something else. In the most sincere and sympathetic way Jade burst into tears. Evan fell to his knees and her tiny arms embraced him.

"I want my mama…I want my mama!" she said, her voice getting louder and louder with each word.

"I know baby," Evan whispered to her. "But your mama's in heaven."

Those significant sniffles from her that echoed through the room, touched every part of me that held sincerity, love, compassion and caring. She was putting out more feeling in just a few words, than I'd seen a lot of people show in a lifetime. And those tears which began to trickle down, made my eyes fill with tears as well. I felt her pain even though I didn't know her very well. I grasped her wants because mine were the same, to be around someone that loves me. She knew her mama loved her tremendously, that was obvious. And knowing she had lost such an important person in her life, pulled at my heart strings to the extent that I wanted to step in and try to be what she needed.

Still sniffling and wiping her own tears, "Where's Heaven?"

"Oh sweetie…it's up above the clouds. It's a wonderful place."

Batting her long wet eyelashes at him, "Have you been there?"

"No baby, but I hear it's the greatest place in the world. There's no pain, no hate, no fear, no violence…only love and happiness. God and souls like your mama are there."

"Will she come back?" she asked, her lovely eyes peering into his that were much the same.

That's when his tone changed. She had posed a question to him he didn't particularly want to answer. His once dry eyes were watery and full of sentiment for his daughter he had just recently learned about. I could tell it was difficult for him to look her in the eye and say, "No, she's not!" That's when I stepped in. I wasn't sure what I wanted to say, but I could tell Evan needed the help. For once, he was speechless and scared.

Coming up behind her, I placed my hands on her shoulders and turned her facing me. With one finger, I gently wiped her face dry, or at least for the time being and tried to explain what was happening in a very caring and sensitive way. She stood there attentively, awaiting the answer to such a difficult question..

"Jade, you remember me right?"

Nodding her head, I wasn't sure if she remembered me or not, but I intended on going forward anyway

"I'm Betty Jean, you're daddy's friend."

"Do you know if my mama's coming back?" she asked tilting her tiny little head to the side wanting the right answer from me.

"Jade, you see, when you die, you go to live with God in Heaven. The sad part is that we don't see them again until we go to Heaven too."

"I have to die to see my mama."

"No baby, we don't want you to die. You gotta wait until God tells you it's your turn. Until then, you'll be with us…me and your daddy."

Her sadness appeared to multiply at that moment. I didn't want to say the wrong thing to her, but at the same time, I wanted to be as honest as I could. She needed to know that her mama wasn't coming back. Taking Lisa's place was not my intention, but I had a feeling that before it was all said and done, she would be calling me mama as if Lisa never existed. With that thought, I almost collapse from an inner fear I had of dying before Cody got the chance to really remember me. I only hoped Lisa made a lasting impression on this little girl who stood before me with the most heartbreaking expression painted across her innocent little face.

"Jade," I muttered softly. "You're mama's always gonna be with you. She loved you."

There was a question on whether or not she was even half-way understanding what I was trying to say. I couldn't tell. There was no smile, no frown, but instead, a blankness I couldn't read. Most doctors would probably say she was still in shock, but for a child her age, it had to be literally impossible to be able to tell the problem. Her tears had ceased and those watery, sad eyes, turned to a different sort. She started staring straight ahead as if she were looking at someone.

"What is it baby?" Evan asked her sweetly, but she didn't bother to answer. She only walked away from us towards the window.

"It was my mama," she muttered below her breath. "My mama!"

That was the moment she lost it. Everything she had built up deep inside of her exploded into a multitude of emotions I knew she didn't quite understand. Her behavior showed fear, pain, betrayal, and above all, a sense of being abandoned by the one person she'd known since the day she came into this world. She felt abandoned by the only mother she'd ever have, and I wept inside for her.

"Evan!" I said, trying to push him to her, but he was just as overwhelmed by everything that was happening.

In the midst of her fit, he picked her up and held her tightly to him.

"No! No! No!" she screamed. "I WANT MY MAMA!"

"She's gone sweetie…she's gone!" he said, still holding her tightly to his chest.

Amidst the anger, a hint of compassion for her daddy came through and she collapsed into him, no longer fighting him, but clinging to him instead.

"Daddy," she whimpered. "Are you gonna leave me too?"

With a smile on his face and a tear finding it's way out, he answered shaking his head. "I'm not goin' nowhere Jade. I'm not goin' nowhere."

Her tiny hand reached over and slid across his cheek, wiping that tear away. Evan didn't say a word, but just his look said it all. Every moment he had lost with her, was being replenished by actions such as this one. Although she was so little, she was sweet, honest, sincere and held a more caring heart than most adults.

I was told once by a teacher that a child sees good in all, but adults try to find the bad. After all we'd been through, I could see how that was true. She was looking into the eyes of the man who helped bring her into this world, but she wasn't judging him, she was seeing him for who he really was…a man who wanted to be a "daddy."

Hoisting her up, she wrapped her legs around his waist and her arms around his neck. They both acted like they didn't want to let go of one another, and I have to admit, for a moment there, I was a bit jealous. Until then, I had him all to myself, but from that day forward, things would be different.

"I need to get her back baby," he said, coming over and giving me a short peck on the cheek.

"Will you come back?" I asked.

"It's a pretty good drive Betty Jean. Why don't you just come to your sister's tomorrow and we'll all ride to the funeral together."

"Yeah, me and Lizzy done talked about it. What time should I be there," I asked, trying to hold my head up high and be understanding to the fact that he was still dealing with his new situation.

"The funeral starts at one, so why don't you come around eleven. It'll take us a bit to get there and I want a chance to visit with the family, not to mention this cutie pie here," he said, tickling her to see if she'd crack a smile.

He had almost made it out the door when I stopped him. I was sure saddness was filling my eyes from the feeling of rejection, but I tried not to let such things show. If anything I needed to show an understanding beyond any.

Pausing, looking down and back up, "I...I love you!"

Stepping to me, his sigh said it all. With all that was going on, he didn't think enough to say those three words that meant the world to me. I saw regret in his eyes momentarily until he replied with a whole heart.

"Oh Betty Jean," he replied, one of his hands resting on my face. "I'm sorry baby. I love you too. Please don't think I don't. It's just that..."

Stopping him before he could go any further, I put one finger over his full, gorgeous lips, "Shhh, I know Evan. I know."

With one last sweet kiss, he and Jade were gone. She was still gripping onto him as if he was going to leave her as well. Soon enough the truck wailed away and I was left standing there alone again.

Suddenly a warmth ran through me. It was so strange. It felt like there was a presence unknown in my midst studying me and my manner. My soul sensed someone else passing through my body that wasn't mine for a split second.

That's when I realized, if it was anyone, it was Lisa. My papa used to tell me that sometimes souls get lost inbetween lives, or that they have unfinished business. I suppose her unfinished business was to make sure Jade was happy and liked being with the man who was absent in the most part of her life thus far. I didn't have an uneasy feeling, but instead a feeling of peace. I felt a sense of something wonderful.

Still in my flannel pajamas, I went on to bed, hoping I'd find the greatest kind of peace…peace of mind. And for once, I found slumber without nightmares to follow. The spot where I laid down, was the exact spot I woke up in, still curled up with my arm wrapped around my pillow as if I were holding my sweet Evan. I only wished as much. But I had no doubt we would have rough times for a while. The transition from what we were to what we'd become, was definitely going to be hard. I was going to be a twenty year old step-mom. I always thought of myself as mature, but I would have to reach such a maturity level to do such a thing, it would take some time.

Cody didn't wake up all night long. He slept like a rock, only moaning a few times when he first laid down. Other than that, he had the most serene sleep. So in the morning, he was wide eyed and bushy tailed with his eyes sparkling the fact he was nothing but happy. As always, when I peeked down into his crib, his wobbly head popped up and he stared me right in the eye. It was as if he knew I was there even though I hadn't made a sound.

"Come here sweetie," I muttered in baby talk, picking him up and cradling him very close to me. His jabbering had started and I couldn't wait until he started talking. But according to Pa he wished the same thing for Douglas when he was a baby, but after he started talking, he wished Douglas was muzzled most of the time. I always took it as amusing, but Douglas never did. For some reason, he thought we were picking on him. But we needed someone to pick on. Luther was an unlikely target since he was so proper.

I hurried to get breakfast ready and get dressed. It didn't take me long to drop Cody off at Ma's. She acted like she wanted me to stay for a few minutes, but I was eager to see Evan. I missed him. Even though

I had seen him the night before, I felt I was missing a part of myself when he wasn't around.

At Lizzy's, I let myself in. Lizzy was sitting at the kitchen table sipping a cup of black coffee. She was wearing a charcoal gray straight dress, with large lapels. The skinny belt that draped around her waist fit her perfectly, and she was dressed more than appropriately for such an occasion. Then I heard footsteps coming down the stairway.

I peeked around the corner and Evan was coming towards me. His black suit illuminated the sad auro of the day. He had on a dull striped tie that was black and gray, and a handkerchief half showing from his pocket. I had never seen him in such attire. His usual look was casual, but at the present, he looked more like a Baptist minister on his way to give a serman.

"Hey baby," I said, grazing his cheek with a kiss. "Don't you look spiffy."

"I never saw you in a dress before Betty Jean. It suits you."

"Why thank you, but don't get used to it. I'm not much of a dress kinda gal. I never did see much use for dressin' up in this neck of the woods."

"Well, in any case, you look very beautiful."

Nodding in thanks, arm in arm, we joined Lizzy in the dining room. There was a tray in the middle of the table with different kinds of fruits.

"Ya best eat a little sis," Lizzy insisted. "It'll be a good while b'fore we get a chance to fill our bellies again."

"I'm not hungry."

"Me either," Evan added, resting his hands on the table and intwining his fingers together.

Dean entered just moments later dressed similar to Evan. They almost looked like twins, in a sense. He stood there tall and handsome, hovering over the rest of us. He had his hands resting in front of him, clasped together.

"It's time to go," he announced. "Or we'll be late."

With no reply from any of us, we stood up. There was a light knock at the door and Dean went to let in Mary, the nanny. She was just as soft spoken as ever and looked thrilled to be there with little Angel.

After they got things in order, Lizzy took Dean's arm and led us out the door. I did the same with Evan, but he was in another world. I didn't even bother to try and get his attention because I knew where his thoughts were. Blinking didn't seem to be something he wanted to do. His stares stayed straight ahead regardless if there was anything there or not. I was worried about him to say the least, but in my mind I knew he was very strong willed. Time would be the culpret and his heart would be the one that needed to be healed.

After the drive, we finally arrived at a house just outside of Fort Smith. It had two stories just like Lizzy's but the shape of it was somewhat different. It was covered in a pale yellow paint and the shutters were blue. And as we got out and started for the door, a woman came out with Jade by her side.

"Evan," she said softly. "I'm so glad you could come."

He went up to her and grasped her hand. Eye to eye they stared at one another until they both started to cry. Jade had her little arms wrapped around this woman's leg while Evan was trying to compose himself for her benefit.

Then he turned to us, "Betty Jean, come here baby. This is Neline, Lisa's mother."

Turning to her, but pointing to me, "Neline, this is Betty Jean, my fiancé. And you remember Dean, my cousin. Last but not least, his wife Lizzy."

"Oh dear," she said sweetly. "It is so nice of you all to come."

"I wanted to," I replied, out of respect for her daughter who died far too early in life. Lizzy and Dean nodded to her with a short grin.

A little voice rang out amidst all of the talk. "Daddy?"

Kneeling down to her, "Yeah baby?"

"Are you sure my mama's in heaven?"

With his dimples poking out from his handsome cheeks, he replied, "No doubt Jade. And better than that…she can see everything you do."

Her look was one of perplexity, but then he allaberated, "You see Jade, there are tiny holes in heaven's floor so the people up there can see their loved ones way down here."

Wiping a tear that had just began to fall down her face, "She can see me?"

"Oh yeah, and always will."

At that moment, Jade walked to the edge of the porch and looked up. The sky was clear and there were few clouds to be seen. Even though it was cold, the beauty above us was the same as always.

"Mama, can you see me?"

There was no answer in a verbal sense, but the same breeze that blew through me the night before, rushed by the little girl not far from me. She took in a deep breath and turned back to her daddy. So much emotion was being transferred in the air around us, that it was almost too much for me to take. I couldn't stand watching Evan see his daughter in so much quandary. I could tell she wanted to believe him, but she was so little, all she wanted was her mama, not just the memory of her.

He lifted her up high then back down just far enough to where she could hold on to him.

"Is everybody ready to go?" he said, noticing the time. It was after twelve thirty and he wanted to make sure we weren't late.

We all nodded, and Neline went inside to tell everyone it was time to go.

"You wanna ride with me Jade?" Evan asked, sitting on the edge of the porch with her.

"I want to go with my mima. She's awful sad."

Feeling my heart break as he took her inside, we loaded back up and traveled the short distance to the cemetery. The mood all around was of wretchedness and gloom, and when we got out, there were people coming towards her graveside from every direction. That's when I thought she must've been a very well liked person. I felt bad for trying make judgment against her without ever knowing what was happening to her. To be honest, it was nothing but pure jealousy that made me do such a thing. I was jealous of a woman who was dying…how terrible is that.

Just a few moments before they started the service, I put my hands in my jacket pocket, but it wasn't empty. There was a folded up piece of paper in it that I didn't know was there. I'm sure my expression changed and Evan noticed it right away.

"What's wrong?" he asked, as I took the paper out and unfolded it quietly.

17

"Here," I answered, handing him the paper I quietly held in my hands.

Lowering his eyebrows, he carefully looked at it, then leaned over and kissed my cheek. "I'll be right back."

Nodding, I stood there and waited for him to return. I felt a little strange being there since I didn't really know her, but it wasn't that at all. I was there so I could show Evan how much I loved him and that I wanted to be by his side no matter what. I saw him approach the preacher standing near the canopy that shaded the coffin Lisa was to rest in from now on. And after a few exchanges of words, he handed the paper to him and came back to me. I could tell he couldn't find a smile if he wanted to, but he was trying for Jade's sake.

Lisa's mother came up beside us holding Jade's hand. Her little face was looking down at the ground. I was sure she didn't understand any of what was happening. I could tell by the look in her eye that she was as confused as a person could be. She stood there without even flinching or moving an ounce. Then the music started. People started to squeeze in closer and closer to where her body lay.

There was an indescribably beautiful spray over her maple casket directly in front of me. There were white, yellow and red roses weaved in together giving it an even softer look with the adding of baby's breath that filled in very nicely. A few carnations were blended in somewhat, but they were overpowered by the supremacy the roses carried as their scent floated all around us.

A few people were talking, but at a low whisper. Evan, on the other hand, had his hands resting in front of him, clasped neatly.

"Shall we bow our heads in prayer?" the preacher said, crossing one hand over the other, clasping them and letting his arms fall in front of him.

The tension in the air danced around every head, most in disbelief. That's when I got to thinking. Being a young woman, I never did give one thought to my life being over instantly. I never did think of not being clearly in my son's memory, but suddenly, the reality of life slapped me in the face more powerfully than ever before. For the second time in my young life I had attended funerals for two young people who died so abruptly, taking away the future that most people take for granted.

The first prayer was completed with everyone saying "Amen," almost in unison, and my weary head rose up and looked around.

"She looks so lost Evan," I whispered, clinging to Evan profusely, afraid to let him go.

Tilting his head towards me, "But we're gonna help her find her way. We have to."

The service was beautiful. The way they honored her, was more than appropriate. There were so many tears that it didn't seem a dry eye was nowhere around. Those nicely dressed ladies in their bonnets kept their heads lowered the entire time. Whispers were coming from all around. They were saying, "she was so young," or "what a shame for the little girl."

Ma used to tell me you could tell the difference between someone who was sincere and someone who was only pretending to be. I saw clean through some of them folks, but others, were fully hurting to the core with sadness and misery for their loss.

Many kind words were spoken of this young woman I had only met a few times, enough to make me think I knew her personally. One after another, people shared their accounts of the sweet and tender way she had about her. It almost made me feel guilty for thinking bad things about her. The green-eyed monster got a hold of me the first time I saw her and it didn't leave until I heard she was sick. Ma always told us jealousy was one thing a relationship couldn't handle. And if wasn't for such a turn of events, I'd probably still be sharpening my claws to tear into what I thought to be a threat to my future.

The silence of everyone around us, was deafening. The only voice heard was the one speaking at the moment, other than that, every mouth was shut and every eye filled with sad, mourning tears. That's when the last person got up. It shocked Evan and I both. Little Jade stood up and her dressed swayed back and forth gently until she reach the podium. Someone had put a chair in front of it and helped her up. She still just barely reached the small microphone, but we all heard her words clear as a bell.

At first her head pointed down. Her uncertainty about what to say was noticeable, but as young as she was, it was hard for me to believe she even understood what was going on. That's when her stillness was broken. Those golden curls rested on her shoulder as she lifted her tiny head to talk. A few tears began to stream down her face, but none the less, that didn't stop her from what she had already started.

"My mommy's gone," she spoke in a low voice, sincerity splendid in every syllable. "She loved me."

If there was a single person who didn't have a tear streaming, at this point, it was unanimous. Every heart was breaking and by the looks I saw, they were all aching with the thought that nobody knows exactly how much time any of us has. Then she continued.

"My Mima said mommy was in heaven. Then she must be an angel," she paused, glancing up to the sky, her gorgeous eyes gleaming like I'd never seen them before. "I love you mommy."

A man standing near her, someone I didn't know, picked her up from the chair and her arms slung around his neck, latching onto him tightly. Red splotches were on her face from crying and when the man handed her to Lisa's mother, her pain was transparent. My heart had dropped from the pity I felt for this little girl I knew I would soon get to know better, but at the same time, pity wasn't all I felt. In an extraordinary way, from afar, she had won my affection as well as Evan's.

With my mind wandering away, I was brought back by the words that were affectionately written by my very own brother. And in closing the service, this was read to all who were there.

ANGEL EYES
The beauty of the heavens,
And the peace of love within,
Are a few things that are in an angels eyes
From the day they first begin.
They see the stars from another view
And place another in the sky,
One to represent their life
Because to them, they did not die.
In an angel's eyes are many birds
Flying as they please,
Not worried for they won't be harmed,

Putting them all at ease.
There are rainbows, lovely rainbows
To line all of heaven's home,
As a symbol that the storm has stopped
And that they'll never be alone.
For now a brand new angel,
Is seeing with new eyes.
She's seeing no more darkness,
In a moody cloudy sky.
But instead she sees the walkway
That will lead her to where she needs to be,
Fulfilling every want and need
As it shows her destiny.
There's a new angel flying
Knowing that she will never fall.
For as it is in heaven,
Through her eyes she sees it all.
She's seeing things through angel eyes.

I held back all of the emotion I wanted to show, but deep down it was welling up tremendously. I noticed Evan wiping his eyes as one after another, tear after tear ran down his gallant façade, stripping him of the manly man attitude he always tried to portray in front of me and everyone else. The softest part of his sincere heart was out in the open and being crushed. The sad part, was that I couldn't do a thing about it. Comforting him on the outside wouldn't come close to healing his hurt on the inside.

One last prayer and another "Amen" by the multitude of people, and it was over. There were a few folks mumbling as they walked away, but for the most part, all I heard was sniffling from those who couldn't hold in the hurt and loss they'd just gone through. I turned with Evan and gently rested my fingers on his arm, showing him I was there but not being too touchy feely. His actions showed he wasn't in the mood to be pawed on by any means and I respected that. My main goal was just to be there.

The mumbling of the people as they passed and muffled crying in the midst of it all, was something I knew I'd never forget. In fact, the air around us, was filled with nothing but pure wretchedness.

Looking up, Lisa's mom was coming towards us with Jade clutching firmly onto her hand. Those tiny streaks down her face were heart wrenching, but understandable. She looked at Evan and I with little expression. It made me wonder if she had slipped back into the denial she was in at first. That was one thing I dreaded. I knew what denial could do to a person.

"Let's go home mima. Let's go home."

"In a minute sweetheart," she whispered in a sweet and caring tone. "But first we have to see when your daddy wants to see you again."

Hesitating, Jade took off running to the car. It was almost like an answer to the unspoken question, "Do you want to spend time with your daddy?" And I could tell Evan was torn into a million pieces.

"She'll get over this Evan."

"I know," he respectfully replied. "I'll be in touch. We'll work somethin' out."

She nodded and went to join Jade. She was leaning against the car with her arms crossed and her eyes staring straight up. It made me think. If I were her, I probably would've been talking to the mother I was just left without. For a moment, I put myself in the mind of a little girl and I felt her pain.

"You ready?" Evan asked, sighing in confusion as Lizzy and Dean stepped up behind me.

"Whenever you are."

With nothing else spoken, we slowly strolled to the car parked a little ways away. He never said a word the whole walk, but he was thinking so hard, I could almost hear his very thought. I started to speak, but immediately decided to leave him be.

Evan opened the door for me and I got in. Climbing in and finding a place next to me while Lizzy and Dean got situated in the front, I noticed he was staring in Jade's direction. The slight wind was blowing her beautiful curls in every direction and her innocence was clearly seen. Ironically enough, she was looking at him as well. As jealous as I was in the beginning of this pint size Lisa, at that moment, it rang clear to me. They were meant to be together. She needed her daddy as much as her daddy needed her. From the day I met him, I sensed this sensitivity about him like none other. His tenderness was unbelievable, and his loving nature blew me away. I got the feeling she was going to be just like her daddy, not to speak ill of the dead of course. But I could see his qualities in her from the start.

"Evan," I said, pulling him out of this trance he was under.

"Yeah, sorry," he replied, shaking off whatever it was that was digging into his thoughts ever so fiercely.

Jade's little hand raised and slightly waved as Dean turned the wheel to head home. And with a genuine smile, he did the same. The look on his face was one of relief. That one small gesture from his daughter showed him that she did care. She was just confused and scared. That was all it took to make him smile. Those sad, dulling eyes he was wearing, brightened up with that one thing, and I too had to smile.

"You think she'll wanna come stay with us?" I asked, hoping not to say the wrong thing.

"I hope."

"I'm sure she will Evan. I saw the way she was looking at you."

"Yeah," he replied. "I'm the one she was wondering where the hell I was all this time."

"But you didn't…"

"I'd rather not talk about it Betty Jean. Let's just get back." His tone changed so quickly, I almost felt like he thought I was his enemy instead of his fiancé

"Whatever you say."

For the first time in a long time, I didn't pay much mind to those grand mountains in the distance. In fact, they didn't have much meaning anymore. To me, if those mountains symbolized God, then why were they still standing to watch a young woman taken away from this world so soon? I sure didn't have the answer and I wasn't bound to ask Evan anything. In some ways, he was acting like *I* was the enemy, when he was only angry at life and himself.

Looking around, trying to occupy myself, I noticed many clustered clouds trying to meet at the center of the sky. I knew if that happened, we'd have a storm for sure, but a storm was the last thing on my mind. Dean wasn't even playing the radio. I figured the radio would change the mood a bit, but I guess I was the only one who felt that way. It was so quiet, I felt like yelling out just to make some noise, but they'd all think I was crazy for sure then.

Evan continued to stare straight ahead, not really looking at anything. That brief smile he showed when we left, was very short-lived and it was replaced with more of a look that spelled uncertainty than anything else.

"We're home," Dean announced after driving a good bit. And he pulled in slowly, parking next to Evan's truck just to the left of the exquisite fountain they had displayed elegantly in the front yard.

Although Evan was clutching my hand tightly in his, it was obvious I wasn't whirling through those thoughts in that mixed up brain of his. I figured he was only doing it to make *me* feel more secure.

Dean jumped out of the car and ran around to open the door for Lizzy. He was always a gentleman that way, but Evan still just sat there.

"Come on Evan," I said. "It's cold out. B'sides, I gotta get Cody. Pa's got an early start tomorrow."

With a nod, he flung open the door, held it open and closed it hard after I had exited. I wasn't used to his behavior being so erratic. I kept telling myself there was a reason, but in the back of my mind, I had my fingers crossed that he would snap out of this inner rage he was sifting out towards the rest of us. I for one didn't know how to handle it.

The door was cracked open when I reached it. I could feel the warm air cover me as I entered, Evan closely behind me.

"Ya'll okay?" Mary asked considerately as she sat rocking my darling niece in the chair in the living room.

"Fine," he replied.

"Thanks for asking," I continued, going over and lightly gracing a short kiss on Angel's forehead as her eyes were fluttering, showing all signs of pure exhaustion.

The fireplace was roaring, its tiny flames creating a display of dancing lights on the walls like a silent movie…dazzling to me. It was enough to create a warmth that seemed to float all around me, warming every part of me that was chilled in the least.

The next thing I knew, I heard the front door open and shut, only to turn and find Evan gone.

18

With my feet sweeping across the floor, I was slowly heading for the window. I was sure my sweet love needed some time alone, but I wanted to be there for him just the same.

My small hand pulled back the curtain and noticed him just standing still, looking halfway up and halfway down.

"Sis, what is it?" Lizzy questioned, joining me as I peered out at the man I'd grown to love so dearly.

"It's Evan Lizzy. I just don't have a clue what to say to him."

"Don't say nothin'," she replied winking afterwards.

Perplexed from her response, with my head half-cocked sideways and eyebrows raised, I asked curiously, "nothin'?"

"Listen Betty Jean. Remember when grandpa died?"

"Sure I do!"

"Then you remember how we both was…Luther too."

"We didn't talk much," I added.

"That's 'cause there wasn't much to be said."

"You're sayin' I just need to let'im work it all out on his own?"

"*You* did. I think he deserves the same…don't you?"

"I suppose," I answered. "But ain't nothin' gonna stop me from bein' there for him."

"Nothin' should," she finished, leaning her forehead against mine and giving me that smile that always lifted my spirits even when I didn't think they could be lifted a hair.

"Thanks sis."

"That's what sisters are for right?"

With a nod, I went outside. I didn't want to leave him alone any more than I had to. Like Ma used to tell me…"sometimes silence screams out your emotions more than talkin' ever could." And once again, she was right.

Amidst the unnerving cold, one step after another I approached Evan carefully. I feared saying the wrong thing to him, afraid he would turn his frustration to me. So, for a few moments I just stood there acting as his shadow. Soon, those clouds I'd seen forming earlier, finally joined, creating a light mist at first. It wasn't long until the drops got larger, making the feel of winter even more unbearable.

Evan crossed his arms. His steady breathing was clearly seen in the white misty smoke hovering in front of his lips with each quick breath he took. Each time I'd start to say something, I didn't. I'm not exactly sure why. He had never given me any reason to fear him, but what I was more afraid of, was the chance he might think I was trying to tell him how to act or what to do. That was the last thing I intended on doing. But through the years I learned men are a different creature.

I learned that no matter what you think men are going to do…they do just the opposite. And whatever you think they're thinking…you're nowhere in the ballpark of what they have squirming through every core of their minds. I used to ask Ma about men. She'd just say, "Well Betty Jean, I can tell ya one thing. Tryin' to figure out a man is like tryin' to put together a puzzle with missin' pieces. You won't ever get the whole picture."

As I let my thoughts take me over, I noticed a short glance from those engulfing eyes I loved so much. It was quick, but he looked at me. Maybe he was seeing if I was going to stand next to him until he decided to talk, but I didn't even want to try to get inside the mind of a man. It'd be no use.

His stance stiffened up suddenly making him portray someone who was callused and scorned. And as I encircled around to his side, his eyes were glossy and staring directly in front of him, not veering off a single bit. In fact, if I hadn't known better, I would've thought he was ignoring me altogether.

"B.J.?" he spoke in a low and questioning voice.

"Yeah Evan," I answered, letting my hand rest on his, caressing his rough, manly exterior that proved his many hard working days.

"You think I'm gonna be a good dad?"

"You already are baby!" I emphasized, resting my chin on his shoulder.

"No," he continued. "Really! I haven't had much of a chance yet. And I guess I'm just scared I won't be any good."

Turning him to me, I placed my hands on his face, feeling each crease, every inch of the handsome man before me, and shaking my head. "You gotta believe in you. I do. But me believing ain't gonna do you no good. Until you believe you can, you never will."

I kissed him on his cheek then dropped my hands to where our fingers laced together momentarily. Eye to eye we were communicating, but there were many words being spoken silently between these two hearts that had grown to be connected somehow by chance.

Without hesitation, I took a step back. It was more than obvious he needed time to think, and I loved him enough to give him that space.

As hard as it was, I didn't want to be in his shadow, but by his side instead. And the only way I knew how to do that for the future, was to leave him alone for the moment.

"I'm goin' home," I whispered, as my voice seemed to stutter because of the cold in the air around us.

With a glimpse of his unforgettable dimples and a slight smile, he nodded, slowly pulling me to him for a brief moment.

"I'll see ya tomorrow," he replied. "You get some rest now and be careful drivin' home."

"Don't worry 'bout me Mr. Bain. I'll be just fine."

"You know B.J., somehow I believe you always will."

I turned to go inside to get my keys and as I turned to handle to the front door, his voice rang loud and clear.

"I love you Betty Jean Cole."

Turning my head half-way back to him, with my hand still clutching the doorknob, "You better," I replied, a bit of attitude gracing my words as they spilled off my lips.

My keys were near the doorway on a table next to the stairway and I picked them up, tossing them up a little. Those few words he said, gave me reassurance, enough to where I felt okay about leaving him. Then, a moment later, he came in from outside, making those noises of how cold it was "burrr." With that, I couldn't help myself.

Tip-toeing over, I walked my fingers up his chest and then let my arms encircle him. "I could take care of you bein' cold."

"I bet you could," he replied quickly, releasing a huge sigh. "But you better get back and pick up that baby. I'm sure he misses ya as much as I'm goin' to when you leave here. And…well, he did have ya first."

Shaking my head at his remark, "You're somethin' Evan."

"Well baby, if you ever find out exactly what…let me know would ya?"

"Go to bed," I said, letting my lips only half touch his.

I said my goodbyes to my sister and Dean, and gave Evan one of my infamous winks before I walked out. It was a silent way of saying "I'll be thinking of you." Of course I was sure he already knew that. I never made it a secret that he was in my thoughts night and day. Even though Ma always said that men like women that have more mystery than anything else, I didn't have enough mystery in me to make him think otherwise.

Slowly, I puttered along up and around the winding curls the road had to offer until I reached the small turn in where I would find my sweet little Cody. It may sound funny, but every time away from him, even for a day, felt like a year. But I knew he was in good hands, 'cept for Douglas that is. I never did know what kind of crazy stuff he was trying to teach my son when I wasn't around. For all I knew, he was tellin' him how to sneak out of the house.

I jumped out of the car and threw my coat over my head, sheltering myself from heaven's tears that had just started drifting down steadily from the dark sky above. When I got to the door, I clearly heard Pa and Douglas nippin' at each other like two rival hound dogs fightin' over a piece of meat. Shaking my head, I felt at home, as it always was…always had been.

"I'm back," I said, opening the door and letting myself in. Their house wasn't as warm as Lizzy's, but it was comfortable enough. Douglas was standing next to Pa's chair with his arms crossed and a look across his face that was all too familiar. But he didn't stop ranting for long. I got the jest of what he was wanting, but Pa was on the opposite side of the fence as usual.

Smiling and passing them by, I waltzed into the kitchen to find one of the funniest sights I ever did see. Cody was sitting in Ma's lap and his face was covered in apple pie. She had placed the pie in front of him, so it seemed, and I could tell he just dug into it whole-heartedly. Those big blue eyes glanced up at me when his hand went in his mouth once more, and I burst out laughing.

"Ma…what in Heaven's name?"

"Oh dear, I made this pie today and I figured I'd let my darlin' grandson try to eat it on his on."

"Looks more like you gave'em a bath in it."

"Well dear, it ain't nothin' a little soap and water won't wash off."

"I swear Ma, you're gonna spoil him to where I ain't gonna be able to keep him."

Grinning back at me, "Then you'll just have to bring'im back to me."

"We really need to get home. A storms a brewin'."

Suddenly, I heard Luther come through the door like lightning. His breathing was erratic and excitement was written all across his face. We all awaited something from him to let us know what was going on and finally he yelled out. "I DID IT!"

Bewildered, none of us knew what he was talking about. In fact, for a moment, it was like he wanted us to guess his good news instead of telling us on his on.

"Come on Luther…tell us," I insisted.

"Okay sis," he said running up to me as if electricity was filling his every muscle. "I got accepted."

"Accepted?" Ma inquired quickly.

"Yeah Ma. You remember that big publishing place Dean's dad was telling us about?"

"Yeah," we all said in unison, hanging on his every word.

"Well, I just got a letter. They love my poetry and want to publish it."

Overwhelmed, Ma's eyes filled with so much joy. She embraced him with enthusiastic arms and Pa came up from his seat and did the same. I was so happy for him I didn't know what to do, but when I glanced over Pa's shoulder, Douglas was standing there with the blankest look. While we were all congratulating Luther, Douglas seemed unconcerned about our brother's new found career.

Soon after, he opened the door quietly, and went out onto the porch.

"What's wrong with Douglas Pa?" I asked, concerned about my mischievous little brother.

"Who knows Betty Jean. I swear that boy comes up with new tricks to get attention every day."

Ma and Pa were still making a fuss over Luther when I slipped outside quietly. I wasn't sure what was wrong with him, but I was bound and determined to find out. He had plopped down on my spot even though the rain was dampening his clothes.

"Alright lil' brother, what's wrong?"

"I don't wanna talk 'bout it!" he insisted rudely.

Crossing my arms, I thought for a moment. "That's great about Luther, huh?"

"WONDERFUL!" he said arrogantly, making it obvious that he was feeling just the opposite.

"You ain't happy for Luther?"

"Sure I am. Ya know, Luther is perfect. He does everything just right...and never does *anything* wrong. And then there's me."

"Come on now Douglas. Do you really think Ma and Pa would ever pick one of their kids over another. Ma's always told us we're all equal."

"So she says! Why is it then, that Luther gets praised for everything he does, and I get scolded."

"It's just that…"

"For as long as I can remember sis," he interrupted. "They've told me…Douglas quit…Douglas don't…Behave Douglas…I said 'no' Douglas. But with Luther, I never heard'em talk that way. It was always 'I'm proud of you son, ' or 'good job.'"

"They love you lil' brother…they do."

He didn't say a word, he just looked up at the mountain. Although the rain was clouding the view somewhat, he continued to stare.

"You think if I made a wish on this mount that they'd be proud of me, they would be?"

Shaking my head, seeing sincere emotion from him for the first time, I replied softly, "Douglas, go ahead, but I can tell you…you're wish done already come true."

Looking at me funny, I continued. "You and Pa are so dang much alike, it's hard for you two to get along. And Ma…well, she just goes along with Pa 'cause that's the way she was brought up. So don't think you're loved any less…just know that Luther ain't much like Pa and you're his spittin' image."

"You're just sayin' that Betty Jean."

"Ma told me a bunch a times. She told me that you and Pa were so much alike it drove her crazy."

"You really think that's it?"

"I don't have a doubt in my little ole country mind brother. Now," I said. "git in there and congratulate our brother. He's been wantin' this for a long time."

Agreeing, he got up, wiped his pants off and followed me inside. He went right up to Luther and stuck out his hand.

"I'm proud of ya Luther."

A hush fell over the room. Ma and Pa seemed shocked Douglas would be so mature and serious. But Luther wasn't shocked at all. I had a feeling them two had bonded some since Lizzy and I left the house. But it was the first time Ma and Pa saw it out in the open.

"Thanks Douglas," He replied. They gripped each other's hand and gave a manly shake. It was a moment I'll never forget. To me, it was a sign that my youngest sibling was learning what life was all about.

Afterwards, I picked up Cody. He was a literal mess, but Ma handed me a clean rag. He looked like an Apple pie himself, and none of us could help but laugh. Douglas did too. I felt like the little talk he and I had, did some good. He took Cody from me and I grabbed the bag I'd left for Ma with the baby's things.

"I gotta go Ma," I said, kissing her on the cheek.

"Be careful dear."

Douglas came up beside me, "I'll take my nephew to the car…if it's okay."

"Fine with me little brother. He's gettin' a pinch on the heavy side these days."

Nodding, he waited on the porch until I got the door open. Then he carefully scurried out and placed my little one in the car. He stood there getting drenched, but he turned and stopped.

"Thanks sis," he uttered sweetly.

"You're welcome…now git inside before Ma whoops you for standin' out here and gettin' soaked to the skin. You know how Ma is about stuff like that."

"Yeah, well, bye Betty Jean," he replied rushing back under the shelter of the porch.

Closing the door, the rain falling on the top of the car was mellow. I knew deep down that it wouldn't take long for me to find my place in slumber land with such a musical sound all around. It reminded me of something Luther wrote several years back. It was called "Tears from God."

Tammy D. Thompson

A single drop from his eyes
From the heavens way up high.
Show to me the sorrow
In this world that he must find.
Then there comes the showers,
Soothing more tears that he does shed.
Tears that show his disappointment
For all his children who have fled.
And finally, there are the storms
With roaring thunder and lightning bright.
Show to me, his anger
That not much is right.
For those who claim to love him,
Abandon him the same.
For within every single storm
Starts with his tears…the rain

I couldn't help but remember every last word of such a lovely verse, and as I started around the curve to my small cabin, a set of lights came suddenly and blinded my sight. I couldn't see the road or where I was going and a tremendous fright filled me. That's when I felt my car start to twist, the rain water under my tires was lifting me up to where it was taking me where it wanted to.

19

The first thing I thought to do was to take a firm hold of the steering wheel and say a little prayer at the same time. Those bright lights of the car I saw, finally vanished and I ended up facing the narrow driveway going to my house. Cody didn't even look shaken up. For all he knew, he just went for a heck of a ride, but for me, it brought back terrible memories.

Not long after we got inside, the rain started even harder, pounding on my roof thunderously. Cody looked around each time the thunder would roar, but he never even flinched. It was like he was fine as long as he was safe and secure in my arms.

The wood burning stove I had was pumping out enough heat to replace the cold that was there, and I laid back on the couch and flipped on that black and white television to see what was happening in the world. It was funny. Everything they were talking about, seemed a million miles away from where I was. Ma used to say that Pa moved us where we were because of the way the world's turnin'. I wasn't sure about that, but I did know one thing. There was a peacefulness about where we lived. Everybody knew everybody. Sometimes that was good, but sometimes there just wasn't a single bit of privacy.

While I was sitting there thinking of this and that, my son had ever so quietly fallen asleep, resting his sweet little head on my chest. His breathing was steady, and every few minutes, he'd wiggle around, moaning each time he did so.

Careful not to wake him, I carried him to bed, covering him just enough to where he wouldn't get a cold. I never could think of anything that looked as adorable as my son falling into the hands of peaceful slumber. In fact, there were times when I just stood there and looked at him, watching him breathe, and caressing his feather soft hair, hoping he knew how much I truly loved him.

He was tucked in nicely and comfortably, and my body gave me signs that it was time for me to follow right behind him. There was no reason for me to be so worn out, but I was. My eyelids kept wavering and there were a few times I dang near just fell over sideways. That was enough for me.

The storm was still tormenting our little town when I laid my head down for the night. The only thing that bothered me, was the lightning. I was always afraid of lightning. My mom's cousin, T.R. used to tell me that lightning can strike clean through the roof and nab you right in your bed when you was sleeping. After he told me that, I never slept a wink on nights when the lightning was raging high. Lizzy laughed at me and Douglas, well, he just laughed.

Pulling the covers over my skin that had goose bumps all around, I pulled my knees up to me and grasped onto the pillow laying sideways beside me. Clutching it tightly, my eyes closed and like Lizzy, I found myself in another place.

Strangely enough, it was a vision of what appeared to be the future. There was a young woman standing in front of a mirror fixing her make-up and finishing that exquisite hairdo she was wearing. That's when a more mature Evan came walking in.

"Honey," he spoke sweetly. "I hope you're happy with this man."

"Jade," I said to myself, but no one seemed to be able to see me. I was like a ghost floating in the room watching what was happening.

Just seeing her so beautiful, I couldn't help but smile the most vibrant smile. Then Jade called out, "Mom, where are you?"

That's when I saw myself walk in and hug her. It looked like she was mine, not anyone elses. Suddenly, directly in front of me, a shadow of someone was being shown to me. "She's my daughter," a voice said.

It didn't take me long to recognize it was Lisa. I could see a pale etching of her face through the vision, but not one that was clear. No matter, I knew it was her. The tone in her voice showed pain and agony of not being able to see her very own daughter marry. And before I knew it, that same shadow begin to move towards me. "She's not yours…she's mine!" it rang out.

When it reached me, I gasped for air and found myself gripping the pillow even tighter than before.

"Dear God," I said to myself. "I'm goin' crazy."

Glancing over at the clock, it said 5 A.M.. Cody was waking up for a feeding and I had a distinct urge to go see Evan. I knew it was a bit on the insane side to go out at such an hour in the cold, but at the same time, there was nothing else I wanted to do. I felt caged there in that small house, waiting on something wonderful to happen to me instead of being encircled by nothing but despair, depression, sadness and disappointment.

I fed Cody and got dressed, layering our clothes to make sure the mountain air didn't get a hold on us too terribly. I went outside and started the car, letting it warm to where I felt comfortable taking my little one out. Then he and I were on the road. It was still dark and there was still a slight rain coming down.

I made sure to cover my son properly, but I was close to drenched . Every strand of my hair was dripping on my heavily layered clothing and my heart couldn't stop racing. Just the look of the road and the rain in the darkness, made me antcy about driving to town. That's when my memory took a hold of me.

I could still see the very moment Lonnie and I had gone off the road. The rain was intense and one small wrong turn caused dissaster for Lonnie and hell for me.

My hands were shaky, but I fit the key in the ignition and started up the car. The engine sounded cold, but after a few moments, it was purring like it always did. Smoke was pouring out from behind me showing exactly how cold it really was, and I just kept rebbing up the engine until I thought it was warm enough to travel. The last thing I needed was to be stuck in the middle of nowhere with a broke down car and a baby.

I waited long enough and backed out more carefully than ever. There were no lights coming from either direction. In fact, the only light I could see, was the light of the distant sun trying to play peek-a-boo with those of us who lived in central Arkansas. There was a faint spray of orange, but it hadn't yet combated the dark of the night. I knew it'd be a while before it actually showed it's illumination.

I drove to town so slow I thought I saw a few turtles passing me, but at least me and my baby were safe. I didn't see the use in speedin' when I didn't have to get nowhere in a hurry. I hadn't been to town many times at that time of day, so I was surprised to see that it looked like one a them lost ghost towns. Few cars were around or seen and I could hear the wind whistling an eerie sound with each brisk of air that passed.

After a few moments of glancing around at this empty looking town, I pulled up to Lizzy's.

Every light was out and the only thing I had to show me the way was the few ground lights they had to show off their lovely year-round plants in front of the porch. By that, I got Cody and snuck up to the porch.

Lizzy always hid a key for me just in case I ever needed to get in when they weren't there, so I found it and hurriedly let myself in, careful not to wake anyone. I knew Dean would kill me if he was woken up. He always had such a long day, starting early and ending late, that sleep was a necessity. Lizzy on the other hand, did as she pleased, except for taking care of that precious little girl of hers. Of course, like Ma always said, that's a job in itself, more than any man would care to admit.

It was nice and toasty in their house and there was not a sound to be heard except for the ones the rain was causing. Cody's eyes started fluttering giving me a sign that he was still tired and I made my way into the living room where Lizzy had Angels swinging bed. I laid him down and propped a bottle up on a blanket next to him. It wasn't but a few moments and he was out like a light. He was lying on his side and his arms were crossed over one another. The sweetness in the way he looked was one that couldn't be spoken about in words. It was just something you had to see…and cherish.

Then a noise made my head whip around. Footsteps were coming from the stairway. Little by little, I inched closer to where it was coming from, hunching down and creeping along like a burglar on a mission to swipe something. When I had just about reached the entranceway, I backed up against the wall and started to peek around the way. That's when my heart stopped. Dean slung himself in front of me and he had a rifle pointing right between my eyes. Funny enough, I raised my hands like he was holding me up or something.

"IT'S ME! It's me," I hollered out, hoping he wouldn't get wild with that gun and accidentally pull the trigger.

"Betty Jean?" he questioned, letting the gun fall to his side. "What in Heaven's name are you doin' out at this hour. My Lord, you scared me plum outa my britches."

"I…I just couldn't sleep and…huh, well, I…"

"Just wanted to come to our house at 5 a.m. in the mornin'?"

"Somethin' like that Dean," I grinned, hoping he wasn't too angry at me for scaring the dickens out of him.

He adjusted his robe making sure he didn't reveal anything to me that I surely didn't need to see, and then leaned the gun against the wall. In a sleepy way, he rubbed his eyes and started into the kitchen.

"Come on," he said groggily. "I'll make some coffee."

"No Dean, that's okay, I'll just…"

"Now listen here," he said interrupted me immediately. "You got me up this early in the morning and God knows if I lay down and go back to sleep, it'll be even harder for me to get up in an hour and a half, so grab a few cups and don't argue."

"Yes sir," I saluted, trying to keep him happy. I sure didn't want to have him against me. He'd been like a brother to me since Lizzy met him and for a change, he was one brother that I was truly close to.

"So," he muttered. "What was on that mind a yours so much that you couldn't sleep?"

"I don't' know."

"You don't know?" he questioned, as if I were telling a story.

"Just things I guess."

"Things like Evan?"

Cutting my eyes to the corner of the kitchen where he was preparing a very early morning pot of coffee, I didn't answer, but just sat there and tapped my fingers on the table.

"You miss'im don't ya sis?"

"I just left him Dean."

Barely shaking his head, he came over with two cups of steaming coffee and sat them down carefully. That's when he started talking. "I remember when I met your sister," he said softly. "I swear Betty Jean, I couldn't stop thinkin' about her for a single moment, much less make it through the night without wanting her near me."

"Let me ask you a question Dean."

"Shoot," he answered, propping his elbow up on the table and peering at me.

"When you asked Lizzy to marry you...did you wanna wait or get married right then?"

Laughing, "That's a silly question. I wanted to marry her the first time I kissed her."

"Really?"

"What's this all about sis? You can tell me, and I promise it won't go any further. I'm close to Evan, but not close enough to betray your trust."

Letting out a deep sigh, "I do love'im Dean, but this whole deal with Jade. I've been havin' nightmares. I'm not her mom. Her mom is gone. I don't think it's right to try and take her place."

Placing his rough hands over mine that were clasped in front of me, "Listen, nobody's askin' you to take Lisa's place. But one thing you gotta do is be there for her like a mom. She needs that right now. As far as Evan's concerned...well, I know you two will be very happy."

"I just don't wanna mess up Dean. I don't wanna do something wrong or say something wrong. I'm afraid she'll end up hating me."

"First of all, nobody could hate you. You're as sweet as a fresh baked pecan pie, and if you ever do say somethin' wrong, change it. Life's not meant to be lived perfectly. In fact, if we don't ever make mistakes, we won't ever learn any lessons."

Grinning and staring at this ruggedly handsome man before me, I said kiddingly, "Now why didn't I find you before my sister?"

He stood up and took my hands, helping me to my feet. "I'd a still fell in love with Lizzy 'cause she was meant for me…just like Evan was meant for you."

"What about Lonnie?" I asked, as if I were talking to the man upstairs.

"You were meant for Lonnie too, but since God took him so soon, he sent you somebody else to love."

"Evan." I whispered, staring to the side.

"Yeah, Evan," he answered, hugging me. It was one of the most assuring hugs I'd had in a long time. He was so nice to talk to, it was like I'd known him my entire life. Lizzy always said the same thing about him, and at that moment, I understood exactly what she was talking about. There wasn't anything he didn't seem to know, but at the same time he didn't talk down to anyone. There was something different about this man who had stolen my sister's heart so quickly.

"Listen sis," he said quietly. "I'm gonna try and get a little more sleep, but if I don't wake up in time for work…IT'S YOUR FAULT."

"Oh just take the day off," I replied in a smarty pants sort of tone.

"Can't…gotta make a livin'. I may have money now, but who knows what tomorrow will bring. Heck, my dad always said to work for your future and the pitfalls will be few."

"Interesting."

"Well," he replied. "My dad's an interesting man."

As he started to walk away, I stopped him.

"What?" he answered, turning half to me.

"Thanks."

"For what?"

"The talk," I answered, winking at him. "For a bit there, I was having a few doubts, but now, well…I just don't"

"I'm glad," his green eyes gleaming. "Anytime."

"Anytime?" I asked hurriedly.

With a little bit of a funny look, he retorted, "Anytime but 5 a.m. in the mornin'."

We both gave a little chuckle and he was on his way back up to bed. The rain was still coming down and it seemed to be pounding even harder than before. My body was weary and I knew I needed to lie down as well, but the only place I wanted to go was next to Evan.

I picked Cody up and he never even batted an eye. It was like he was still in the same place. I took him upstairs and placed him in the same bed as Angel. Side by side they were adorable. They were both such beautiful babies, it was hard to believe Lizzy and I were moms. Just five years ago we were immature and not thinking the least bit of the future. And suddenly, time flew by and we took the place Ma always had to us.

I watched them for a few moments, making sure Cody wasn't going to wake up and very carefully, I treaded softly to the door and closed it, leaving just enough of a crack to where I could look in on them.

Trying not to make a sound, I tethered down the hall and found the doorway that led to the bed that Evan was lying in. Just the thought of being next to him made me crazy. And knowing I was only steps away, made me insane with eagerness.

Slowly turning the knob, I eased open his door. I could see the outline of his body under the covers and his breathing was more intense than usual. That was one thing that told me he was in a very deep sleep. I didn't want to wake him, but in another sense, I did.

The closer I got, a bigger smile came on my face. Making my way around the bed, I slipped off my shoes and laid down next to him, covering myself with the same covers as he had blanketing him.

He was warm to the touch. His muscles from all of the military labor he had been through, were literally irresistible, and it was all I could do not to wake him from such a wonderful sleep. He wasn't even moving. His stillness reminded me of the way Cody looked when he was asleep…completely peaceful and without worry. Although I knew Evan had plenty on his mind, at that moment, it didn't seem to be the case.

After a few moments of contemplating what to do, the decision made was simple. There was no way in the world I wanted to bother him in such a state. So I rolled over, my back to him and scooted to where we were touching. As long as I could feel him, that was enough for me.

I could still hear the rain. It had come on like a magnum force, deteriorating the dryness the earth around us had turned to. And just as my eyes were getting weary enough to take me away for a while, I felt him moving behind me.

20

He began to twist and wiggle around, making low, sleep enhanced noises the entire time. Finally, after all of his flopping around, he ended up facing me. With a slight sigh and release of a deep breath, his hand found its way to me. Unconsiously, it rested on the curve of my hip. A mere touch from him was satisfying to me, but I did my best not to move. I didn't want to wake him until he was ready to greet the new day.

The pillow under my head didn't seem to be just right, so I lifted it slightly and repositioned it, lifting up a hair in the process. And although I was trying tremendously not to do anything to arouse him from such a long snooze, my attempt was failed. Glancing back at him, I saw one eye of his slightly open. Then the other followed soon after. He looked more than surprised to see me lying in the same bed as he was, considering when he laid down, I was at home in my own bed. But his surprised look, wasn't one of disappointment, but joy instead.

"B.J." he said sleepily. "What are you doin'?"

"What does it look like I'm doin' Evan…tryin' to get some rest, but dog gonnit, you just keep squirmin' around."

Laughing, he cleared his throat then continued. "No, I mean, I thought you was at home."

"I was."

Tilting his head sideways a hint, I could tell he was waiting for me to continue, but I left that as it was.

"But…"

"But…" I hesitated. "I missed ya that's all."

His hand that was motionless, started to make its way around my waist, sneaking its way to where he could get a good hold of me. All of the sudden, he pulled me to him, our bodies blending together like the colors of a rainbow, unable to distinguish one color from the next, me from Evan. Both our legs were bent exactly the same way, but the only difference, was that he had his linked in between mine, making the position we held even more intense. There was an odor in the air that smelled of passion…a sweet and enduring smell. And as his fingers inched their way all over my stomach, I was beginning to wonder if he wasn't going to try and explore to places he hadn't been.

"Evan Bain!" I declared. "If I didn't know no better, I'd think you was tryin' to take advantage of me."

"Hmmm," he sounded, pressing against me even more firmly than before. "And what if I was?"

With no answer to his question, I placed my hand on top of his that was creating a map on my stomach, and held it still. I liked the way it felt being that close to him. Truth be known, I wanted more than anything to be with him, but I was always taught better.

The heat of his breath got closer and closer until I could feel it readily warming the back of my neck, tickling the area that drove me utterly out of my mind. And in slow motion he let his soft, warm lips touch the curve from my shoulder to my earlobe.

Still holding his hand firmly, I couldn't help but close my eyes, imagining what the future held for the both of us. And the cool sheets against my skin was comforting. Evan just kept on caressing different places until he made me let out a few low moans beneath my breath.

"You know I love you?" he asked, kissing down my shoulder and making his way down my back, slightly pulling my shirt down to be able to see all the flesh he could.

"I love you too Evan."

Forcefully, but with silent permission, he laid me flat on my back to where I could look him in the eye. The sun had started to rise and it was clearly seen through the double window to the right. There were many different sprays of colors reflecting in the room like an amazing rainbow that had been sent down just for us. And that only made the moment more romantic.

Evan removed his hand from my stomach, and for a moment I thought he was going to withdraw his advances, but I was wrong. He was only trying to entice me even more. Before I knew it, I felt sweet caresses on my leg, moving up slowly. With that, I couldn't keep my heart from dang near jumping out of my chest.

"Evan, I don't think it's the right time."

"No," he said, kissing me very sensually, slow and easy.

"No," I answered, kissing him just the same, feeling my entire body starting to shiver from pure expectancy.

I gave no more objections and after a while of nothing but kissing and heating the room to such a degree that it was steaming hot in there, he sat up. His strong hands grasped mine and lifted me to where I was sitting up. I wasn't sure what he was up to, but I knew it had to be something totally erotic and sexy.

He hovered over me, shadowing my entire body and grasped a hold of the bottom of my shirt, lifting it off with ease. I sat there with my chest barely covered by the lacy, narrow bra that I bought to be sexy. Ironically enough, I had it on the perfect day.

Lying back down beside me, he rested on his side rubbing across my arm as soft as a feather, then he outlined my breasts with his touch, not handling them, but he seemed to be admiring them instead.

"Evan, I…"

"Shhh, don't talk," he said quietly as he began to unveil to him what was beneath the pants I so tightly wore.

With a little help from me, they were soon off and lying on the floor. That's when my nerves took me over, making me doubt the certainty that this was a good idea. But still, my brain didn't overrule my heart. On the contrary, it kept on letting all of the good feelings he was giving me, go on and on, taking away any form of self-control I may have had previously.

Although the light from the sun started to let itself in more vibrantly, that didn't affect anything that was happening. If nothing else, it helped me to see those brilliant eyes of his glaring back at me like two black onyx stones, looking more magnificent than ever. The scruff on his face was so very masculine and the dimples he so gallantly wore in the unique light of the new morning, made him the most attractive me in the world to me. I was hoping he could see it in my eyes, but then again, my body language said it loud and clear.

He and I were pretty darn close to lying there in the buff, but there was still a little left for our imagination. I liked it that way. I could tell he was imagining me utterly naked, but I was doing the same about him as well. As much as I hated to admit it, I was going against everything I'd been taught moral wise. In fact, the desires I had welling up inside of me were just about to explode to where everyone in the whole house, maybe even clear into town, would know them.

With no further hesitation Evan climbed to where he was completely covering me. I could feel his manhood pressing up against me as he finally begin to put together two pieces of a puzzle that were meant to be joined. Although nothing was happening actually, it felt like the greatest pleasure I'd had in so very long. Just feeling him in that manner, was too much to describe in words, and as he took that final step to unpeel the remainder of my clothing…the door opened slowly.

"Evan?" Lizzy said, realizing what she had just walked in on once she got the door fully open. "Oh my Lord…oh…my. Heaven's I'm sorry."

I could tell she was embarraced, but to be honest, I was even more so. I was in her house and trying to make out with her husband's cousin just a few rooms down from her. I was sure she was still red faced because I was definitely.

"I'm sorry Evan. I need to get downstairs and apologize."

"We didn't do anything B.J."

"We didn't, but if she hadn't come in, we probably woulda," I said, hurriedly putting my shirt and pants back on to go and talk to my baby sister.

"Hey," he said, grabbing my hand before I could get away.

"Yeah?"

"That was nice," he smiled, looking satisfied even though we didn't go any further than we did.

Giving the same look back, "Yeah, it was."

"Come'ere," he said, pulling me back to him.

"I really need to…" I started to say, but he interrupted me with one long, tongue-lashing, passionate, dreamy, make me want to faint, kinda kiss before I knew it.

I was speechless when his lips ever so slowly left mine alone. I remembered what one of my friends told me a few years back. She said that some men can kiss to where it's just as good as doing the real thing. And with that one single kiss, he made me a devout believer. He put more excitement in that one kiss than I'd had my entire lifetime of kisses.

"Now," he said in a sly voice. "you can go now."

Biting my bottom lip slightly, I stood there quietly. I could do nothing but stare at him. His bicepts were bulging out to the extent that I wanted to do nothing more than just feel the intensity his strength intales. But I knew I needed to run down and explain everything to my sister.

Shaking my head, I went towards the door, but before I left, I turned back briefly.

"I love you baby."

With a sheer look of delight, he returned those words ever so sweely and blew me a kiss as I left.

If there ever was a time when I was floating on cloud nine, this would've been the moment. In a short time, he drained my fears, comforted my insecurities and reminded me of how it truly feels to be in love.

Gliding down the stairs, I could hear Lizzy in the kitchen. I figured she was making breakfast for Dean, but then again, I never knew of Lizzy to be much of a morning person. And when I turned the corner where she was, the look she gave me, said curiosity was getting the better of her.

"I'm so sorry Betty Jean," she started rambling. "I didn't know that you were…I mean, Dean said you were here, but I didn't know you were sleepin' in…"

"Calm down sis. Remember, I'm your elder. It's okay. B'sides… nothin' happened."

"Come on now. You don't expect me to believe…"

"NOTHING HAPPENED!" I insisted.

"Then what was goin' on when I walked in."

Shrugging my shoulders, "uh, well, we were just."

"Oh my Lord," her eyes getting bigger and bigger. "I stopped it didn't I."

Taking her hands and leading her to the table, we both sat down. "Don't worry 'bout it sis. It probably wasn't the right time anyway. There'll be more chances."

"Yeah…the rest a your life."

Unable to keep that smile from creeping out, she could do nothing but stare at me. "You're happy aren't ya?" she said, sighing like she'd just seen an adorable puppy or something.

"I am sis. I really am."

"What are you two ladies talkin' about," Dean said, entering the room before I knew it.

She and I both laughed and I got up to help her with breakfast. She had started some bacon before I came in and by the time I made it over to the stove, it was dang near about to burn.

"That's my Lizzy," Dean said. "The best dang cook in Arkansas."

She ran over to him and he whisked her up in his arms suddenly, twirling her around in circles until she was about to get dizzy. About that time, Evan came strolling in, his plaid robe barely tied in front. Dean and Lizzy suddenly stopped and the moment seemed frozen. It was unspoken, but I was sure they both knew what had been going on in Evan's bedroom. In fact, I thought I saw Dean give a wink to him as if to say "nice job."

"Mornin'," I said in a sexy tone, going over and kissing him on the cheek.

"Mornin'." he replied, lifting me straight up and hugging me tightly, his face just about buried in my chest until he released me enough to let me slide back down to where my feet were touching the floor.

Dean was still standing there with Lizzy up in his arms and they could do nothing but peer.

"What do you think you're lookin' at?" I asked, still clutching this man that I never wanted to release.

"Just two people in love," Dean said. "Just two people in love."

Lizzy poked him slightly and he put her down. She went over to the stove and I joined her, both of us chattering the entire time in a whispering voice. I was sure the men were probably trying to hear us, but we were careful not to disclose anything we didn't want heard.

"Breakfast is ready boys," she said, taking both Dean and Evan a plate with Bacon, eggs and homemade biscuits.

"mm…looks good," Dean said, diving into it without hesitation.

"Hold on a minute. We ain't said grace."

He stopped, swallowed what he already had shoved into his mouth and put his hands together. After we got our plates to the table, we sat down and Lizzy nodded to me to do the honors. Nodding back I began.

> *Dear Lord,*
> *We thank you this fine morning for this wonderful breakfast to start the day. Thank you for our family, friends and those who love us and that we love back. Give us the strength to go through the day and serve you Lord. In Jesus name I pray.*

In unison we all said "Amen," and dug into the first meal of the day. Ma used to say that was the most important meal. Although I used to never heed those words, on the days I did, I felt better. And before too long, Dean and Evan had their plates cleaned spotless. I didn't even think they needed to be washed after they ran those biscuits across that yoke like it was gravy.

Dean was already dressed for work. And with a hug, a kiss and a wink, he was gone in a flash. Evan on the other hand, sat there gaping at me like a love sick puppy dog not wanting to look away for a single moment.

"Well, dishes are done," Lizzy said, drying off her hands and going into other room, glancing back before she was completely out of sight. Her nosy side was taking over and I was sure she was probably standing on the other side of the wall listening in on what Evan and I were going to say to one another. But I suppose I didn't mind. More than likely I'd tell her what was said anyway.

"You full?" I asked, tottering over to where that handsome man sat.

"Too!"

"Me too. I feel like goin' back to bed."

His eyebrows raised and he got this look in his eye that said, "let's go." I knew then I should've had a better choice of words.

"I need to get in the shower," he said, stretching his arms up high in the air.

"Go ahead. I'll be here for a bit."

"Wanna join me?" he said playfully.

"Get goin' Mr. Bain!" I replied just as playful.

Grinning, he went back upstairs. It was only a minute until Lizzy came back in and rushed over to me, sitting down and demanding the entire story.

"There's really nothin' to tell sis. We started to, but then we stopped. End of story."

"But ya'll aren't married Betty Jean. You know what Ma said."

"I know, but it's so dad blame hard not to. Didn't you see how sexy he looked this mornin'."

"Personally I was lookin' at my own man sis…not yours."

We laughed and talked for a bit and I knew I need to run. I remembered I had left my shoes upstairs in Evan's room, so I ran up to get them. For the first time in a while, I didn't have a care in the world. The sun seemed to shine brighter than usual, the air seemed cleaner, and the happiness scale in my heart was all the way to the top. In fact, it was overflowing rapidly with each minute that passed.

When I got to the top of the stares, I decided to check on the babies first. It was still early and they were just now opening their eyes for the day. Cody was reaching over and holding Angel's hand in such a cute way, I wished I had my camera there to capture the moment.

A few baby words to them and I was on my way to get my shoes so I could get ready to go back home.

Unconsciously, I started humming a tune that suddenly jumped into my head, and when I opened the door into Evan's room, my heart completely dropped. Evan was standing near the bed. His clothes were lying on the pillow, and suddenly the towel he had wrapped around him came untied and dropped to his knees.

21

I could feel my entire body turning red from embarrassment, but I was sure I wasn't the only one that felt that way. I'd seen many sides of Evan, but this was one side I didn't think I'd see, at least not yet.

As he hurriedly reached down to grab his towel, I turned around closing my eyes trying not to keep seeing that image of him in my mind over and over. Although it made me want him even more, I waited until he gave me the word that he was finally decent enough for me to come inside.

"You can come in now," he said, his voice cracking.

"You sure."

"I'm dressed, come in."

Slowly turning back in the direction I was before, my hands were tightly over my eyes as I carefully removed them little by little. When I did so, he was standing there in a pair of sweat pants and a T-shirt. His hair was wet and messed up, giving him an even greater sex appeal than many other times I'd seen him.

"Come on," he motioned to me.

Inch by inch I crept over to him, still incredibly humiliated for walking in on him without knocking first. Truth be known, if it'd been me, I'd a felt violated, but then again, he *was* a man. Men and women are completely different creatures. I learned that the first time I liked a boy years earlier.

I looked up and he ran his fingers through his somewhat dripping hair and made what little he had stand straight up. Words were hard to come by. I didn't want him mad at me, but then again, it was an accident. I never would have walked in if I'd known he was…well, completely exposed. Shoot, I wouldn't want anybody doing that to me.

"It's alright," he whispered, making me sit down near him.

"I'm so sorry. I don't know what I was thinking."

Reaching up, he kissed my forehead, "It's…" then my cheek. "O…" lastly my lips, "kay."

That simple gesture was enough to ease my mind enough to where I wanted to put that recent memory and set it aside. He always had a way of making me feel like that…comfortable no matter what was going on. And to anybody that knows me, that's a pure and natural talent.

"So, what are you gonna do today?" I asked knowing I had to go to work.

"Hadn't thought about it, but I guess I could come help you out at your job."

Laughing, I replied spirited like, "I don't think we'd get much done Mr. Bane."

"Is that right?"

"Definetely…besides, you need to start thinkin' about the wedding."

"What about it?"

Hunching back away from him, I'm sure the look I directed was one of half anger for him not even worrying about such an event.

"You know Evan…the place…the time…the invitation list."

Shaking his head, "I thought's we'd just do it here in this house. It's so dang cold, it'd be crazy not to. As far as the time, B.J., that's no matter. The sooner the better. And last, the invitation list. I'd just a soon have a small simple wedding. I mean, all that matters is the fact that we get married, what difference would it make if we got a ton a folks here."

Tilting my head sideways I thought about what he'd just said. To be a man, he made some sense. It sounded like he put forth a lot of effort in thinking about it.

"That's fine," I answered. "I guess we can talk about it after while when I get off."

"You want me to be waitin' for ya but naked when you get home," he laughed.

Slapping his knee, "I told you that was an accident now Evan Bain. Don't be aggravatin' me or I won't give another thought to bein' you wife. Besides, I'm sure I'll see you like that plenty after we say 'I do.'"

"And I bet you're on pins and needles to say them two simple words."

"Me?" I asked, looking surprised he'd say such a thing. "What about you? You was pretty touchy feely yourself this mornin'."

"Didn't have no complaints now did ya?"

"I gotta run," I said, pecking a short kiss on his cheek and heading for the door.

"No," he demanded in a playful voice. "I want an answer."

"I gotta go," I replied in an equally playful tone, then running down the stairs, hearing the pitter patter of his feet trampling after me.

With both of our laughter taking over the house, none of us could barely hear the phone as it started to ring. Lizzy ran out of the kitchen to answer it before it stopped and she put her finger over her mouth trying to get us to quiet down. We did as she wanted, but Evan was still tickling me and playing around the way I loved for him to do.

"Evan," Lizzy said in a clearly questioning voice. "It's for you."

"Well, who is it?" he asked, still dancing around me energetically.

She put her hand over the phone, "I don't know, but it sounds important."

Kissing me on the run, he went to where Lizzy was standing and took the phone. "Hello," he answered almost out of breath.

That humorous look he just had across his face turned. His eyebrows lowered and his stance became still and serious.

"Uh huh…yeah…okay, I understand," he muttered lowly. When he was finished, it seemed like it took him ten minutes to put the receiver back where it belonged.

There was an extreme glassy look in those coal black eyes of his that I couldn't read. All I could read was the fact that he seemed to need further clarification of what was just told to him by whoever it was on the other end of the line.

His silence was perpetual. Lizzy and I just stood aside and waited to hear what was going on. Then, without a clue, Dean comes in from outside in a rush.

"I forgot somethin'," he stated. Then he noticed the thickness the air had taken on. "What's goin' on?"

Lizzy and I shrugged out shoulders, then he looked towards Evan. "Cuz?" he asked questioning. In one word, Evan knew Dean was asking him a question.

Evan turned away from us for a moment, and when he turned back looking me directly in the eye.

"That was Lisa's dad."

"What'd he say?" I jumped in, worry seizing my whole being… afraid something had happened to Jade.

"It's Neline, her mom. She's not well."

"Terrible sick or..."

"No," he cut in. "But not well enough to care for Jade any longer."

Feeling like a ton of bricks had been lifted from my shoulders, I went to him and smiled the sweetest smile I knew how.

"We can just go get'er Evan. That's what you want right?"

"Sure, but what if she don't wanna stay with me?"

"That's ridiculous baby," I encouraged. "What child wouldn't want you for a daddy."

"I suppose."

"I tell you what? Why don't we go ahead and set a day for the wedding and your darlin' little baby girl can be the flower girl. If ya ask me she'll be prettier than that sunset over them mountains. What do ya say?"

"Are you askin' me to marry you Ms. Cole?"

"I guess I am. Will you marry me Evan Bain?" I asked, getting down on one knee and acting like that was the first time it was ever brought up, giving the moment a hint of theatrics.

"Oh, well, I don't know," he said, talking like a woman, playing along. "Yes...yes!"

We couldn't help but laugh, but in all seriousness, he did just agree to go ahead and get married sooner. I thought it'd be best for me, Evan, and especially for Jade. She needed something stable, something wonderful. She needed more love than she ever thought was possible. She needed us.

I figured since I raised his spirits, I needed to go. Ma was at home waiting for me to bring her precious grandson to her and I needed to time to change for work. After the short lived uncertain look Evan portrayed about Neline and Jade, suddenly it was gone. I could tell he was thinking of the future as I was. And it made me more than happy to know he was wanting it as much as me.

Bundling Cody back up, I went to the door where Evan stood waiting to help me to the car, as if I needed it.

"Thank you baby," he said tenderly, kissing both me and Cody on the cheek.

Squinting my eyes, "What for?"

"For lovin' me...just for lovin' me!"

One soft, slow, lip to lip, heated breath kinda kiss, and I was gone. He left my whole body wanting more, but as Ma always said...there's a time and a place for everything. I figured our time to prove our love for one another, to show our conjugal love, was nearing. I was like a kid in line at a candy store...anxious to get my sweet reward for waiting. And I knew when the time came, it would be more than well worth the wait.

The rain had stopped, leaving a magnificently colorful rainbow in my view, starting at the beginning of town and ending at the mountain. It looked like you could find the end of the rainbow just on the other side of that mount and it made me smile. All those years my dear sister went on and on about that huge hill in our midst, I never listened, until it showed me its true power.

When I got to Ma's, I scurried out of the cold into their little nook of a cabin set back in these woods. That's when I saw the woman who brought me into this world. She was sitting in the kitchen sewing on a quilt that she swore she'd finish six months earlier and didn't, but she kept on sewing. It was at that moment I saw her as something different. If I ever thought there were angels on this earth, she'd be one for sure. The twinkle in her eye and the love in her voice was enough to tell me that me and my son were very lucky to have her.

I'm not speaking ill of my Pa, not at all, but he was more the rough, tough, do what I say type…that is, until you place one of his grandkids in his arms. Then all that manly man stuff turns to mush.

"Oh dear," Ma said, glancing up from her work after a few moments. "I didn't hear ya'll come in. Bring my doll to me dear."

Shaking my head, knowing she was spoiling him tremendously, I did as she asked and his arms automatically reached out for her. With that, the smile she normally wore, got even brighter, even more illuminating. She always loved the attention my baby gave her, making her look younger and younger just from the pure joy she got from receiving such love.

"Ma," I said softly.

"What is it dear," she said, while baby talking to Cody at the same time.

"I'm gettin' married."

"I know dear."

"Soon Ma!"

Her head popped up quicker than a rattlesnake about to strike. "When?"

"Don't know yet. Evan and I was gonna talk about it after work. Oh, by the way, he's gonna go get Jade. Neline her grandma ain't feelin' well enough to care for her proper."

"Instant family Betty Jean."

"Yeah, well, I feel like the luckiest girl this side of the Mississippi. B'sides, ain't no sense in waitin'."

"I suppose not," she agreed.

"You mean it's okay with you?"

With a smile, that was all the answer I needed. I gave her and the baby a kiss and went home to get ready for another day of work. I was flying higher than an eagle above the clouds. Shoot, I was so anxious about bein' a wife again, I didn't know what to do. There was a time I thought I was a hex, but with Evan, he taught me I was a prize instead.

It took me a bit to get cleaned up and fixed just so. Soon enough I was gone again, ready to make a few more dollars to add to the few I already had saved. It was rewarding to know I was making my own way, but it was going to feel even more so, knowing I was helping take care of a family of four very soon.

Kim was the only other one working that evening, so we were swamped. I suppose not many folks wanted to cook that evening because just about every drive-in slot was full. I didn't normally perspire, but running back and forth, cooking and taking food out to each car waiting, made my brow look like the grass after a morning dew. I felt sticky even though the cold was getting worse. Going in and out over and over again made me wonder if I wasn't going to catch my death a cold.

"Kim look!" I said enthusiastically.

"It's Mr. Wonderful," she said grinning, noticing Evan's car pulling in to the only empty spot out there.

I had been at work for hours and I was ready to see a face that would make it worthwhile for me to finish my shift. I handed Kim my orders that were up and I made a special trip outside to see my husband to be.

When I reached his car all I could do was beam from just viewing his handsome face. But to my surprise, he wasn't the only one in the car. Jade was sitting next to him with her hair fixed just perfectly…every curl in place, and her long eyelashes were batting showing the beauty of those eyes she would one day catch her own husband with. The sweetness of seeing those two together, was unexplainable.

Her things were in suitcases in the backseat, and she was warmly covered in a red coat with a colorful scarf that was neatly wrapped around her neck.

He reached out to me, "Hey sweetheart," he said, it being the first time he ever called me by that nickname and it sent electrical like shocks all through me, touching the most sensitive parts.

Leaning down, "Hey sweetie," I uttered, looking over at Jade.

"Hi," she replied, not looking either happy or sad, but somewhere trapped in between the two.

"Ya'll hungry?"

Evan looked to his daughter and placed his bare hand over hers that was nestled warmly with a cotton winter mitten. "Jade...baby, you hungry?"

She didn't say a word. The only reply he got was the shrugging of her shoulders and her beautiful eyes looking back up to him.

"How about two burgers and two fries?" he asked, still looking at her, hoping she'd feel the need to respond.

"How 'bout this?" I asked. "Why don't ya'll hold off a bit and when I get off, I'll cook a real nice supper."

"Don't you get off late?"

"Kim'll cover for me. She'll be busy, but after a while it slows down. She can handle it."

"Say 6:30," Evan added.

"How about 7:00? You know I gotta get all prettied up for you."

"You wake up pretty!"

Laughing in a flattered manner, "You say that *now*."

Kissing my hand, "And I'll say it forty years from now."

Bending down, "Love you."

"I love you too," he replied, lightly kissing the corner of my mouth, then leaving.

Cloud nine carried me back inside where it was warm and I continued working, trying to come up with a good way to ask Kim to cover for me the last part of the night. Of course, when I did ask her, it wasn't near as hard as I made it out to be. In fact, she practically told me to go ahead and leave. More than half of the people that were there had already left and little traffic was moving anymore.

I took her advice and after another hour or so, I turned in my apron, said a sincere thank you and was on my way. The evening was a pleasant one and after I picked up Cody, we were home lickety split. I had picked up a few groceries and was ready to cook a wonderful meal. And although I didn't know what Jade liked to eat, I tried my darnedest to fix a little bit of everything most kids love. I wanted to make a good impression on her. It didn't matter to me that she was so little. The only thing that mattered, was me and her getting to be close. I didn't expect her to look at me like she did her mom, but I did hope she'd want to.

As I started preparing supper, I noticed the little booklet of poetry Luther had given me. For once, this particular one wasn't those he'd written, but instead, ones he loved to read himself. He told me once that there is a poem in there for every occasion and for every person. So I stopped what I was doing briefly and scanned through it. Finally I ran across a poem about daughters. It was called, "Innocence"

Hair of beauty, eyes of hope,
A smile for all to see...
Strength of a lion,
And love of humanity.
For in a daughter is forgiveness,
There are treasures in her ways.
A daughter with her tenderness,
Wishes for brighter days.
Hair of beauty, eyes of hope,

*It all makes perfect sense.
For a daughter's strength and love are great,
But greater is her innocence.*

I could feel the right side of my mouth raise, smiling to myself. I could see all of that in her. I saw how strong she was when she lost the most important person in her life, and I almost envied that strength.

Putting the book down, I continued with my cooking, then went to change to where I would look more than presentable to the man I was so wonderfully anxious to marry. I put on a hint of rouge and a salmon colored, glossy lipstick that was just enough color, but didn't overpower the natural look I was trying to obtain. I didn't want to look like I was going for a night out on the town, but then again, I wanted to be desirable.

I was almost finished with supper when I heard his car pull up. The headlights blinded me for a brief moment until they were shut off, and I hurried to get everything set on the table before he came knocking. I wanted things to be perfect. But as someone once told me, "if you strive for perfection, you might as well give up."

As soon as I laid the plates on the table, a faint knock came at the door. I could tell it wasn't Evan's robust knock, but Jades instead. I figured he was trying to make her feel more wanted and needed.

Straightening my clothes as if it were the first time meeting this man, I felt silly, and opened the door. There they both stood, Jade close by her daddy and Evan with his hand on her shoulder patting her sensitively.

"Oh, come in…come in. Get outa that cold air."

A quick hello kiss and I kneeled down to where I was eye to eye with this little golden haired doll before me. Her stare was serious, but questioning, silently asking me a million questions and silently, I was doing my best to answer them all.

"I bet you're starving," I asked, squeezing her hand, trying my best to make her feel at home.

With a nod, I took the answer to be yes I led her into the kitchen and lifted her up, putting her down in a chair that I cushioned high enough to where she could reach the table. Evan found a seat next to her and began to bring the food over.

"Mmm, looks delicious Betty Jean."

"Thanks Evan. You know I'm not one to make big meals. I hope it's plenty."

He made her plate and slowly she fiddled with every bite. It was like she was in some sort of deep thought about something neither Evan or I would understand.

"Is it good sweetie?"

Again, she nodded, still not speaking, but instead, I could tell she was looking my place over like the time before when she was there. Evan shrugged his shoulders. I knew he didn't know what to do to bring her out of her shell and to be honest, I wasn't sure myself. That's when I got an idea.

"Jade, I don't gotta work tomorrow. You wanna go meet my Ma and Pa?"

"You have a Ma?" she muttered lowly.

"Yeah, I do. And you're gonna love her."

With another nod, I let out a breath just glad I got through to her a little and Evan's smile proved I'd done something to take a step in the right direction.

Dinner was good and after visiting for a few hours, I knew they would have to leave. He told me he wanted to make sure she stayed in a routine of a distinct bedtime and a schedule she can get used to. But something else seemed to be bothering him.

"What it is?" I asked, grasping his arm before they left.

22

Pausing for a moment, "I just don't wanna intrude on Lizzy, Dean and Angel. I know they got a family of their own. They sure don't want me bringin' somebody else over there to take up more room."

Grinning and placing both my hands on his face, "Baby, you must not know them two very well. Dean's the most caring, helpful and loving man I know…besides you *that is*. And I know Lizzy would love to have Jade around."

"You don't think they're gonna mind?"

"Not one itty bitty bit. B'sides, if they do, you always got a place here. There's an extra room next to mine. It's small, but then again, she she's small too."

With a sigh, "Why is it that you always know just what to say to me?"

"Maybe I learned from the best…you."

"Now you're bein' the sweet talkin' one."

Thinking of something out of the blue, I blurted out, "Hey, why don't you let me come get Jade tomorrow and take her to meet my Ma and Pa."

"And Douglas."

Laughing, "I don't wanna put her in shock."

"Why not. And I'll watch my Code man."

"Sounds good to me. I'll come get her as soon as I get dressed tomorrow. I'm off so we can spend some time together. Maybe it'll help her to loosen up and get used to me."

This whole time she was standing there looking at both of us as if to say, "I'm right here."

Bending down to her, "Night sweetie. You have nice dreams okay? And if you don't, your dad's real good about scarin' 'em away."

Nodding, I gave her a short hug.

"Night Betty Jean…and thanks."

"For what?"

"For bein' you."

So Jade wouldn't feel too weird about me, he just gave a wink and was on his way. She clung to his hand with hers like she was afraid if she let him go, he'd be gone forever. And I'm sure that was probably the way she saw things. But the one thing I wanted to accomplish was making sure she learned to trust me as well as Evan. Being as young as she is and losing someone so close to her, I knew it would be a challenge, but one I was sure we could handle.

After they left, I drank me a large glass of warm milk. Pa always said that it made him sleep better, and as fast as my mind was turning, I needed something to slow it down enough for me to get a good nights sleep. It didn't take long for it to kick in and when I opened my eyes, I was catching a glimpse of the morning sun in my sleep filled eyes.

Happily, Cody was looking up at me with a smile as he always did. I couldn't think of a better way to start the day than a look like that from my son. He had no worries and to him, the world was perfect.

After eating and dressing, we left. Cody's coo's from the back seat were soothing to me as we traveled down the winding road to town, and I totally looked forward to spending a day with my soon to be step-daughter. I wanted to be like a mom to her. She needed it desperately.

Just as the car started getting warm and cozy, it was time to get out. That was always the case as small as our town was. Cody was still just as happy as he could be with his toboggan and gloves on to protect from the cold that seemed to worsen as each day passed. That's when I saw Evan walk out on the front porch.

Wearing his red and black plaid flannel shirt, faded blue jeans and boots, he reminded me of Dean, trying to look rugged and used to living in such a place. But regardless what he had on, he was still the most striking man in my eyes.

"Look who we got here," he said, coming around and carefully taking my son out of the car.

"Yep," I replied. "He's ready to spend a day with his new…"

Looking at me, knowing what word was going to come next, "You can say it Betty Jean. I am gonna be his daddy. I wouldn't want to be anything else to him."

Grinning, I nodded and graced his cheek with my very cold lips.

"Come on," I said, motioning to him. "I can't wait to see Jade. Is she ready to go."

"I guess as ready as she's ever gonna be."

"She been talkin' much."

Shrugging his shoulders, "Ah, a little, but I figure it'll just take her some time to get used to all a this."

"I suppose, " I replied. "Maybe all it's gonna take is a girl's day out."

Looking iffy, "I sure hope so B.J. I can't seem to get through to her."

Going inside, there she was right in front of me. She was sitting on the bottom step of the stairs and she was dressed so adorably. Evan had dressed her in a dark pink pant suit with cartoon characters on the front of the shirt. But it was the first time I'd seen her without a bow in her hair. I figured Evan just didn't know how to do such things and he sure wasn't going to get Lizzy to do it. Heck, I had to teach Lizzy all that stuff myself.

"You ready to go sweetie?" I asked nicely, going over to her and sitting down.

All she did was nod, but that was enough of an answer for me. In a way, she acted scared of me, but I wasn't so sure that it was her being scared or if she was just afraid to get close to me for fear she'd betray her mother who was now gone.

"Well, tell your daddy bye and we'll see'em later on…K."

Without a word, she ran to him and wrapped her arms around his legs. He still had Cody, so I went and took him just long enough for them to say their good-byes. He stroked her shiny, soft, blonde curls and in a fatherly way, kissed her cheek.

"See ya after while sweetheart," he said tenderly.

After handing Cody back to him and giving them both a peck, Jade took my hand and we were on our way. She was so tiny, but when she did talk, she seemed older than she truly was. That gave me the impression that Lisa made sure she taught her daughter all she could before it was too late. Heck, I didn't recall Douglas talking that good until he was at least six.

She climbed in the front seat with me and I buckled her in tightly, making sure she was safe.

"Betty Jean," she said in a whispering voice.

"What is it sweetie?"

"We goin' to see your Ma?"

"That we are. And my Pa and brothers too."

She nodded again and turned her head facing the front even though she couldn't see over the dash just yet. And as I started to make the turn to go back up those twisting roads, I noticed a new little shop that had just opened to the right of me, across from the market.

"You feel like shoppin'?" I asked.

Motioning yes, I pulled in and jumped out, trying not to stay in the chilling wind for too awful long, and got her out. The sign read, "Ginger's" Although it didn't give me a clue what sort of things she had, we went in regardless.

Jade kept close by me, but no sooner did we step in the place, a bell rang and this woman came out from behind the counter in a flash.

"Well, well, well. What a precious little girl," the woman said, bending down to her. "Now what might your name be?"

Jade just looked down, but I answered instead. "It's Jade."

"You must be proud of her."

"I am," I replied as if she were my own flesh and blood.

"By the way, " she said, acting like she'd forgotten something. "I'm Ginger."

"Nice to meet you," I responded. "You live around here?"

"Do now," she continued. "I just moved here from Texarkana. I used to teach school down that way, but I heard so many folks talk about how nice it was here that I packed up my things and off I went."

"Neat store."

"Oh, it's just a little bit a this and a little bit a that. I love kids, so I made a decision to sell stuff kids would like. It is getting 'bout near Christmas ya know."

"Yep," I replied. "Not far off."

She stood there happily, gleaming a smile that I assumed she carried around most of the time, and her glasses were resting on the middle of her nose. She smelled of the most wonderful perfume. I didn't know the fragrance, but I sure wanted to ask. Then Jade went over to a table that was filled with stuffed toys. The one she picked up was a feather soft bear with a bright red heart on his chest. Her tiny arms wrapped around it and embraced it so tightly that I thought she was going to squeeze the stuffing out of it.

"You like that Jade?" I asked, caressing her silky hair.

"Uh huh," she replied, actually answering me. To me, that was a step in the right direction.

"What a doll, "Ginger said, shaking her head, unable to take her eyes off this beautiful little girl.

Backing away from Jade a hint, I explained to the woman what had happened. "Her mama died not long ago, and I'm engaged to her daddy."

"Poor, poor dear," she sighed, shaking her head side to side, showing the pity most folks showed for her when they found out the truth.

"She don't talk much, and I just don't know what to do."

This woman I just met looked at me with the most sincere eyes, and replied, "You don't have to do anything dear. Just be there. Show this little girl you care about her and before too long, she'll be fine."

"I hope so."

Jade walked up to me and held the bear up in the air as if she were reaching it out to me, "What is it sweetie?"

"Kiss him," she demanded in a childlike way.

Instead of just taking the bear, I picked her up instead, kissing the bear on the nose, then Jade as well. It was at that moment when I actually saw a tinge of a smile try to creep out from her often sadden face.

"Did I see a smile?" I said, slightly tickling her, trying to see if she'd loosen up. "Did I?"

With a short giggle she muttered, "Yes," squirming all around in my arms.

Turning to Ginger, "We'll take the bear. How much do I owe ya?"

"Okay," Ginger said, ringing me up, then reaching into a box next to the register. "Now let's see if it's the right color."

She had pulled out a gorgeous hair ribbon that perfectly matched the pink outfit Jade so preciously wore and begin to place it neatly in her hair.

"Oh, but I can't…"

"It's on the house sweetie. I figure this little one deserves a special gift…don't you?"

"Yes ma'am. Thank you," I replied, grinning and paying her the price I owed.

"Thank you," a tiny voice said to my surprise, as she felt of the bow that the nice lady had ever so sweetly placed in her hair.

"You're very welcome sweetheart."

Jade and I both left there with a bit of a smile. It felt good to know that she had it in her. For a while, all I thought she could do was look gloomy and miserable. But for the first time, I saw a light shine on this little girl's face. It wasn't a bright light, but it was a start. Like Ma told me once, a journey of a thousand miles starts with a single step. And to me, the first grin from Jade, was the first step in our journey to happiness as a family. There's nothing I wanted more than that.

Slowly roaming up the swurvey road towards Ma and Pa's, I noticed Jade staring around at the scenery. It seemed like it was the first time she ever saw such a view, but I was sure it wasn't. Maybe it was the first time she'd seen anything just as lovely. But in any instance, she was in a trance. She wasn't blinking or moving an inch, just staring out at God's gift to us.

"Well," I said, pulling in. "We're here."

She looked confused. Maybe because she'd never been to such a run-down place before. From what I saw, all she was used to, was a nice, roomy place to live.

I hoisted her up in my arms and held her close as I could. I knew the more affection she received, the faster she would come out of this shock she went into when Lisa died.

"What a great surprise Betty Jean?" Ma said, coming up and lightly kissing my cheek. "And who is this lovely little girl you're totin'?"

"This is Jade Ma. You know, Evan's little girl. I just thought I'd bring'er out to meet ya'll and see what a fun family I got."

"You're just as pretty as Betty Jean said you were," Ma said, pinching her cheeks just a hair like she always did with cute kids. Although I never understood that, I suppose it just ran in the family. "I'm so glad you did."

"Somethin' smells awful good."

Giving that look, she replied, "Oh dear, I just baked a fresh batch a homemade chocolate chip cookies."

"Mmm, sound good."

"Sit her down right in here dear and I'll pour her up a nice cold glass a milk to go along with 'em. And take off that bundle some coat you got her in."

Again, Jade's face lit up slightly, as I sat her down in the kitchen and she climbed into the chair closest to her.

"You her Mama?" she mumbled, trying to talk with a big bit of a cookie in her mouth.

"Why, I sure am little'en."

Changing the mood, she replied, "My mama died."

At that moment, I saw a rush of sympathy in Ma as she came over and sat down next to Jade.

"That's what I heard dear, but do you know what?"

"What?" she asked, gulping down a drink of milk.

"There's a story about those who die."

"A story?" Jade questioned, raising her tiny eyebrows in wait of the answer.

"Oh sure dear. You see, when people die, you might not be able to see'em but they sure enough can see you."

"Betty Jean told me that."

"But I'm sure Betty Jean didn't tell you about what people do in heaven did she?"

"No."

Laughing, "Ah, dear, they don't have no more pain. They can run and play and watch over folks they love dearly...like you Jade."

"She's still gone."

"Just not here, but I can guarantee she's made a spot for you right next to her when God finds that it's time for you go leave this world too."

"When I leave here, I'll be with her?"

"That's right dear. But until then, she's your special angel...keeping you safe."

While they talked, I bet Jade ate three of those big homemade cookies and drank almost a whole glass of milk. I was sure she had to be full as a tick or at least just about there.

"What's your name?" she asked Ma.

"Gertie," she replied.

"Gertie?"

Ma nodded and ran her hand through Jades soft hair, looking into that little girl's eyes like she was hoping she helped with such a talk.

"Yes dear, but if you want, you can call me Nana. Your dad and Betty Jean *are* gonna get married, so you might as well say I'm gonna be a grandma to ya child."

She had crumbs and chocolate all around her mouth from eating Ma's delicious cookies so quickly, and I grabbed a rag and wiped her face clean. It felt so natural with her. Even though I hadn't known her for very long, she and I were bonding slowly but surely.

"Come with me Jade," I said, putting her coat back on her and buttoning it up warmly. "I wanna show ya somethin'."

She picked up her bear that she laid in the chair next to her and followed me outside.

"She'll catch her death a cold out there Betty Jean!" Ma demanded, trying to stop me.

"We'll just be a minute Ma."

Taking her to the edge of the porch, I sat down where Lizzy always sat and I picked her up and put her next to me. The sun was high in the sky and the mountains were so very beautiful. Without me saying anything yet, she started glaring up at the same spot my sister always did. It was like she was drawn to it.

"You see how beautiful that mountain is?"

"uh huh."

"Well, my sister Lizzy once told me that if you come out here and make a wish on this mountain, it'll come true. She said that it was like talking to God. And since the mountain is so high, you're closer to God just by bein' here."

She didn't say a word, nor did she flinch or move an ounce. That's when Ma came out, picked Jade up and took her back in. "I told you it's too dad blame cold out here to be sittin' on the porch."

Shaking my head, I followed them inside. After a few hours of visiting with Ma and eating up most of the cookies and drinking all of the milk, we had Jade talking non-stop. She rambled on about things we had no clue what she was talking about, but we humored her and would nod and shake our heads just so she would know she was the center of attention.

Before I knew it, suppertime was approaching faster than I thought. I was hoping Cody didn't give Evan much trouble, but I was sure them two were just fine. And when we were leaving, Ma stopped us.

"Now you come back and see me again…ya hear?"

"K" she replied, letting her spellbinding eyes glimmer in Ma's direction.

"See ya later," I said, waving as we climbed in the car to head back where we came from…Lizzy and Dean's. Truthfully, I was hoping Lizzy made enough for an army. I didn't really feel like cooking and as much as she'd been in the kitchen feeding Dean, I assumed she was learning more and more as each day passed.

It wasn't a very long drive and when we pulled up, Jade unbuckled herself and jumped into my lap.

"Carry me?" she asked.

"Sure enough," I replied, lifting her up in my arms once again. I didn't see Dean's vehicle, but I was sure Lizzy was home.

As usual, I let myself in and the place was utterly quiet. I saw Lizzy on the couch asleep with the bassinet next to her. Angel was sleeping as well. Jade and I looked at one another and tip-toed upstairs slowly. I wanted to make sure I didn't make a single sound. From what Lizzy told me, she didn't get much sleep as it was, and when she could catch a few z's here and there, I sure didn't want to disturb her.

"You're daddy must be in here," I whispered, tapping the door slightly, but not loud enough to be heard downstairs.

There was no answer, so I slowly pushed the door open, making sure I didn't catch another view of the Evan the streak. But when it was open, that's not what I saw at all. In fact, the living picture in front of me, was something I wanted to keep in my mind forever.

23

Evan was lying on his side with the covers half pulled over him and his hand was resting on Cody's back. They were both asleep and looked more peaceful than ever. It looked like that was the way God meant for things to be. Hearing them breathe almost in unison forced me to sigh a huge sigh.

"Daddy," Jade said, running over to him and slightly shaking him.

Grumbling as he was torn from his slumber, he turned to find his darling little golden haired daughter staring at him with big comforting eyes. I, on the other hand, went on the other side of the bed and laid down, sandwiching my son between the two of us.

Cody was still snoozing like no one was around, but when Evan picked up Jade, I moved him over near me so there would be room. Smacking his lips and moaning, he half opened his eyes then closed them the same as they were moments earlier.

To my surprise, Jade got this curious look on her face. She raised her hand and began to stroke Cody's head, petting him so sweetly. She never took her eyes off him. It appeared she was making a connection with my son for no reason at all, and then she turned to Evan.

"Is he my brother?" she asked Evan, cutting her eyes back to him briefly.

"He will be sweetheart."

"When?"

Evan looked at me, "When Betty Jean?"

"How about next week?"

All smiles, Evan appeared to gleam all over. From his eyes to his smile, he showed nothing but utter happiness from the answer I game to him.

"Oh, but there is something we have to do first."

Lowering my brows out of curiosity, "What's that?"

Pulling Jade closer to him, "We got a little girl that's gettin' ready to have a birthday."

"ME!" she exclaimed.

"Yes…you. How old are you gonna be Jade?" Evan replied, asking her a question he already knew the answer to.

"Four," she replied in a very country way. "I'm gonna be four."

"Four, well, we best get your party in order before you turn twenty."

She laughed at him and I could tell he was glad to see such a reaction from his daughter that didn't seem to be happy before then.

"You tired sweetheart?" he said to her, glancing down.

The funny thing, was that she had already passed out from the day we had. Her arm was around Cody and they were both far, far from where we were, probably dancing around in their own dreams.

Motioning with his head for us to leave the room and let them sleep, I carefully got up and followed him out the door. My insides were smiling as well as my outsides, and Evan was looking just the same. All my worries from before began to dissipate with that one sweet scene with me, him and the kids. It practically reassured me that our family would be one of the happiest anywhere around.

Closing the door with a small crack to where we could look in on them, hand in hand, we went downstairs. The feeling in the air couldn't have been any lighter. In fact, for the first time since we found out about Jade, I felt like things were truly coming together.

"How was girls day out?" Lizzy asked as I made it to the bottom of the stairs.

Smiling and sighing hugely, "Wonderful sis. I think I'm finally gettin' through to her. In fact, I ain't got a doubt that we're all gonna be just fine."

Slightly shrugging her shoulders and giving me that look of agreement. "I never thought otherwise Betty Jean."

"Come on now sis," I added, following her into the living room where the fire was blazing, warming every inch of the place. "Tell me that you didn't think it was gonna be hard to get her to trust us."

"Nope," she replied, plopping down on the couch and crossing her arms as if she could see the future.

Standing in front of the fire, I found a spot on the floor where I could feel all of the warmth it was illuminating. Then, like follow the leader, Evan was next to me, wrapping me up in his arms ever so sweetly.

Lizzy sat there staring at us with the most unusual look on her face. I could tell she was studying the affection we were giving one another and hoping I never lost it again like I did with Lonnie.

Amidst all the quietude, the silence was abruptly broken when Dean came slopping through the door covered in mud. He looked like a swamp monster.

Bursting out immediately in laughter, the scowl he pointed in our direction was one that made us hush at once.

"I just had the worst day I could've possibly had."

Trying to let the sensitive side of her immerge, Lizzy went over, careful not to get too close. "What happened baby?" snickering beneath her breath with her hand covering her mouth slightly.

He let out a huge breath and started explaining, "Well, first of all, we ran outa gas in the middle of nowhere. Then, when we get goin' again, we got stuck in a mud hole not too far down the way. Henry, well he thought he could steer a little better than me, so he told me to get behind it and push."

Again laughter prevailed, filling the entire room, all of us knowing what was coming next. And after a few moments of laughing at him, he began to laugh with us. I suppose he saw the hilarity in it just as we did.

"Come'ere Lizzy…gimme some sugar," Dean said, sticking out his lips to her and motioning with his fingers for her to come to him.

"You get away from me Dean Thomas…I mean it!" she said, backing away from him steadily. "Besides, you're getting mud all over the place."

"Don't you want a kiss," he continued towards her.

Lizzy stopped, put her hands on her hips and glared at him mean like. "You turn right around and go outside. You wash yourself off. I don't care how cold it is out there, then get back in here and act your age."

He half turned away from her, but as soon as she glanced over at me and winked as if to say "he does what I say!" he whipped back around and picked her up, getting her just as soaked in that stuff as he was. I swear, I thought I was gonna pee on myself just from laughing so hard. Evan was amused too. I could tell by looking in his eyes that was also the sort of thing he'd do to me as well.

"Put me down," she kicked, making sure he knew she was making her madder than a wet hen.

Finally he did as she asked, "Now darlin', we can both go outside and get washed off...*no matter how cold it might be,* and then come inside and take a shower."

She mumbled all the way outside. I knew it was far too cold to be wettin' yourself out there, but I couldn't imagine him going upstairs, leaving muddy footprints the whole way up. After a few moments, they both came back in soaked to the skin. I had grabbed a couple of towels from the downstairs bathroom and wrapped it around them one at a time as they came back.

"Thanks sis," she grumbled, shivering all the way up the stairs, glancing back at her fun filled husband the entire way.

Dean remarked the same and they were off to the showers.

"Hey," Evan blurted out. "You hungry?"

"Starved. 'bout all we had today was some of Ma's homemade cookies and some cold milk."

"And you didn't bring *me* none?"

"Jade ate 'em all mostly. Shoot, I think she left half the cookie in the glass of milk every time she tried dunk it like me."

"That's alright then."

"I tell ya what," I said. "Let's get the kids up and go as a family. How does that sound?"

"You were readin' my mind sweetheart. Just readin' my mind," he said, taking my hand and directing me to the room where we left our two sleeping babies.

Peeking through the tiny crack we left open, Jade was squirming around, but Cody was still in the same spot. It looked like them two belonged together as brother and sister.

"I hate to wake 'em up Evan," my eyes looking drooping, trying to appear sad.

"I'm sure they're as hungry as we are."

Getting them up was a chore, especially Cody. I swear, he was the soundest sleeper I ever did see. A war could be going on right next to him and he'd still be living in slumber land. But somehow, Evan found a way to get to him. When he lifted him up, Cody had these tiny streaks down his face from the covers and that side of his face was beet red. It looked like he had fever from one side and normal on the other.

If nothing else, it got a grin out of both of us.

"Come on you two," he said in a fatherly manner. "Let's go grab a bite somewhere."

Of course Cody didn't say anything. He was still rubbing his tired little eyes, but Jade was all for it.

"Are you hungry Jade?" he asked her.

She nodded a definite yes, then "nana gave us cookies."

He immediately looked back to me and grinned, "Nana?"

"Yeah," I replied. "That's what Ma said she could call her."

"Ohhh," he said, looking back at her. "Did you like nana?"

"Uh huh. She's nice."

I took Cody and Evan elevated Jade up clean to his shoulders. She clung to him tighter and tighter the further up he placed her, but once she was there, the smile showed enjoyment.

We were coming out of the bedroom with the kids when Lizzy and Dean came out of the bathroom with their neatly matching robes. All the mud was gone and Lizzy looked more like she was in a better mood than when she charged up the stairs just a bit ago.

"Feel better?" I asked, snickering still.

"Much," she answered, steadily working the dry towel through her dripping hair as she spoke. "Where are ya'll goin'?"

"Oh, just to grab a bit."

"I can cook!" she insisted, then Dean wrapped his arms around her waist and cut in.

"Darlin' you ain't cookin' tonight. It's my turn."

Trying to look mad, she answered sternly, "I suppose you owe it to me for pullin' such a dirty trick. And I *do* mean dirty!"

Dean commenced to laughing and we joined him. It didn't take long for Lizzy to find the humor in the whole situation, but she still gave him one stiff elbow in the belly for it anyway.

"Have a good time sis?"

"We will Lizzy…oh, and by the way, Evan and I are gonna get married."

"We know that already Betty Jean," she replied as if I had lost my memory or something.

But before we walked out, I finished my sentence, "SOON!"

Closing the door, I could still hear her hollering back at me to come back. I could tell that she couldn't stand not knowing the details of the whole thing, and I wanted to leave it that way until Evan and I made a decision ourselves.

"We're all set," he said, firmly placing his manly hands on the steering wheel. "Where to?"

"Hmmm, don't matter to me. I'm easy to please."

Laughing as if I had just told a story, I scooted over and nudged him. Jade and Cody were nestled in the back seat and a few moments later he pulled into Sally's. Since the last time I was there, they had added something to it. I was told there was a woman who had so many books that she rented the back part as a used bookstore, buying, trading and selling all sorts of books.

When we went in with the kids, everything looked the same, but the doorway that used to lead to an extra room, now read, "Judy's books." After sitting down and ordering, I left the kids with him long enough for me to go and check it out. There were only a few people eating, and I wasn't so sure that many folks around our little town read much, but I was curius.

Going through the door, it led me into a little nook. There wasn't much space at all, but Good Lord, there were more books than I'd ever seen at one time in my entire life. I suppose they were separated in some form or fashion, but if they were, I couldn't tell it. And when I began to gaze around, looking to see if there was anything that would suit my fancy, a woman came out from around the corner.

"Hi!" she said robustly, smiling like a oppossum, from ear to ear. She was a little heavy set, but attractive, her slightly rough sounding voice echoing through that tiny area where she had a million books back to back...one on top of the other. "What'cha lookin' for young lady?"

Hunching down a bit, I replied, "Nothin' inparticular. I was just curious why you'd put a bookshop here. It's so small."

"Well, the way I look at it dear…it's not the quantity, it's the quality. And I got a ton of quality books in here."

Looking to my left, there was a row of childrens books and unconsciously, I started to browse. I suppose the motherly instinct in me began to roar like a lion because I picked one of them up and asked how much it was.

"Nickel," she replied, giving a half smirk. That old me she was giving me one heck of a deal.

"You're kiddin' right?"

"No young lady," she retorted nicely. "You got a little girl."

"Not yet, but I'm fixin' to."

"Well," she clapped her hands together. "Congrats."

Realizing what she was thinking, "No...no, I'm not expectin', just getting married to a man who already has a daughter."

"Hmmm, how old is she dear?"

"Four in a few days."

"I got just the thing," she said merrily, marching around the small maze until she stopped at the last corner of the store. "Here."

Taking it from her, the title read, "Branches of a Tree." I didn't quite understand what she meant by giving me that book, so I asked.

"Oh, I didn't mean anything by it dear, just that maybe it'll help her understand the meaning of family if you read it to her. It sure did help my kids."

I dug down into my purse and pulled out a shiny nickel, handing it to her. With a gleaming smile, she took the book and neatly slid it in a small bag. Although it was hard to even turn around in that crowded room with books surrounding me, I felt comfortable. It felt like I'd known this woman for years just by the way she talked to me.

"Thanks for your help," I said, starting to leave.

"I didn't get your name," she said hurriedly.

Turning, "Betty Jean...soon to be Betty Jean Bain."

With a nod and wave, I walked out of that tiny shop that was nearly hidden in the back room of one of the busiest eatin' places in town. And when I walked out, I saw Evan glaring at me. I wasn't sure if it was an angry look or if he was just trying to act that way, but none the less, I scurried over to find out.

24

That evening with my soon to be husband and the kids, was wonderful. The bonding went far beyond what I thought it would at that point, and Jade appeared to start feeling at ease with me and Evan.

The following day, we did a quick job planning Jade's birthday party, as well as making a few arrangements for the wedding. The party was easy, but the wedding part, well, that was one he and I disagreed about. I got the feeling he wanted to wait until after Christmas to tie the knot, but I didn't want to wait. I had a desire to go ahead with my life, not wasting a single day, and after some talking, he agreed.

Jade's party was going to be at her grandma's in Ft. Smith, and everyone she was used to being around was invited. I didn't have a clue how many people cared about her until folks started flooding in from every direction. She had more presents stacked up than I ever remembered getting in my entire life, and she, just four, didn't know how very lucky she was to have so many people on her side.

Standing in a chair directly in front of the birthday cake, Neline lit the candles. Jade took one huge breath in and blew as hard as she knew how.

"What'd you wish for Jade," one of her cousins asked.

"To be with my mama."

The room went silent briefly. I think Evan was a hair stunned because he thought she had gotten over the whole ordeal somewhat, but with that one huge remark from such a tiny little girl, everyone turned their happiness for her birthday to sympathy for her feelings.

One present after another, she tore through them all. From dresses to hair things, to every toy you could imagine…she got it all, and in the midst of everything, she seemed to fall back into the same daze she was in the first time I saw her. Her look was of a blank sort, staring passed everyone to something else.

"Mama," she said, getting up and going towards the window.

"Jade honey, come here," Evan pleaded, trying to get her to snap out of whatever state of mind she had fallen into.

"But my mama was there."

"Where sweetheart?"

"There," she said, pointing at the ray of light that almost looked like it was a pathway to the world above.

"No one's there," he replied sincerely, trying not to upset her.

That's when something happened that hurt me deep down. The bear I had gotten her was lying on a chair near the window. She picked it up and hit it repeatedly then dropped it, running to the room that used to be hers before Evan went to get her.

"I'll talk to her," Neline said sweetly, slowly making her way with amble steps towards the room Jade resided.

I couldn't hear what she was saying to her, but I was sure it was something wise. I only hoped it was something that would make her want to leave with me and Evan. I knew if she didn't want to, his heart would be destroyed totally.

Shortly after Neline left, out came Jade, one slow step after another. And she didn't stop until she reached her daddy, staring up at him.

"Can I be with my mama?"

"One day sweetheart...one day you will be."

Embracing him, she let out her emotions as she did the day of the funeral, but this time it was different. Although I couldn't pinpoint it...it was different.

After all the 'thank you's' were said and the place was cleaned up, we loaded up the many boxes of things she had gotten. She didn't look particularly happy...or sad for that matter, but woman's intuition told me something was wrong.

On the way back to Lizzy and Dean's she fell asleep in the back seat. She looked especially innocent at that moment. Her golden blonde hair flowing down and that soft gorgeous complection of hers making her look more like an angel than anything.

"She's got somethin' on her mind Evan."

"She'll be fine."

"No really...you need to listen to me. Somethin's not right."

Cutting his eyes, "I said she'll be fine. I'll make darn sure of it. Now...what about the wedding."

Although he was changing the subject, I was glad it was one I didn't mind talking about. "Well, we decided to do it soon. It's only a week till Christmas. How about day after tomorrow? I already told my folks and the few people we want to be there, won't be hard to get in touch with."

"You wanna have it at Dean and Lizzy's?"

Griinning, "That'll be perfect, but I've gotta go get Jade a beautiful dress. She *is* going to be my flower girl."

"I wouldn't want nobody else for the job."

We started to pull in at my sister's when I told him to keep going. He looked at me kind of funny, but did as I asked.

"I want ya'll to stay with me tonight. She's already asleep so she won't no any difference, and when we get up, I'll take her shopping for a dress."

Very agreeable, he headed up the winding hills to my house. I went in before they did so I could make her a warm comfortable place, and in Evan's arms she was brought in tenderly.

"There we go," he whispered as he laid her down, stroking her hair before he left the room.

"She's somethin' else Evan…I gotta say."

Looking in her direction, "She is ain't she?"

"Listen, I'm tired…why don't we hit the hay and get some rest. I gotta get up early and call in to work. The girls there are gonna have a wall eyed fit when I tell'em we're gettin' married in two days."

With that, he coiled his masculine arms around me and lifted me slightly off the floor. Suddenly, I could almost hear a voice speaking to me. It sounded like someone was telling me to be happy. Like echoes from heaven, I swore to myself it was Lonnie talking to me from another diminsion…another place.

"What's wrong?" Evan asked, feeling me tense up briefly.

"Nothin' at all…nothin' at all."

Arm in arm, he led me to my room and in a gentlemanlike manner, tucked me in as if I were a small child needing such an actin done for me. And after a kiss on the forehead and a stroke on my cheek with his slightly callased hands, he walked out, starting to close the door behind him.

"Evan!"

Stopping for a moment, "Did I forget somethin'?"

"Yeah, you did."

I got up and mashed my body next to his as much as I could as I planted a very intense kiss on his irresistible lips. He followed my lead, but after a moment or so, he stopped.

"There's plenty of time for this Betty Jean…when you're my wife," he said honestly. "In the meantime, remember how much I love you."

"You do the same Mr. Bain," I said, honoring his wishes and leaving him be for the night. As difficult as I knew it would be, I wanted to stay apart from him until it was proper for us to be together.

Although I assumed I'd never get to sleep in such a circumstance, I was completely wrong. As soon as my head hit the pillow I was out like a light. No dreams graced my mind and no nightmares haunted me…only peaceful happy sleep.

The following morning came very quickly, and I hopped out of bed so I could whip up something wonderful for my future family to feast on, but when I went into the kitchen, it was too late.

"Goodmornin' sunshine!" Evan sang, forcing me to see a side of him I hadn't seen before. He was standing there in his boxer shorts and a white T-shirt, in front of a pan that was cooking bacon and eggs. "I made some homemade biscuits too."

Grinning, "You did not!"

"I did too," he declared. "Homemade right outa the can."

"You are some kinda crazy."

"Good crazy though…right?" he asked, leaning backwards, half kissing me and half watching the food.

Shaking my head, I noticed one little girl was already up. Cody hadn't made a peep yet, but I was sure it wouldn't be long until he did. He never was one to sleep too awful late.

I lifted Jade up and sat her on my knee. Her messed up morning hair was something I'd never seen and I was excited that I was going to get to fix her hair for the very first time.

"We're gonna go get you a dress today sweetie."

"For what?" she asked, still rubbing sleep from her eyes.

"Well, me and your daddy are gettin' married tomorrow and I want you to be my flower girl."

"Flower girl?" she questioned, making a face as though she had no clue what-so-ever…what I was talking about.

Trying to explain, "You're gonna walk ahead of us and sprinkle flower petals on the floor."

"Why?"

"Well…"

Evan jumped in, seeing I was having a lot of difficulty explaining such a simple thing. "It's like this sweetheart…you're gonna wear a beautiful dress, carry rose petals for us, and look beautiful for everybody to see."

"Okay," she replied, as if his explanation was incredibly better than mine.

Breakfast was great even though the bacon was a tad on the crisp side, and I got Jade all dressed and warm while Evan stayed at home with Cody. He told me they were bonding. I hoped it was true, but more than that, I wanted to bond with the little girl I truly wanted to call my daughter.

With a wave and a blown kiss, we were off to find the perfect thing for Jade to wear, as well as for me. Of course, the place we had to go to was Lulu's Bridal Shop. She had the most beautiful dresses I had ever seen even though I hadn't been many places…but they were still beautiful none the less.

When I walked in with Jade next to me, Melynda's bright blue eyes lit up.

"Oh my," she cried out. "Look at this little lady you got with you."

"What's your name?" she asked, bending down to her kindly.

"Jade."

"What a pretty name," she continued. "I'm Melynda Posey. And I'm guessin' ya'll are needin' dresses."

"Second time's the charm I suppose."

"You're not...You are! Gettin' married again," she excitedly stated, dancing around trying to find something unique. "Now this is a privelege."

Looking around, I stopped at one rack of little girl's things. "I'm lookin' for somethin' sweet and frilly for this little one here, but for me...traditional."

"Traditional...you, well alright then. Let's see what I got."

That tiny thing jumped from rack to rack and finally, after a while of looking and trying on, I found the two most perfect dresses. In a way Jade and I would look almost identical. I thought it would be sweet if I made her a miniature version of me, and so I did. She tried it on and I swear, it almost made me cry just looking at her.

"I assume these are the two you want Mrs..."

"Bain...soon to be Bain."

"Alright Mrs. Bain."

We got all rung up and Jade went over staring at herself in the mirror. It always seemed funny to me how little kids did that, especially girls. I remember when I was younger...fourteen maybe. I used to stare at myself and pose like I was some sort of model or something, knowing I was nothing but a poor ole country gal who was lucky if I had one pair of shoes that had a purse to match. That was my thing...matching.

"She's a cutie," Melynda said, staring at her as well.

"Yeah, she is."

"You ready sweetie?" I asked, going over to her and kneeling next to her.

She didn't answer, but nodded instead, and we were headed back home to where Cody and Evan were doing some sort of male bonding thing. Of course, I didn't know how much bonding Cody could do. He wasn't old enough to put a sentence together, but then again, some men can't do that either.

I stopped off at the market to get a few groceries and Jade stayed right next to me. I had seen other kids in there asking their parents for this or that, but she didn't ask for anything. It just didn't seem normal. Shoot, I remembered when we would go to the market with Ma. I did my share of askin' but Douglas...he went way overboard. Heck, he'd cause a scene in there to where everyone knew what he wanted, not just Ma. With Jade though, she was different. Most little girls her age would tromp around trying to find something to get into. In her case, she did all she could not to cause one iota of trouble.

I did everything I could to make her feel at ease with me, and there were a few times when I thought I had succeeded. There was a complete turn around in her. That pitiful looking expression painted across her innocent little face, was breaking my heart.

"Hey," I said in a spry voice. "How 'bout we go say 'hi' to Ma for a minute."

"Okay," she nodded, but I could tell she was only doing that to pacify me and to keep me from asking her any questions about what she was thinking.

For the first time I could recall in some time, nobody was home. I knew Luther had gone out on an adventure to meet the publisher interested in him, but I was sure somebody would be there. From what I remembered, Ma didn't go much of anywhere anymore. She told me she didn't have any need to. She said that if she needed somethin' she'd tell Pa and he'd run to town.

"Well sweetie...nobody's home it seems."

With no remark, she just looked at me, those dazzling eyes of hers steady and direct, being completely attentive.

"Button your coat Jade and put on that tabogin. I'd hate for you to catch your death a cold."

She did as I asked and waited for me to come around and get her after I got out of the car at home. The sounds around us were mesmerizing. Each whisk of air that blew by felt like it came directly from the South Pole directly, and the way the tree limbs clacked together, made the perfect surrounding for me and my new family.

But just before I opened the door, Jade tugged on my arm enough to get my attention.

"What is it sweetie?"

"Daddy was sad when mama went away."

"Yes he was."

"Would he if I went away too?"

Sitting down the groceries on the porch next to the door, I picked her up and held her close to me, our eyes peering at one another.

"We don't ever want you to go away Jade."

She looked down and put her head on my shoulder. That motion alone boosted my thoughts that she would, one day, see me as her second mama. I wanted that more than you could ever imagine. It's like told me. She said that raising Lizzy and me was the best experience to her. She loved the boys, don't get me wrong, but she said there was something about being able to primp and dress a little girl in frill and bows. Even though she never could get Lizzy to dress much like that, I was one that wanted it more than Ma. In my mind, silly now that I think about it, I thought I was a beauty queen waiting for her king to come and take her away. And I suppose I found two kings.

Evan scared the dickens out of both of us when he opened the door rather abruptly. For a moment I lost my breath.

"What in the world are you two doin out here. It's colder than a…"

"Evan," I demanded. "Don't say it. Just grab these bags. I'm carryin' a special package inside."

She glanced up at me, then laid back down resting her head in the nook of my neck. I went into the living room and laid her down on the pillow placed near the armrest.

"What'd you ladies buy…the store I bet." he joked.

"Nooo…" I answered, sitting down. "But we did get two very gorgeous dresses if I do say so myself… and at a good price. Melynda was a sweetheart."

He nodded and winked, then leaned down to kiss Jade on the forehead. About the time he reached her, her eyes opened and crinkled up from where she gave him a quick grin. It was only moments later, she fell into a sleep that lasted for several hours.

Watching her lying there like that made me realize how lucky I was to be at such a place in my life. When Lonnie died I never would have guess I was going to meet such a wonderful man, not to mention extending my family a little further with a gorgeous new daughter to boot.

"What'cha thinkin'?" he asked, handing me a ladel, helping me cook.

"Oh, I don't know. I guess I was thinkin' about somethin' Jade asked me earlier."

With his eyebrows slanting inward from inquisitiveness, he asked me what I was talking about.

"She asked if you would be sad if she went away just like you were sad when her mama went away. I don't know…it just struck me as odd."

"Oh, maybe you're overreacting Betty Jean. You know kids are full of questions."

"I know Evan, but this question was different. The look in her eyes when she asked, was more serious than just a kid asking a question."

"I wouldn't worry about it. She's tryin' to adjust to the change...we all are."

"Maybe," I said, showing my worry that was running coarse all throughout my body.

Kissing my cheek, he took the pot of freshly cooked pinto beans and I followed him carrying a pan of homemade, sweet cornbread that Ma taught me to fix. I was sure it wasn't nearly as good as hers, but then again, I didn't have the years of experience behind me either. I figured by the time I got her age, I'd be equally as good...maybe.

Dinner was nothing fancy, but adequate, and about the time we got everything set, I heard Cody crying, in turn waking Jade up in the other room.

"I'll get Cody," I said hurrying in to calm my baby boy as quickly as I could.

"Let me help," he said, showing me how much closer he was getting to my son as each day passed.

A knock came to the door and I handed Cody to Evan so I could answer it. Of course, I had no clue who it could be. Not many folks came out my way. In light of that, I opened the door and saw Ma standing there shaking a bit.

"Come on in Ma,"

"Thank you dear. I just brought ya'll over some fresh baked bread. I know how you used to love it so."

She sat it in the kitchen and when I turned to tell Jade to come and try some of nana's bread...she was gone.

25

Remembering all of the comments she had made to me, my panic was extreme. Ma wasn't sure what was going on, but when I yelled for Evan, she figured it out quick enough.

"I've gotta find'er Evan," I said, throwing on my coat and rushing outside in a frenzy.

Ma stayed there while Evan came with me. Neither one of us knew where to start and for a moment or two, we turned in circles yelling for her to answer, but there were no sounds except for those that the wind provided.

"Okay," Evan said, trying to calm down. "Why don't we split up. I'll look down by the pond, between here and your Ma and Pa's house."

"I'll go up the hill on the backside of the house."

Stopping me before we went any further, Evan could tell my frustration. "We'll find her."

Nodding, we went our separate ways, scowering every place we thought she might go. But after I got passed the house and started up the hill that steadily went up and up, I began to get more and more nervous. It was so very cold outside and there were so many dangerous places around there, especially for a little one like her.

"Jade!" I yelled, hoping she would hear me and answer, but nothing. Finally, after hollering for her over and over, I did hear something.

"No! Go away," I heard, faintly in the distance.

Just that glimpse of hope lifted me up enough to where my speed picked up, climbing the hill that began to get more steep with each step.

"Jade!" I hollered once more.

This time when she responded, I could tell where the noise was coming from and I took a sharp right and ended up on this narrow trail that led to a sudden drop off. That in mind, the same panic I had when I noticed she was gone, was multiplied by a thousand, hurrying best I could to reach her before anything terrible were to happen. I feared Evan would blame me, but most of all, I had learned to truly love this little girl as if I had given birth to her myself. And the thought of losing anyone else overcame me.

Grabbing a hold of the top of the hill to help me up the rest of the way, I stood and there in front of me, was this tiny darling staring back at me. She looked so very petrified. Her eyes were glassy and affixed on me, but her mind was obviously somewhere else. She was only a few feet from the drop off and where she was standing wasn't that steady.

Reaching out my hand to her, she muttered to where I could barely hear her, "I wanna be with my mama."

"Oh baby," I replied, feeling a tear slowly trickle down. "No. You need to be with us right now."

Realizing what she had been talking about the entire time, I felt like an idiot. Why didn't I see it coming. She was thinking of what Ma told her about being with her mama, but I never would've guess she was intelligent enough to think up doing such an act of taking her own life.

"Jade sweetie, just be still. Let me come get you."

"No!" she bawled, taking a tiny step backwards.

Inching closer and closer without making her aware, finally I was only arms length away. When reached for her, it seemed she lost her footing and with one small movement, the foundation under her collapse.

My heart stopped, but my thinking didn't for a second. As her tiny little body started to fall, I grabbed her, only catching her hand.

"Help me!" the little voice cried, echoing throughout the air around me, sounding like echoes from heaven, repeating itself one time after another..

"I got ya baby…I got ya," I replied, trying my best to pull her up.

After a moment or two, I lifted her until she was in my arms. And in the cold, I laid back on the hardened ground with her in my arms tightly.

"You scared me to death," I cried, never letting go of her.

"I just wanted to…"

Sincerely, I added, "Be with your mama."

Nodding at me, wiped my tears and hers. Then I scooted back far enough to put us both out of danger.

"Jade you can talk to your mama anytime you want, but she wants you to be with us."

Burying her head in my chest, I felt the emotions that she'd been holding in since we got her and it was a wonderful moment to know you finally got through to someone so very special.

"I know what it's like to lose somebody. I lost a husband, but when I hear the bird's song echoing through these hills, I hear him. It's like he's talkin' to me from Heaven."

"Echoes from Heaven?" she asked

"Yes baby...echoes from Heaven."

"My mama too."

Smiling at her, "You're mama too. She'll be talkin' to you too."

Another tear ran down her round cheeks, but I wiped it away with a kiss.

"Come on...let's go home."

"Okay," she replied, her arms around my neck as I carefully made it down the hillside.

"Betty Jean!" I heard Evan yell.

"We're here Evan...HERE!"

Through the brush, he poked his head through. The relief showing on is face was one that couldn't be described. I don't believe he ever smiled so huge and for me, I don't believe I ever felt so humbled.

"Here," he said, trying to take her.

"I got 'er,"I responded quickly, making sure he knew that I needed to hold her. It made me feel like, with every step, we were bonding.

When we got back to the cabin, Ma was waiting inside anxiously to see if everything was alright. And when we came through the door, she let out a sigh.

"Land sakes, ya'll must be frozen clean to the bone," she said, grabbing a few blankets and wrapping them around us as we went and found a place in my old, sunk in couch.

"Thanks Ma."

Then Jade looked up at her, "Yeah," she said. "Thanks Nana."

I saw the joy she felt in the glimmer of her eyes. Jade had just taken a step forward. And I believed it was time for Evan and I to do the same.

"Let me make ya'll some nice hot soup," Ma muttered walking towards the kitchen.

"No really Ma…we're fine. Besides I made some beans and cornbread a bit ago. It's probably still a hair warm."

She stayed for a while making sure we were all okay and then left. She said Pa would have him a wall-eyed fit if she didn't get back quick like. Besides, it was nice to be there with Evan, Jade and Cody. Before Ma left, she put Cody in Evan's arms. He wrapped that cover over my little one just as it was around us. It was cozy, but that didn't take away from the fact that what happened was any less serious.

Things kept going through my mind about what could've gone wrong. Then I realized something. If I spent the rest of my life thinking of things that could go wrong, they probably would.

"Do I get to wear that dress Betty Jean?" she asked sweetly.

"You sure do Jade…tomorrow."

She smiled and leaned against me. "I like you," she replied.

Grinning an unmistakable grin, "You know what? I like you too."

All of us laughed and turned something that could've been tragic into something wonderful. I was finally feeling that carefree emotion I had before so many terrible things happened to me one after another. And, as most fairytales go, the princess meets her handsome prince and lives happily ever after.

"Now what are you thinkin'?" he asked, noticing how my mind was wandering away.

I didn't answer verbally, but acted out my answer instead. With my finger, I told him to come closer. And when he did, our lips locked together like two pieces of a puzzle that were meant to be together.

"Hmmm," he replied. "I like that answer."

"Yuck," Jade said, making a face.

I couldn't help but horseplay around with her after that. And when we warmed up enough we finally ate the dinner I cooked earlier. She ate like she was starving to death and Evan, well, he ate the same…as usual.

"We really need to go," Evan said, picking up Jades new dress and laying it over his arm. "You know, we wouldn't won't any bad luck just because I saw the bride before the wedding."

"We wouldn't want that."

With a short good-bye, our hands let go and they left. All I could do was stand there and sigh. I was filled with the most happiness I ever remembered feeling. It was like I was the princess in that fairytale. The only difference was that there wouldn't be a happy *ending*. Because to me, it was only the beginning.

That night drug by, minute by minute, hour after hour, until the moon hid itself from the sun who was ready to rise. And I, soon to be Mrs. Evan Bain, greeted the light with a gigantic smile.

Trying to wake fully, I picked up the booklet that Luther had given me. I always found inspiration in the poems in there. And when I opened it, I didn't have to turn anymore pages. "The Fate of Life," was the first poem I ran across and it so happened that it was written just as if I would have if I were a writer. It read:

> *One knows not of tomorrow,*
> *But yesterday is clear.*
> *One knows not the future*
> *Day to day or year to year.*
> *Instead no matter what*
> *The fate of life prevails.*
> *It'll cause you to succeed,*
> *Or even so to fail.*
> *Fate sends you saddness,*
> *As it sends those happy days.*
> *It Foretells the future*
> *In many curious ways.*
> *The fate of life is definitely*

Not predictable at all.
One moment you may climb a mountain,
And the next, you may fall.
One knows not the future,
Of your happiness and strife.
For the only one who knows such things...
Is the fate of life.

Those words filled my heart, re-energizing my belief in the things that are meant to be. In fact, the reassurance I needed were in those few simple words. You know, I never understood why my brother was so fascinated by poetry, but after really paying attention, I knew why. I was so glad he introduced me to something that was so wonderful, but simple. Those words ran through my mind as I got up and started to get ready. Afterwards Cody and I ate breakfast.

It was strange to think that later that day I was going to be married. What was even stranger, was the fact that he and I had so many rude confrontations when we first met. I never would've thought in a million years he would be the man I would sincerely, truly and utterly fall in love with.

"Knock knock," Lizzy said, letting herself in.

"Well just come on in sis, " I shook my head, aggravating her. "What do I owe this early mornin' visit."

"*I* am gonna get you all fixed up."

"*You* are gonna get *me* fixed up?" putting my hands on my hips. "From what I remember, I taught you how to fix up yourself to catch that handsome husband you got."

"First of all," she replied boldly. "Me bein' all fixed up ain't what caught Dean. It was just me. Second of all, it's my turn to pay you back for showin' me how to look like a lady."

So far, all I had done was dry my hair and put on a tad of foundation. And after Cody ate, I laid him down in the living room floor on his blanket while Lizzy *tried* to do some of her wedding magic.

"You sure you now how to…"

"Shhh," she interrupted. "Close your eyes now. I gotta make you look perfect."

I sat there while she did her thing, as if I couldn't do it myself, but from what she said…it was my day and I deserved to be pampered. I didn't argue one ioda. In fact, I sort of enjoyed being made a fuss over.

"So sis, ya'll goin' anywhere on your honeymoon?"

Tilting my head, "Don't know. I suppose we didn't much talk about that."

She kept on until she was finished. I grabbed a mirror and examined what she did to me. Surprisingly enough my cheeks were rosy, and it looked dang near as good as I would have done it.

"Let's talk sis." she asked, putting her arm in mine making a chain and leaning us back on the couch.

She and I went on and on, jabbering as if we were still kids talking about anything and everything. Soon, it was about time for me to go to her house. That's when my nerves took over every cell of my body. In fact, I was so nervous, I couldn't put my shoes on.

"Good Lord Betty Jean…what have you got to be nervous about. You should be impatient."

"I am…but nervous too."

"It's just the jitters. Ma said most folks gettin' married, get'em. B'sides, Evan's got 'em too."

Standing up, "You mean you think he's havin' doubts?"

"Are you havin' doubts?"

"Why no!"

"Just get your coat and I'll load up this handsome nephew of mine."

I made sure I had everything and followed along behind my sister. Ten or so minutes later, we were at her house.

"I'll keep an eye out," Lizzy whispered. "And you go upstairs in my room and put on that weddin' dress."

"Keep an eye out?" I questioned.

"I'm just gonna make sure you don't see the groom before you're supposed to. Now go ahead Betty Jean. The guests are gonna be here any time now."

Scurrying up the stairs, I made it to my sisters room. I closed the door and went over to lay the dress down on the bed. I felt itchy all over. The anticipation of becoming Evan's wife was greater than ever. So I put on my dress and went over to the mirror. Ma used to say that when you pull your hair up, it makes you look more like a lady, so that's what I did. After pinning it up, leaving a few wavy hairs resting by my face, I looked at the image staring back at me.

"You're gettin' married," I said to myself, almost thinking I was crazy for doing so.

A soft knock came at the door and then it eased open. "You dressed sis?"

"Yep, and ready to do the wedding thing."

"Not yet," she said, coming in with Jad, Neline, and Ma. They all looked so very lovely and when Lizzy stepped up to me, she laid a medium sized brown box on the bed.

"What's that?"

First Ma came up and reached in, pulling out an old heart shaped pin. In fact, I remembered seeing her wear it a few times. I always admired it so.

"Since you need something old...I want you to wear this. My mother told me that any bride who wears this pin will surely keep the love she's found...forever."

"Oh Ma, thank you."

"Now it's my turn...something new," Lizzy jumped in, also putting her hand in the box. Next thing I knew, she lifted out a bracelet that was silver and gold. It had the four names on it...mine, Cody's, Evan's and Jade's. "I hope you like it. I thought it'd be somethin' you didn't have."

"I love it Lizzy. I do!"

Lizzy stepped aside, and Neline, Lisa's mother walked up. "I haven't known you long dear, but I've known you long enough to know that you're going to treat my granddaughter good. I know what happened last night and I have something for you."

She stuck her hand in the box and, in her hand, was a small blue corsage with tiny white flowers on it. She tied it on my wrist and lightly embraced me. And lastly, Jade came up. She had on the lovely dress I had gotten her and it looked like it was made for her. Each side of her hair was pulled back with a tiny bow that matched her dress perfectly, and the smile she wore, completed her look.

"You're beautiful sweetie," I said, stroking her golden blonde curls.

"You ready," she said, taking my hand.

"I sure am," I said.

The music started and we were all on our way to join the guests for the day I'd been waiting for. Ma, Lizzy and Neline went ahead, but Jade and I took our time. I'm sure everyone thought we looked like a mirror image of each other, and to me, that would've been a compliment.

"Come on Jade," Neline motioned, holding out the flower basket.

As she went on, I had to breath in and out...in and out. I was so nervous, I almost couldn't think. It wasn't doubts mind you, but just the idea of getting married. Something about it seemed to have an effect on everyone who's ever gotten married from what I was told, and I was no different.

When Jade was out of sight, Neline nodded and the music for the bride started. I let out one more long breath and preceeded down the stairs. Each step was an anxious one and I couldn't wait until I was officially married to this man who turned my life from a living hell to Heaven on earth. It seemed like a long walk getting to him, but it wasn't at all.

Reverend Cline performed the ceremony. It was short and sweet, just the way I asked for him to do it and everyone I cared about the most was there. Evan looked very attractive in his navy suit and I could see the sparkle in his eyes the moment I said "I do." I felt the same when he agreed to love, cherish and honor me from that day forward, til death do us part. I didn't particularly like the last part of that, but none the less, I was sure he loved me enough to want to be there for me from that day on.

"So Mrs. Bain," Luther said, coming up behind me.

Astounded to see him, thinking he was out of town, I hugged my baby brother. "What are you doin' here?"

Turning, "I'll leave if you want."

Laughing, "No…no."

While we were talking, Evan quietened everyone down and raised his glass of wine. "To the woman I love, I would've never thought the day I met you, that you and I'd be standing here doing what we're doing, but what can I say…you put a spell on me."

Then I raised my glass, "To the man that I love. I was taken by you at first sight although you never knew it, and even though I tried to fight my feelings from showing…my feelings won. So here we are."

"Here…here," everyone hollered out, raising their glasses with us.

As far as the honeymoon went, well, it was probably different than anyone would've imagined. In fact, since Jade had just moved with us, we thought it would be a little uncaring to leave. So we just stayed home. Evan, me, Jade and Cody were together on the first night I was legally Mrs. Betty Jean Bain. And as soon as the kids were asleep, the honeymoon officially started…if ya know what I mean.

It seems like only yesterday since we vowed to one another, but time has gone by. Ma and Pa are just the same as always, pinching pennies and being who they've always been, country to the core. Lizzy and Dean still act like they did when they first met, hugging and kissing every chance they get no matter where it might be. And Douglas, well, what can you say about Douglas? He's doin' his best to grow up. But if you ask me, when he's fifty, he'll still act the same as he does right now. I don't know. I suppose change is inevitable, but sometimes not so welcome. In my case, change was what I needed.

Luther started making his way in the writing world and we were all so glad to see it happen. I would hate for a God given talent like his to go to waste. And he was gonna darn sure make sure his didn't.

It's funny, there was a time when I thought life was being so horrible to me. I thought nothing would ever go right. I thought I was doomed to years of misery just because of a few misfortunate happenings. I learned something though. Most people spend a lifetime trying to find one person to love and that love them back. I was lucky…I found two. To me, that's a miracle in itself.

As far as my family goes, we're all gonna be just fine. We're the *Coles*…and I suppose that's all that needs to be said.

About the Author

Tammy D. Thompson is the author of *Buried, But Not Forgotten*, and the *Dream Mountain* series including *Dream Mountain*, *A Dream Come True, Lessons of the Heart*, and *Echoes From Heaven*. Her next book in the making is *The Beggar*. From her hometown in Arkansas, the simple things in life are the most important. "When you write from the heart, you can't go wrong," she says. "Writing is my passion, but touching someone's heart is my goal."

Please contact the author by e-mail, authorthompson@yahoo.com, or by visiting her website at www.tammydthompson.com.

Printed in the United States
87272LV00005BA/89/A